THE NEW ANGELS
EARTH832

I0564273

L FERGUS

Copyright © 2021 by L. Fergus

@FallenAngelKita

http://FallenAngelKita.com

ISBN: 978-1-949789-07-2

Cover art by Mark Gardner and Mrinmoy Kar

ALSO BY L. FERGUS

Angel of Yorq
(Available in paperback version of *Birthright*)

Birthright

Razor's Pass

Project Omega
(Available in paperback version of *Razor's Pass*)

Fall and Rise

Return

Sarin's Heart
(Available in paperback version of *Breakout*)

Breakout
(Coming Summer 2021)

The Legion
(Coming Winter 2021)

Rebirth

Clouds

Sarin's War

Li've

THE NEW ANGELS

Earth 168

BykeChic

Earth 832

NON-KITA BOOKS

Warmache

PATREON EXCLUSIVES

Return of the Fallen Angel Series

Return of the Fallen Angel: Book 1

Return of the Fallen Angel: Book 2

Return of the Fallen Angel: Book 3

Return of the Fallen Angel: Book 4

Children of the Emperor Series

(Coming soon to www.patreon.com/FallenAngelKita)

Rescue

Children of the Fallen Angel

Sacrifice

Irruption Series

(Coming soon to www.patreon.com/FallenAngelKita)

Unbalanced

Fusion

Retreat

Sins

Reformation

Metamorphosis

For the women in my life,
You taught me strength, courage, and sacrifice.

CHAPTER ONE
KAREN AND ZHI

"ANY QUESTIONS, LADIES?" KAREN SAID, ADDRESSING the briefing room of pilots. She stole a glance at the Angel Kita, standing in the back, having arrived partway through the briefing. She wasn't dressed as the Vicereine, so she wasn't here in an official capacity. *Probably checking in on her favorite pet project.*

A hand went up. "What if the rest of the Navy doesn't show up after we bomb them?" said Harlequin. "I don't remember *run like hell* being taught in Angel School."

The other pilots laughed. They were all graduates of the elite Superior Air Tactics and Combat School Karen helped Kita establish a year ago. The punishing sixty-day course pushed pilot and machine beyond their limits. The school's washout rate was ninety-nine percent and already claimed the lives of seven pilots. Graduates earned more than a tab for their jackets. They received the basic Angel package—a bionanite injection that increased their physical and mental stamina and gave them special abilities like regeneration, super strength, enhanced vision, and invisibility.

Karen didn't think it was funny. "If you run, I'll shoot you down myself. You only bail if we run out of missiles and bullets."

"Forget running," said Anastasia, a pilot from Ukraine. "I crash plane into them. If they survive, I kill them with bare hands on ground."

"That's why you have a pistol," said Pepper.

"Beat them with rock."

"Ok, ladies, we have ninety minutes until we cross phase line x-ray. Get to your fighters."

The pilots gathered their tablets and helmets and climbed the steps out of the briefing room. Each gave Kita a nod as they went by. Karen went last with her wingwoman, Shen, a new pilot from China. Kita stepped in front of them as they reached the top.

"Hi, Karen," said Kita from under a large hood that hid her face.

"Hey, Kita. No problems to report. Everything is a go."

"I prefer they not kamikaze the planes," said Kita. "The technology in them is beyond classified."

"I will tell them to make sure, but I think she was joking."

Kita looked at Shen. "How's the new girl?"

Shen bowed. "I'm ready to serve, honorable Kita. Death will come fast and swift to our enemies."

"Call me Kita. Save the pleasantries for when I'm Vicereine."

Shen looked confused. "You plan to be Vicereine someday?"

Kita chuckled. "No. I am the Vicereine, but only when I wear the dress. I prefer my day job as an assassin. How are you adjusting to the fighter, Shen?"

The 154th Strike Fighter Squadron flew customized versions of the F-22 Raptor. It was faster, turned harder, out-climbed, and was more heavily armed than any other fighter in the world. The wings were fitted with gravity wells allowing for higher speeds and high-g turns that would kill a normal pilot.

"It's a superb aircraft. I will get many kills."

Kita smiled. "The sky will be full today, but I'll leave that to you girls."

The door opened, and Empress Apocalypse entered. She pushed her hood back and stuck her face in Kita's hood to get a kiss. "Hey, angel. Chelsea's down for her nap."

"No fight this time?"

"The swaying of the ship helps. We should find a bed that rocks. Hi, Karen."

"Hi, Kimmy." Karen had spent the last eighteen months living with the Angels. She was at ease with them, even Apocalypse. When Shen moved to kneel, Karen pulled her elbow to stop her.

"Who's your friend?"

"This is Lieutenant Zhi Shen. She joined the Fallen Angels three weeks ago."

"Hi, Zhi."

"Y—Your High— ness."

Apocalypse laughed. "You're one of Kita's girls; call me Kimmy."

"How is Chelsea?" said Karen. "I haven't seen her in months. She must be huge."

"Like a potato with wings," grumbled Kita.

Apocalypse elbowed Kita in the middle. "What she means to say is she is adorable and is getting bigger all the time. After the mission, you'll have to come see her."

"You have a child?" said Shen in surprise.

"Closely guarded secret," said Apocalypse. "I was only pregnant for seven weeks. No one noticed when I disappeared for a month."

"Last I saw her, she looked like a little cherub," said Karen.

"All she does is eat," said Kita.

Apocalypse gave Kita a loving look. "The sociopath hasn't warmed up to her yet. You should see her trying to hold Chelsea. The look on her face is utter terror."

"She could erupt at any moment. I don't want to be covered in baby puke."

Apocalypse rolled her eyes. "It wipes off."

"And smells."

"Anyway, is the mission ready, Karen?"

"The only thing left to do is drop the bombs and pile up the bodies."

"Excellent. This will be a good warm-up for our forces. Europe is protesting my declaration of world nuclear proliferation."

The networks had played the thirty-minute speech repeatedly for the last week. Apocalypse's simple message was only the Empire of the United States would be allowed to have nuclear weapons. All others were to be handed over, taken, or destroyed by force.

"Have they gone on alert?" said Kita.

Apocalypse shrugged. "So far, no. I told their

ambassadors that we would be running military exercises around the Middle East. They protested, but that's all."

As an Angel, Karen knew some of Apocalypse's plan. The first step to conquering the world was to eliminate the rest of the world's nukes. France, the UK, Germany, Spain, Italy, Sweden, and the Arab Alliance were the only countries left. Europe was deemed a minor threat. The unpredictable religious dictator that led the Arab Alliance was the top priority and the target of today's mission. Karen and the Fallen Angels, the 154th's nickname after the Battle of Moscow, were to go in and bomb the facilities and silos, removing the threat.

"Kita and I will be observing in the VIP Combat Information Center," said Apocalypse. "If you have any problems, contact us."

Nothing like having both your bosses looking over your shoulder. "I don't see any problems. Everyone's concern is getting back out, but I know the rest of the Navy will meet us in the middle."

"Don't try and take the Alliance's air force on by yourselves," said Kita sternly. "Blast through to friendly lines. I know your pilots are itching to fight, but you're no good to me dead."

Karen bowed her head. "Yes, Kita. I will make sure they know."

Kita touched Karen's upper arm. "We can't win the war today, so now is not the time for foolish risks. Planes can be replaced. You can't."

Karen never dared to ask Kita how old she was, but she always spoke with wisdom and experience. "I'll make sure everyone comes home."

"There will be plenty of air battles in this campaign," said Apocalypse.

It's like they don't want us to kick ass. We haven't trained this hard not to. "The squadron will be ready."

"I know," said Kita. "That's why I put you in charge. Now, go lead your squadron to glory."

"PHASE LINE DELTA CROSSED. EXECUTE," SAID THE Airborne Warning and Control System controller Sky Fortress. Four AWACS aircraft patrolled outside the Arab Alliance airspace providing command and control for the various Naval and Air Force assets moving around the region.

Karen's squadron broke formation into six pairs. Each pair had a target—missile silo, assembly plant, and enrichment facility—around the country. Special Forces teams had infiltrated the country over the previous weeks and were now in position to mark the Fallen Angels' targets.

"Fallen Angel Lead, turn to zero-four-three. Use your discretion to avoid the SAM sites," said Sky Fortress.

The F-22 was a stealth aircraft. On radar, it returned the same amount of energy as a bee. Thanks to the improvements to their eyes, Karen and the Fallen Angel pilots could see the violet domes of radiation formed by the beams emitted by the Surface-to-Air Missile sites' active radar. Karen guided her fighter around them or above them. Their modified F-22s could reach eighty thousand feet, higher than any SAM could reach.

Karen and Shen passed into the Iranian mountains.

Thirty years ago, the Empire of the United States fought a bloody war here against an Arabian army backed by the Soviets and their allies. Unable to counter the alien threat and the Arabs, the EUS had withdrawn and lost access to the Middle East's valuable oil reserves. The Soviets set up the Arabian Alliance as a puppet state. After the Soviets joined the EUS, the AA fell to religious zealots.

"Approaching target," said Sky Fortress.

Karen checked her computer. She could see the nuclear enrichment facility on her screen and a bright dot of energy on the building's side coming from the laser aimed by the Special Forces team. Her bombs would follow the laser energy to make sure it hit the target.

This was the most dangerous part of the mission. The doors to her internal bomb compartments would open, ruining her stealth signature. She would be exposed for a few minutes, but the risk was considered minimal by Command. The AA flew outdated MiG-25s and didn't have advanced air-to-air missiles.

"Target identified, Sky Fortress," said Karen.

"Sky is clear. Start your run."

"Adder, Hedgehog," Karen said to Shen, "We've a green light. Starting my run."

"Roger, Hedgehog. I'll follow you in."

Karen pushed a button turning on autopilot so she could prepare the bombs. After arming them, she opened her bay doors. Karen waited for the bombs to locate the laser from the ground units. Instead of getting the steady tone announcing the bombs had a lock, she received the angry warble of an enemy missile lock.

"Hedgehog, something's lit me up," said Shen.

"I've got it, too. Sky Fortress, what is out there?"

"We're searching. Continue with the mission."

A steady tone went off in Karen's ear. "I've got tone. Dropping now." Karen pulled the trigger and dropped the two thousand-pound bombs.

"Dropping," said Shen.

The warble in Karen's ear became urgent. "Break, break, break," instructed Karen as both fighters took evasive action to break radar lock. Karen rolled, closed her bay doors, and dove. The maneuver should easily counter any missiles the AA used.

"Hedgehog, I'm not shaking it," said Shen.

The warble in Karen's ear was becoming insistent. "What the hell is out there, Sky Fortress?"

"We're being slimed, Fallen Angel Lead. Take evasive measures."

The AA doesn't have the capability to jam an AWACS. Whoever does isn't firing average missiles either. "Adder, we have to break lock. Execute stairway to heaven."

"Roger, Lead. Coming at you now."

Karen executed a high-g turn and flew at Shen. The warble in her ear stayed constant. The two fighters approached collision. Both pilots pulled back on the stick, making a sharp turn straight up. They flew belly to belly and entered a vertical roll in hopes to confuse the incoming missiles' radar lock.

The warble in Karen's ear disappeared. "Break, break, break," ordered Karen.

After climbing five thousand feet, the two fighters rolled out of the climb in opposite directions. Karen debated what to do. She could run and let the AWACS figure out what was going on, or she could turn on her radar and find the enemy herself. She wasn't about to be chased away by a near miss. Flipping on her radar, it lit up with a cloud of contacts. *Oh shit.*

"Sky Fortress, I've got a dozen contacts bearing zero-three-three. Not squawking IFF."

"Roger, Fallen Angel Lead. Orders are to return home. Mission's accomplished."

The angry warble returned to Karen's ear. She shut off her radar, but the warble remained. Karen performed a series of high-g turns to shake contact. When that didn't work, she turned toward the missile to give it the smallest cross-section she could. Still, the warble sounded.

"Adder, I'm lit. I can't shake it."

"I'll get them."

"Don't go after them!"

Karen couldn't worry about Shen. She dove to make one last attempt to break lock. She accelerated toward the ground. The warble was almost a solid tone, then a new beep sounded.

"There's too many!" yelled Shen.

What the hell did she do? With the new beep becoming a constant tone, Karen's ejection seat fired automatically. The canopy of her F-22 flew away as she was launched into the sky. Under her, the F-22 went up in a ball of flame.

KAREN AWOKE STRAPPED TO HER SEAT IN A WIDE ravine. Letting the woozy feeling pass, she hit the release on her harness and slid to her hands and knees. After giving her body a chance to recover, she stood and opened the emergency compartment in her seat. Karen removed the rations, map and compass, flares, and locator beacon. After pocketing the items in her flight suit, she hit the self-destruct on the seat and hurried out of the ravine.

"*Zhi? Did you make it back to the carrier?*" Karen called over her comm, a biological communication suite that was part of the basic Angel package. She had a limited range but could connect to anything she could get a frequency for.

"*Karen?*"

"*Zhi, where are you?*"

"*I went down north of you. I dislocated my knee when I landed. A group of villagers captured me.*"

"*I will come find you. Stay put and let your body heal.*"

"*Ok.*"

If one person's comm has the range to reach me, it would be Kita. "*Kita?*"

"*Karen? Are you ok?*"

"I'm *fine. I was shot down over the mountains. I have my locator beacon.*"

"It's *going to be a while. Some European countries have sent aircraft to the AA. We won't be able to get a helicopter to you until we establish air superiority.*"

"*Understood. I've talked to Zhi. She's injured and captured. Can you give me her location, and I'll go get her?*"

"*It might be better to wait until we can send a retrieval team.*"

"She's *injured, and I don't want her in their hands.*"

"*Ok. I've got her location, and I'll send it to you.*"

Karen received a grid coordinate in her mind. "I'll *get her.*"

"*I have every faith,*" said Kita.

Karen opened the map and plotted the grid coordinate. Shen was ten clicks north over a series of steep ridges. Karen put the map in her leg pocket, took a bearing with her compass, and started jogging.

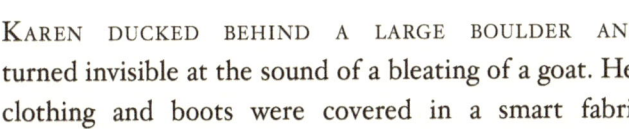

KAREN DUCKED BEHIND A LARGE BOULDER AND turned invisible at the sound of a bleating of a goat. Her clothing and boots were covered in a smart fabric capable of changing colors or turning invisible. It was technology from Kita. She gave it to the unit six months ago when Karen took command. Ahead of her, a herd of goats passed by traveling on a rocky trail.

The goat herder guided his flock down the rocky valley. *I must be close to the village.* According to the map, it was over the next ridge. After checking to make sure the area was clear, Karen crossed the narrow valley and climbed the ridge's summit. Tucked between two ridges was a cluster of mud-brick houses with a well on the north side. A pair of rickety trucks sat parked to the south next to a set of dirt tracks leading down the valley through the scrub grass. A man wearing an old military fatigue top, dark pants, and a newsboy's cap stood outside a house holding an AK-47. *This must be the place.*

Karen traversed the slope to the village, approaching from the east. She moved through the houses and over some low stone walls that divided the open spaces. As she went to cross another wall, she froze. A pair of dogs lay in the dirt near a doorway. Karen was invisible to the eye, but she still had a scent, and a dog could bite her—she was invisible, not a ghost.

How am I going to get around them? I could find another way around, but if one house has dogs, won't more? I need to keep them busy with something smellier than me. It might have been a mistake to use the apricot conditioner this morning. Pulling her rations from her pocket, she tore open a packet of peanut butter and emptied the small bottle of hot sauce into it. She whistled lowly and tossed the packet between the dogs. They sniffed it and growled at each other as both tried to get the packet at the same time. Karen hurried across the open space and another rock wall. On the other side was the man with the AK-47.

The man was pacing impatiently in front of the doorway, swinging the rifle back and forth. Karen pressed herself against the house, preparing to slip behind him when a woman's voice from the doorway made the man turn and say something. Two old women in colorful skirts, white long sleeve blouses, and headscarves stepped out of the house. They told the man something, and he yelled at them, shooing them away with his rifle. The old women hurried past Karen into a neighboring house.

When the women went inside, the man entered the house he was guarding. Karen followed him. The floor was dirt, and a cooking pot was on a stand in the corner. A wooden table and stools sat against the opposite wall. A small doorway led to a back room.

Karen went into the back room. Shen lay in her underwear and t-shirt on a dirty Persian rug with a goatskin under her head. She was gagged and her wrists bound above her head. A crude splint was on her right knee. Her flight suit and boots were in a pile next to her.

The man was kneeling over Shen running his hand over her exposed leg and leering at her with a lewd look. Shen's eyes were wide as she squirmed under him. Karen grabbed the AK-47 propped against the wall.

"Hey, asshole," Karen snarled as she swung the rifle by the barrel like a bat. The buttstock hit him in the face, knocking him into the dirt. She didn't know how to use the rifle but struck him again across the face. Satisfied he wasn't getting up, Karen knelt next to Shen and undid her wrists.

"*Zhi, are you ok?*"

"*Creeped out, but fine. I landed on my leg. They straightened it, but it still hurts.*"

"*Depending on what's wrong, it might take a day to heal. But we have to get out of here.*"

Shen pulled the gag from her mouth and undid the splint as Karen grabbed Shen's clothes. Working together, they got Shen into her flight suit and boots, then to her feet.

"*I can't stand on it,*" said Shen.

"*Do you know how to use this?*" said Karen holding up the AK-47.

Shen took it, chambered a round, and flipped the safety off. "*All Chinese pilots are soldiers first.*"

"*Good, because I don't think I could find the safety on an M-16.*"

Karen put Shen's arm over her shoulders and her arm around Shen's waist. It gave her the leverage to almost carry the smaller woman.

As Karen ducked Shen into the front room, a hand grabbed her arm and yanked her back. Karen let go of Shen as the man spun Karen into the wall. She caught herself and pushed herself back into him, knocking him off his feet. Karen landed on top of him. She drove her elbow into his ribs with a satisfying *crack*.

"*Karen, move!*" ordered Shen.

Karen rolled off the man towards the doorway. The *chatter* of the AK-47 was deafening in the tight space. As the man crumbled with a hole in his forehead, Shen leaned against the doorway with the rifle. Karen climbed to her feet using the wall.

"*Wow. I've never killed anyone up close before,*" Karen said, feeling a lump in her throat.

"*Neither have I, but I wasn't going to let him up,*" said Shen.

"*Good call. Let's get out of here.*"

Karen supported Shen as they exited the house after ensuring no one came to investigate the rifle shot.

"*Where do we go?*" said Shen after they turned invisible.

"*Kita says they can't get a helicopter in to pick us up. The nearest friendly line is Turkmenistan to the north.*"

"*That's a long walk.*"

"*It's the only option. We should find a place where you can heal first. That will make getting out easier.*"

Karen guided Shen between the houses out of the village and up the valley deeper into the mountains.

KAREN DUCKED INTO THE SHALLOW CAVE SHE AND Shen had found during the night. It wasn't far from the village, and Karen didn't think the man's killing would go unnoticed or unpunished. She spent the night and morning outside scouting the area and watching for pursuers.

"How are you doing, Zhi?" Shen sat leaning against a rock wall cradling the AK-47.

"It only aches. I can bend it and put some weight on it. I can go if we need to."

"I'd rather wait until you're a hundred percent. It's rocky and treacherous footing. I haven't seen anyone come this way."

"*Karen. Kita.*"

"*Yes, Kita?*"

"*It's still too dangerous to get a rescue helicopter in. How are you girls holding up?*"

"*We found a safe place to hide while Zhi heals.*"

"*Ok, good. When she's healed enough to travel, I want you to go north. It'll be easier for us to get a helicopter in from Russia than from any of the carrier groups. There is a road north of your position. I want you to follow it toward Turkmenistan and find a safe spot for pick up. It might be a couple of days.*"

"*Understood. We'll get as close to the border as we can,*" said Karen.

"*Do your best and try not to get captured. Leaf isn't interested in visiting Iran.*"

Karen wasn't sure what that meant. Kita wouldn't leave them here if they were captured. *Would she? No, it's not like her to leave a friend behind. Leaf wouldn't hesitate to get us. Kita's telling me to make sure I don't make her job harder than it already is.* "No problem. We'll find an extraction point."

"*Good luck.*"

"Something up?" said Shen.

"Kita called. She wants us to follow the road north and find a safe spot for evac. It might be a few days. The Europeans sent fighters to help the AA."

"And we're stuck on the ground."

"We'll get our turn, but we have to get out first."

There was a voice outside the cave. Both pilots turned invisible. Karen pressed against the side of the cave as two male teenagers entered. One held a shepherd's staff, while the other wielded a worn hand pick. They saw the AK-47 and said something excitedly.

"*We can't let them leave,*" said Karen. She turned visible and grabbed a teen from behind. Lifting him, she spiked him into the ground knocking his staff from his hands. Karen jumped on his chest, grabbed him by the face, and slammed the back of his head against the rock until his eyes rolled up in his head.

Shen became visible and whipped her good leg around, knocking the other teen from his feet. She rolled to her knees, placing her leg against the teenager's throat. She struck him twice in the face. The teenager clawed at her leg until he passed out. Shen grabbed the AK-47 and pointed it at a teen.

"No," said Karen. "We might need the bullets."

Shen made a face but lowered the rifle. "Acts of mercy can come back to haunt us."

"I don't know if mine is alive or not, but we might run into real soldiers, and we'll need every bullet we have."

"Thirty rounds of nine-millimeter and eleven rounds of seven-point-six-two isn't much use against real soldiers. Better to use it where it is most effective." Shen nudged a teenager with her foot.

"They're out. We need to leave." Karen turned invisible.

Shen tucked the AK-47 into her flight suit and joined Karen.

Karen adjusted her eyes to thermal viewing so she could see Shen and waved her to follow.

INVISIBLY, KAREN AND SHEN WALKED ALONG THE shoulder of the dirt road heading north. The road was improved with drainage and decent bridges. It was also the main artery for traffic in the region. All types of vehicles—motorized and otherwise—used it. They traveled all morning, and no place looked out of the way enough for a helicopter to land.

Behind them, the blasting of horns caused them to turn. A convoy of military vehicles—a jeep followed by trucks and giant eight-wheeled vehicles with missiles— was coming up the road. The rest of the traffic pulled onto the shoulders giving the military room to pass.

Karen and Shen jumped down the shoulder and watched the convoy go by.

"*You know what those are?*" said Shen.

"*No idea.*"

"*Those are scud missiles capable of carrying nuclear, chemical, or biological payloads. They can't reach the states but can reach Ukraine.*"

"*We should follow them and see where they go. Kita will*

want to know. We can't have that kind of weapon sitting on our doorstep."

Shen sprang up the shoulder onto the road.

"*What are you doing?*" cried Karen.

"I'm *catching a ride.*" Shen jumped ten feet into the air and landed on the back of a scud carrier.

Shit. Karen hopped onto the road and jumped onto the next scud carrier.

Karen made her way up the side of the carrier to the left side cab. She climbed on top and counted five scuds. *Where are we going?* Karen sat down, feeling the cab's top was a safe and out of the way place to hitch a ride.

THE CONVOY PULLED OFF THE ROAD ONTO A GRAVEL and rock-filled creek bed. The jeep and trucks pulled into the center as the scud carriers parked along the creek bed.

Someone from the jeep yelled, and soldiers exited one of the trucks. Karen jumped from the cab and found Shen standing on the back of a scud carrier. She climbed down and joined Karen.

"*What do we do?*" said Shen.

"I'll *contact Kita and tell her where we are. I*—"

Several soldiers and the scud drivers ran by them and deployed the support legs of the carrier. On a scud parked farther down the creek bed, a missile rose into the air.

"*Are they going to launch?*" said Karen.

"*If the missile is up, they can launch at any time,*" said Shen.

"Our side isn't going to get here in time. We need to stop them."

"How do we do that? I'm not an expert shot with this rifle, and there are over thirty of them. We aren't super soldiers."

"We're better. We're Angels. Kita and the others would find a way to stop them; so, will we."

"What do we do? I have no idea how to stop a missile without my fighter."

"Come on." Karen led Shen around the back of the carrier to the missile with large. Fixed fins on the bottom. A cradle held the missile in the upright position. Under the missile was an exhaust nozzle and control fins that came to points under it.

We covered missiles and rockets in training. There must be a weakness we can exploit. *"Look,"* said Karen pointing to the control fins and nozzle. *"Heat and gas come out the end, right? And it has to be just right or—"*

"Boom," said Shen. *"How do we mess it up? We could rip off the nozzle, but that would be noisy."*

"No, even simpler. Help me grab a big rock and stick it in the control fins. That should block the gas and cause heat to build up, keeping it from going anywhere or make it go off course."

The rocky creek bed offered plenty of large rocks. They found one and, with a little effort, balanced it on the control fins.

"Good," said Karen. *"Let's do the rest."*

The operators were in the cabs while the soldiers roved along the perimeter, ignoring the launchers. Karen and Shen moved between carriers, loading rocks into the bottom of the missiles.

A shout to some of the men on patrol came from the jeep. The soldiers ran over and saluted.

"*Get it in. Then we'll deal with them,*" said Karen.

They finished placing the rock, and Shen picked up her rifle as Karen drew her pistol.

"*Do I shoot the one in the jeep?*" said Shen.

"*Yes. He's got to be the leader.*"

Shen raised her rifle and fired, hitting the leader in the chest. Karen aimed at the oncoming soldiers and fired two rounds. She hit one soldier, and the others dove to the ground. The soundwaves from the firearms disrupted the bionanites in their invisibility matrices, causing Karen and Shen to become visible as they moved along the carrier's left side to the cab. Shen opened the door and pulled the operator out of his seat, dumping him onto the ground. She smashed the butt of her rifle into his face.

From the back end of the carrier, two soldiers appeared. Karen fired at the closest one, her round sparking off the side of the carrier. The soldiers brought their rifles up to fire as Karen and Shen backed around the carrier's front. They moved to the right-side cab. The operator opened the cab door with a pistol drawn. Shen slammed her shoulder into the door, pushing the operator back in. She yanked the door open and pulled the operator out by his boot, landing him hard on the rocky ground. With a *crack,* she stomped down on his neck.

A *beep* from the cab caught Karen's attention, and she climbed inside to investigate. An amber light was blinking on a panel, but the label was in Russian.

"Something's happening," said Karen looking down at Shen.

"What?"

"I don't know. It's in Russian."

"Let me see."

Karen hopped out of the cab.

Shen handed her the AK-47 and climbed into the cab. "Just pull the trigger."

Karen backed away, looking at both ends of the carrier.

"It says LAUNCH DATA RECEIVED. They're in the process of firing the missiles," said Shen.

"Can we stop it?"

"I don't see how. All the controls are for the deployment of the missile, and they're locked for launch. The process appears to happen remotely."

"I—"

The two soldiers pursuing them appeared from around the front corner. Karen fired the AK-47 from her hip. The rifle fired faster than she expected and fired four rounds. The first two hit the first soldier in the chest. The climb of the rifle sent the others high. The second soldier raised his AK-47 and fired two rounds into Karen—one round in her stomach, the other in her chest. She fell to the ground out of breath and her chest on fire.

Shen jumped down from the cab and landed in a crouch with her pistol drawn. She fired twice, hitting the soldier both times in the chest, then scrambled to Karen.

"Karen, are you ok?"

Karen pressed her hand against the wound in her stomach. There wasn't much blood. "It stings, but I feel ok." Kita told Karen about getting shot in front of Walter Reed Army Medical Center after getting the

Axiom. She said it hurt, but she was fine in fifteen minutes; her body had pushed the bullets out and repaired the damage. "We should get away from this thing if they're going to launch it."

Shen helped Karen to her feet. It was painful to move, but Karen grit her teeth and pushed herself forward. A loud rumble and a bright light came from the back of the carrier.

"They've ignited the missile," said Shen to Karen.

"We need to get out of here."

They ran from the carrier and climbed the bank of the creek bed. Yellow grass and rock covered the ground from the creek bed to the steep slope of the valley. Scrambling over the boulder field to the top of the ridge, more rumbles and bright lights came from the other missiles.

The first missile roared and vibrated in its launcher before it rose into the air.

"It didn't work," said Karen, feeling her heart sink.

"Maybe the soldiers removed the rock. The others haven't left yet."

Karen grimaced. She wasn't used to failure.

As the missile cleared the launcher, it spun wildly and exploded. A shockwave followed a wall of heat up the side of the valley. The explosion engulfed the carrier and knocked the neighboring carrier and missile on its side. The missile fell out of the launcher and flew forward, skipping along the ground into the third carrier, exploding on impact. The third carrier's missile detonating in a catastrophic ball of fire that engulfed the fourth carrier. The fourth carrier's missile fell out of the launcher and cartwheeled into the fifth carrier, detonating both missiles almost simultaneously.

Karen stood dumbfounded as the heat and shockwaves washed over them. Orange and yellow light illuminated everything as shadows flickered in the firelight.

"Did—did we just do that?" said Karen to Shen.

"Hollywood would be proud. Let's get out of here."

Karen and Shen ran over the crest of the ridge.

"We need to get back to the road," said Karen, "and keep scouting."

"Which way to the road?"

Karen pulled the map from her flight suit's pocket and folded it to what she thought was their location.

A trio of fighters screaming up the valley just above the ground caused both of them to drop to a knee and duck their heads.

"What the hell was that?" said Karen.

From their left, a pair of planes flew across the ridge and made a tight u-turn ending with a roll to show the EUS NAVY on the underside of their wings.

"It's the Fallen Angels!" cried Karen.

"*Adder, Hedgehog—you girls, ok?*" said Harlequin.

"*I took a few bullets, but I'll be fine. What are you girls doing here?*"

"We're *escorting your pick up.*"

The rhythmic *thumping* of helicopter blades came across the far valley as a twin-rotor Chinook rose above the ridgeline and angled toward them. It climbed into the air as it approached.

There's no place to land. Are they going to drop a basket?

The back of the Chinook opened, and five Angels

glided out. They spiraled down and landed next to Karen and Shen.

"Karen, Zhi—are you ok?" said Kita.

Karen grimaced at the pain in her chest. "I'm ok. I need a little time."

"Those holes say otherwise. Kimmy, Leaf, you want to help her?"

"They don't have to. I barely notice the pain."

"There's no need to be a hero—now," said Apocalypse as she placed a hand on Karen's chest as Aspen placed a hand on Karen's stomach.

Apocalypse made a face. "How much does it actually hurt?"

Karen gulped. "A lot. My chest is on fire, and it feels like something is squeezing my heart."

"The bullet nicked your heart, and you have fluid in your chest cavity." Her hand glowed until she pulled it back, holding the bullet. "Hold still." She extended a barb from the heel of her hand and pushed it into Karen's chest.

The pressure in Karen's chest lessened. Apocalypse took her barb out. Karen took a deep breath and let out a long sigh.

"Better?" said Apocalypse.

"Much. Thank you," Karen said sheepishly. She couldn't conceal the embarrassment of needing the Empress to heal her.

Aspen removed her hand, holding the other bullet. "*Nothing serious here. The adrenaline in her system kept her from passing out.*"

Apocalypse hugged her. "Don't worry. We take care

of each other. You no longer need to be tough. Now is the time to heal."

Kita folded her arms. "When I sent you north along the road, I hoped you would find the scuds and report their location. The Fallen Angels came loaded to take them out, but you beat the other girls to it."

"I, ah, we—they were going to launch, and we were afraid our side couldn't get here fast enough," said Karen feeling like Kita was unhappy with her. "We—I did what I thought you expected of Angels. Stop them no matter what."

"It's not just her fault," said Shen. "I helped."

Kita pulled back her hood to expose her face. "That's what I expect of winged Angels. How did you stop them?"

"Rocks," mumbled Karen. The fact they used such a simple and low-tech way of defeating the missiles seemed undignified.

"What?" said Kita.

"We used big rocks to block the exhaust nozzles and overheat them," said Shen. "It was Karen's idea."

"You helped?"

"I was the muscle."

Kita nodded. "I expect Angels to work together, just like you do when you fly. Some Angels are specialists. Others are brutes who can hand out the punishment. I'm impressed. That was a boom worthy of Lizzy."

"Beginners luck," said Sapper with a laugh.

"There was a time when you thought a quarter stick of dynamite was a big boom," said Kita.

"And now you spoil me."

Kita rolled her eyes at her on-and-off girlfriend.

"I'm sorry," said Karen.

"Why?" said Kita. "I mean, you are grounded."

"We are?" cried Karen. "But—"

"It's going to take a few weeks to build fighters that you can fit in."

"Fit in?" said Shen.

Kita reached out and touched Karen and then Shen on the nose. "Boop!"

Karen and Shen screamed. The pain between Karen's shoulder blades sucked the air from her lungs and made her fall to her knees. A spasm caused her to contract into a ball. The pain increased as something tugged on her back. A sharp pain extended from her shoulder blades into the air. A burning sensation followed. When the burning ended, so did the pain. Her back was heavy. She looked up at Kita.

Kita pointed at Karen. "Rise Poison."

"Poison?" she whispered.

Kita pointed at Shen. "Rise Venom." She offered both hands to them.

Poison took Kita's hand and stood up, nearly falling over backward.

"Careful," said Apocalypse as she caught Poison. "You've got ten extra pounds hanging off your back."

"My back?"

Apocalypse pulled a wing around so Poison could see. Her feathers were orange, with a purple top edge and a black bottom edge.

"I—I have wings?" said Poison, unable to breathe.

"I hope you understand why I couldn't give you Hedgehog," said Kita.

"Yes, of course. I know your daughter had it first."

Kita's daughters Spike and Quill had affectionately named themselves after the pointy critters hedgehog and porcupine.

"Yes, that's it," said Kita with a sideways look.

"I'm an Angel?" said Venom. She had bright green feathers with blue insides.

"Yes," said Velositi. "You both have impressed us. Your ingenuity and dedication have been exemplary. I look forward to seeing you around Area Fifty-one."

Above them, the Fallen Angels roared overhead.

"*Congrats, Hedgehog and Adder,*" said Pepper. "*Now get back in the air! Those European bastards need their asses kicked back across the Mediterranean.*"

"They're *going to the Advanced Angel Course,*" said Kita. "They'll *be back in the air soon. Harlequin, you're in command until Karen gets back.*"

"*You got it.*"

"Ok, let's get out of here," said Kita. "Time for your first flight, girls. Spread your wings, flap, and think up. Lizzy, Velositi, you want to help?"

Poison did as instructed. When she lifted off the ground, her heart raced. *I'm flying! I'm flying on my own! I'm a real Angel!*

CHAPTER TWO
ANNA

THE JUMP IN TEMPO WAS LIKE A PHEROMONE FOR THE dance floor. Club goers migrated to it as the nightly ritual of alcohol, smoke, and drugs took hold. The rhythm would call the king to his throne. Anna took a drag off her cigarette while keeping her perfect smile in place. Tonight was her turn, and she could wait a little longer.

The heads of the clubgoers turned toward the door. *Vítek never uses the front door. Who commands such attention?* Anna followed their gaze. She pressed the cigarette tightly between her lips. *AC Metro* was a famous night club that attracted a certain level of patrons and allowed Vítek—the owner—to have his pick of girls. But even it was not worthy of the six gorgeous women making their way in from the door.

They walked with grace, gliding—almost floating— across the room on heels that would make the cutting edge of fashion in nearby Paris and London look decades old. Their dresses clung to their every curve, accentuating and teasing. *Why would Vítek pay girls to come to his club? The club was doing fine financially. Maybe he's paying for a fantasy. Not tonight. I will show him the best things in life money can't buy. But they shouldn't go to waste...*

A surprise, warm feeling filled Anna. She rarely felt emotions. The fantasy of being in the arms of one of those girls excited her. Women were tantalizingly sensual—unlike men, who only had one thing on their mind. The right woman could make her feel alive. Tonight—after Vítek—she would reward herself.

The angelic group moved to the bar. The taller pair made room for the group with a look and a wave of the hand. *Where are you from that you command such authority? Not even Parisians have such an aura of entitlement.* The tall blonde with floor-length hair held in combs acted and moved like she had a royal linage. The tall brunette wearing a silver and red dress commanded the area around her. *A night with them would be superb.*

Anna didn't doubt her ability to seduce. She was a master, no matter the sexual preference. They would test her skills, not of seduction, but planning. She must gain the attention of both Vítek and the girls without arousing the suspicion of the other. Vítek would need to be dealt with out of sight.

The group of exquisite girls pushed another lesser group from a tall table. The little one pulled over a stool and sat. Even though she was tiny, she appeared to have the same status as the rest. They talked and laughed, touching and sharing affection—it was difficult to discern if any were a couple—as they sipped their drinks and swayed with the music. *Who are they? I have never seen a group act in such a manner.*

Movement in the VIP box made Anna shift her eyes. Vítek took his usual seat in the middle of a black couch. His trio of bodyguards stationed behind and around him. Like clockwork, the server appeared with his favorite black label champagne from a private family-owned vineyard in Champagne, France.

Vítek took a glass, sipped, and scanned the dance floor. His eyes lingered on a few girls. He waved at the DJ booth. The music tempo increased. The dancers rose to the challenge and the dance floor pulsed with raw energy.

Anna snubbed out her cigarette and tossed back her drink. Vítek was hungry, and she would feed his carnal appetite. She stole one more glance at her herd of unicorns. *Soon. Work before pleasure.*

As she crossed the club, she let her hips, shoulders, and arms find the rhythm of the dance floor. Others just followed the beat, moving instinctually en masse. They were not dancers. When Anna's heel hit the dance floor, her body came alive, capturing the music and turning it into her partner.

The other patrons seemed to sense she was more than a member of their mob and made space for her. Anna took over the center of the floor, flowing with the music, daring any to join her. Her eyes found her target as she spun. Vítek looked on with interest.

A surprise came through the crowd. Her six beauties gracefully danced their way around Anna. They encircled her, and she found herself facing the tall blonde. Her black and baby pink accented dress emphasized her body and her moves. Her smile reminded Anna of a cheetah daring a gazelle to outrun it.

Anna licked her lips seductively as she accepted the girl's challenge. She had no choice if she was to be with Vítek tonight. Anna twisted, moving her arms and feet seductively with the music inviting the other girl to follow with her eyes.

The other girl matched her—perfectly. When Anna thought she was done, the other girl added her own additions—moves Anna had never seen before. She refused to be upstaged. Dipping, swiveling, and spinning, Anna repeated the other girl's moves back to her and adding her own while sliding across the floor like on a cloud.

The sultry look Anna received from the other girl made her head swim. The girl repeated the entire display with grace, copying Anna's movements flawlessly, ending in a spin that put her behind Anna. The air escaped Anna's lungs when she felt the girl press against her and the girl's hands on her hips. Suddenly, they were moving together as one. The girl's warm breath on her shoulder made all her hairs stand up. They danced together for what seemed like forever, Anna lost in the other girl's touch and movement. Anna caught herself. She was supposed to be doing the seducing here.

Before Anna could regain control of the pair, the tall brunette in the silver and red dress moved in and claimed the other girl. Anna was left struggling to maintain control of the situation and why she was there. The group of girls decamped from the dance floor back to their table. Anna spun and regained control of herself and the dance floor. She moved around, making sure she was the main attraction.

The tempo of the music changed, signaling it was time for a pairs dance. Glancing at the girls' table, Anna hoped to attract attention, but they ignored her, busy talking and petting each other. Not showing her disappointment, Anna slipped from the dance floor toward the bar.

Space opened for her.

"Hello, Miss Zelda," said the bartender.

For the last four months, Anna spent every night at *AC Metro*. "Roland, a cosmo, please." She knew hundreds of drinks and their contents and never ordered the same spirit in a row. As she kept a happy face on for the bartender, the back of her mind was in turmoil, wondering if she had done enough to secure her place on Vítek's couch tonight.

Turning to glance at her table of girls, her view was blocked by a large man wearing a cheap suit trying to disguise the gun under his jacket.

"Miss, Mister Vítek would like a word," he said in a deadpan voice.

Anna smiled. "Of course. I would love to."

Anna followed the bodyguard through the patrons to a darkened staircase and up to Vítek's VIP area. Vítek didn't bother to stand to greet her. *If I was that fat, I wouldn't want to have to stand very often either*.

"Aren't you a curious thing, my dear," said Vítek. "You've graced my club for months, and only tonight have you shown how delectable you are. I feared you a wallflower, but you move like a goddess."

Anna smiled and bowed lowly. "You humble me,

Lord Vítek. I have been enjoying your wonderful club for all this time and felt I should repay your hospitality."

"It was a beautiful display. I've never witnessed anything like it. Have a seat."

Anna did as instructed, taking a seat on the couch, crossing her legs, and pushing out her chest. She knew what Vítek liked. The fact that his were bigger than hers didn't seem to cross his mind.

Vítek stretched out a chubby hand and stroked Anna's short blonde hair. "Nice and soft. Care for a drink?" He motioned toward the champagne.

"I would love some."

Vítek motioned to the waiting server. "I have this imported from France. It's the only place you can get it."

Anna's smile didn't waver. *All champagne comes from France, idiot. It's the only place you can get it.* She took the flute by the stem and took a sip. She suppressed a cough from the sweetness. *It tastes like American soda.* "It's wonderful."

"Drink your fill." Vítek stretched his arm across the back of the couch around Anna.

She took the signal and cuddled up next to him. Keeping her smile firmly in place, she fought the wave of nausea from the cheap cologne that smelled like a men's room. She settled her stomach by admiring her group of girls. They were laughing and smiling about something as they sipped their drinks. Anna drank more champagne and let her hand wander around Vítek's chest and gut, unbuttoning his jacket in the process.

Vítek lowered his arm around her, running his hand down her exposed back and onto her butt. He gave her a hard squeeze. Anna leaned into him and purred in his ear. "You have nice strong arms. It feels good to be protected. It makes me horny."

"I can keep you safe. If you can do things for me," he said in a low, lustful growl.

Anna ran her hand down his front. She couldn't reach around his gut to get between his legs to fondle him. *Not that I mind. I wonder how long it's been since he's seen it.* "I think I can think of a few things." She leaned in and kissed his bearded neck, leaving a trail to his ear. With her tongue, she played with his lobe and nibbled on the edge. The hair on his neck stood up. *I bet you've never had anyone like me...*

Vítek let out a light groan. "You are a treasure."

"That's what I can do to your ear. Imagine what I can do to other things. Over and over..."

"Lots of girls promise..."

"I can deliver. You just have to do one thing for me."

Vítek turned and looked at Anna. "And what is that?"

"Make me the only one, and I will do whatever you want whenever you want. My skills will be yours."

"Talk is cheap."

"Then let me show you. I will show you such pleasure you'll want no others." Anna kissed the tip of his cheek and traced it with her tongue. "You saw what I can do on the dance floor. Imagine what I can do on top of you."

Vítek reached across and pulled the sparkling strap off Anna's shoulder and down her arm, exposing her breast. He fondled it roughly and squeezed her painfully. He finished by tweaking her nipple so hard it made her gasp in pain. "You have nice, round perky boobs. I am also very good and know what women want. Perhaps we can come to an arrangement. You make me a happy man, and I can make sure you are well taken care of. But first, your *mouth* must prove it's as good as you say."

Anna batted her lashes as she fixed her strap. "Of course. But, not here. I am not a common whore. I am a lady, and I will be treated like it." In her many visits, Anna explored the club learning the layout. Vítek kept an office with a bed in the back when he wanted more than a blow job in full view of the club.

Vítek smiled. "I have a place in the back. I hope you are prepared."

"I'm as smooth as silk."

Vítek pushed Anna to her feet and, with several grunts, stood. He fixed his coat and pushed Anna around the couch, through a black curtain, into a narrow hallway. A bodyguard led them to an intersection. They took a right and stopped in front of a door. The bodyguard opened it, and Vítek pushed Anna inside.

The bed was to the right, a door to a bathroom next to it. Under a window was a desk with a laptop. Two bodyguards remained by the door while a third followed them in. *So much for just walking out...* Vítek took off his jacket and draped it over a chair. He faced Anna and crossed his arms. He gave Anna a look that she could start anytime.

"I need to freshen up first," said Anna, motioning to the bathroom.

Vítek waved her away.

Anna turned on the light and closed the door. She pulled the straps of her dress down exposing her left side, revealing a plastic film stuck to her ribcage. After fixing her dress, Anna pressed her lips to one side of the plastic, covering them in a protective coating. She removed a plastic cling on the other side and covered her lips in a potent poison. Tossing the plastic into the toilet, Anna flushed and ran the sink. She checked herself in the mirror and hiked her dress up a bit. Satisfied, she opened the door.

Vítek stood where she had left him, but he had a scowl on his face. Anna smiled seductively as she took a few steps toward him, slipping the straps of her dress off her shoulders, and gave him a flirty look. "You look like you need to relax. Sit."

"Hurry up and get naked," huffed Vítek.

Anna didn't flinch. *What a pig. He cannot even appreciate the art of seduction.* "Don't worry, I will...like I said, I'm not a common whore. I can bring you pleasure in ways other girls can't. Sit, watch, experience..."

The bed let out a groan as he sat on the corner. *What an idiot. How am I supposed to do anything with him sitting like that?* Anna didn't let Vítek's stupidity get to her. She didn't need both sides to do what she needed.

Anna took small, measured steps as she approached him, moving her body to a silent rhythm, slowly working her dress down. Normally, she would just bend down in front of her object of seduction to show off her breasts, but with Vítek's girth, she ended up lying on top of him. Improvising, Anna undid several buttons of his shirt with her tongue. She rolled over and pushed her butt into his lap, doing her best to work underneath his gut and between his legs.

"Silly girl, what are you doing?" demanded Vítek.

Why do I even try? You uncouth pig. You do not want a girl. You want a milking machine. Anna spun from between his legs to his right side. She took his hand and pressed herself against his arm. Rubbing her breasts against him, she kissed his neck, hitting the spots she had earlier. Vítek responded the same way. She kissed his cheek, turned his head toward her, and kissed his lips.

Anna had been kissed by dogs with more skill. Vítek put out his lips like he was whistling. Anna used a series of kisses and tongue movements to separate his lips and draw his tongue out. She stroked his with hers, feeling him quiver under her. When she was sure he wouldn't resist, she coaxed his tongue into her mouth, sucking on it gently—slowly moving up and down, spreading her saliva activated poison. Anna sucked all the way to his tip before letting go and rolling away from him.

"Where—" Vítek broke into a coughing fit. His eyes bulged as the poison attacked his central nervous system. He spit foam down his chest as he rolled off the bed.

"What did you do?" yelled the bodyguard.

"Nothing!" cried Anna, acting scared and upset.

The bodyguard leaned down to check on Vítek.

Anna spun, bringing the back of her heel down on his neck. The bodyguard slumped forward onto the dirty shag carpet. Anna tapped the heel of her shoe twice on the carpet, ejecting a blade. Taking the knife, she slashed the bodyguard's throat.

"Everything ok in there?" said another bodyguard as he knocked on the door.

"Everything's fine," cried Anna, "just a little excited." She went to the laptop. Reaching up her dress, she pulled a micro-USB drive taped to her inner thigh. After plugging in the drive, she turned the laptop on. The drive booted to a special program. Anna selected the correct settings and hit OK. The program scanned the laptop and wormed its way through Vítek's private network, downloading his arms shipments' records. When the program finished, she tucked the drive into the lining of her dress and grabbed the blade, hiding it in her hand.

Slowly, she opened the door and stuck her head out.

"What is the problem?" said the bodyguard to the left of the door.

"Nothing," said Anna as she stepped into the hallway, closing the door. "I'm finished."

"Where's the boss?"

"Dying a pig's death." Anna slammed her heel on the instep of the bodyguard on the left. With her right hand, she thrust her hidden blade into his throat. Spinning back to the left, Anna raised her leg over the crippled bodyguard. Slamming her legs shut around his neck, she flexed and twisted, popping his skull from his spine. Anna let him fall to the ground, letting his vacant eyes stare up at her as she fixed her dress and hair.

After a breath to center herself, Anna retraced her steps back to the VIP box. The dance floor was still full, but the table full of girls was not. Frantically she searched, but they were gone. *Bathroom?* It wasn't big enough for six. Anna hurried down the hidden stairs back to the main floor of the club.

Pushing her way through the patrons, she waved to a bouncer standing by the door.

"Roman, did you see where that group of girls went?" There was no question on which group of girls she was referring.

"When they left the club, they went south."

South? There's nothing south, except factories. "Did they say why they were going that way?"

"They didn't say a word. That was the direction they went. I thought they were meeting a car."

"Thank you, Roman." Anna pushed through the door of the club into the cool night air. Steam rose from manholes and lingered, shrouding the Prague night air.

She hurried south. The factory district wasn't safe at night. *Why would they go that way? All the clubs are to the north. Maybe someone told them there was a party in an old factory. If that was true, Roman would have said something.*

Anna followed the street around a shallow curve. In the fog, she saw a figure with long hair that went down to her ankles disappear between buildings.

"Hey!" cried Anna. "Wait! It's me, from the dance floor." She hurried down the street and found the narrow alleyway.

Prague was an ancient city with narrow streets and even narrower alleys left over from medieval times. Anna hurried up the dark alley. A figure stood in the darkness. It wore a witch's hat. *Is someone playing a joke? Halloween was last month. Maybe there is a party I don't know about.* "Hello? Did you see a group of girls go this way? I think they were headed to a party."

The tips of the girl's fingers glowed as she chanted, "Onca uncia pardus!"

The alleyway was bathed in light, revealing the girl. She was one of the girls Anna was trying to find, but she now wore a full-length skirt with two slits up the front to her belt full of vials, a black lace top with a black bra underneath. Behind her was a pair of towering orange, purple, and black wings.

What kind of joke is this? Is that what these girls are? Playing pretend? Anna knew of the Angels like everyone. She knew their wing colors, but not their faces.

"This is not a funny joke," snarled Anna, letting frustration show that her plan for the night was ruined.

The Angel moved her glowing fingers in a pattern. "Onca uncia pardus!" She grew taller and bigger, transforming into a giant rock golem. It thumped its chest several times and roared.

Anna jumped back, turned, took two steps, and ran into someone. She looked up into the eyes of a Chinese woman. She had been with the group, too.

"Where you going in such a hurry?" said the woman. Something on her back moved.

Wings. More wings.

"There's nothing to be scared of." The Chinese woman wore a sleeveless denim vest with fur-lined armholes. Hundreds of black widow spiders grew from her exposed skin.

Anna shrieked. "This isn't funny."

"This is not a joke," said the Angel.

The golem walked up behind Anna with heavy footfalls and picked her up around the waist.

"Let go of me!" Anna screamed.

Another Angel dropped in from above and landed between the others. "Ok, I think that's enough. She's no good to Kita scared to death."

Anna recognized the Angel called Sapper, with red and white wings. She had been with the others in the club. "You're real Angels?" whispered Anna.

"What? Speak up," said Sapper. "Just kidding. The witch and arachnid queen didn't give it away? Come on. Someone wants to speak with you."

The golem put Anna down and transformed back into an Angel. The Angels lifted into the air.

"Where are you going?" said Anna.

"You think I'm walking?" said Sapper. "Kita's that way." She pointed down the alley. "We'll see you there." The three Angels flew down the alley and disappeared in the fog.

Anna wasn't happy. She didn't like games, and it felt like they were making fun of her. *Why me? What did I do?* She now had to endure this humiliation on top of having her night ruined. It was almost enough to bring tears. *If I could cry. But I'm not playing their game.*

Anna hurried back out of the alley but didn't go back to the club. She turned toward the factories in hopes of finding someone to take her frustration out on.

She found a hole cut in a fence that surrounded a factory. Vagrants and the homeless liked this area because of the warm ducts and easy hiding spots. She stepped through the hole with practiced ease, not catching her dress on the protruding wires. Swiftly covering the distance between the fence and the building, she searched for anyone.

Anna kept moving, even after she discovered that someone was following her. The way they hid in the shadows and moved without a sound said they were professional. Only a puff of breath had given them away. She stopped at a pair of rusty barrels with handled lids shrouded in wispy fog. She placed her hand on a lid as she looked behind them.

Spinning, Anna brought the lid up to block a sword strike. She tried to punch her shadowy attacker, but a swift kick put her on the ground. She rolled, bringing the lid up like a shield as a series of strikes bounced off. Anna whipped her legs around, trying to knock her attacker down, but the attacker jumped into a corkscrew roll and landed on her other side. Anna rolled to her right; a blade hit the ground where she had sat. Anna twisted up to her feet, holding the lid out to protect herself as she searched for her assailant.

The attack came from her left, but instead of blocking the blow, the top of the lid came off. A split second later, the bottom was gone. *Nothing is that sharp!* Anna's toe hit a pipe. Using the sole of her shoe and toe, she tossed it up to her hand. She turned, searching.

She spun, blocking the attack from behind with what was left of her shield. With her pipe, she attacked. Her attacker blocked her strikes with the pipe with ease. A gust of wind blew the steam from her attacker. She was the short girl from the group, but she wore a white sneak suit. Her wings were white with golden tips.

"Leave me alone," screamed Anna. "I've done nothing to you. Why are you tormenting me?"

"Just a little hazing is all," said a pleasant voice.

Anna turned to watch the two tall girls from the club appear from thin air. Their wings matched their dresses. But they weren't wearing dresses now. The tall one with black and pink wings pulled back her hood.

"You," Anna whispered, looking into the tall girl's eyes.

The black and pink Angel stepped up to Anna, took Anna's face in her hands, and kissed her. Not even

Anna's trainers could kiss so well. She felt like a student again as their lips and tongues danced.

"Ok, break it up," said a sweet but artificial voice.

Anna looked over the Angel's shoulder to find a robot with wings looking down on her. "My girlfriend," the robot asserted.

"I might have to veto this one if this keeps up," said the Angel with red and silver.

"I think it's a sociopath thing," said the witch, landing with Sapper and the arachnid queen.

The tall Angel looked into Anna's eyes. "Hi. I'm Kita. I think I owed you that."

"Good. Mine," said the red and silver Angel as she grabbed Kita by the arm and pulled her away.

Kita laughed. "Just having fun. I think it's cute both of you feel threatened."

"What do you want with me?" said Anna.

Kita cocked her head. "I want my data." She held out a hand.

"Your data?"

"I sent you on that mission, as well as the last six. You haven't wondered why you've gone from seducing low-level diplomats and military personnel to assassinations, seek and destroy, and asset recovery?"

"I thought the CIA was doing what the Kremlin would not—put my training to use."

"I was a little disappointed when I discovered the Kremlin's Cardinal School graduates were being wasted finding out the next unit deployment timetables. But you are the best, and I want the best."

"You already have me."

Kita's smile twisted. "You've had your life stolen to

be this world's greatest assassin. I reward devotion, service, and loyalty. It's time you got your life back." She reached out and touched Anna on the nose. "Boop!"

Anna gasped, followed by a scream. The muscles in her upper back contracted painfully, twisting her, making her fall to her hands and knees. A burning sensation between her shoulder blades exploded outward. It felt like she was boiling. A searing pain climbed up her back. Suddenly there was weight, and the pain stopped.

"Rise, Cardinal," said Kita offering her hand.

"What?" said Cardinal.

"Come," said Kita. "The night's still young. We still have plenty of time to do what your heart desires."

CHAPTER THREE
NICOLE

THUD! NEMESIS GRIMACED AT THE IMPACT OF A BULLET and rolled out of the air to her right, landing hard on the dirt road's shoulder. She slid into the tall green grass and turned invisible while drawing her sniper rifle.

"Damage?" she asked the VI that controlled her suit. The layered graphene weave was impenetrable, but it didn't stop energy from transferring.

"Suit integrity is one hundred percent. Contusion detected on your left side between ribs four and six. Non-life threatening."

It still hurts. Damn. Nemesis crawled up the gravel shoulder to the edge of the road. She scanned the neighboring field looking for the shooter. An elderly man and a young boy ran toward her. The man held a Soviet World War II Mosin-Nagant rifle. *Where did you get an antique like that? Better question, where did you find ammunition for it?*

As they approached her, the VI translated Kashmiri into English.

"The bird was huge," said the boy. "I bet it will feed us for a week."

"Calm, Amit. We haven't caught it yet," said the old man.

Just because I have wings, I look like a bird?

The pair clambered up the shoulder on the far side of the road. Amit jumped into the grass near Nemesis and searched the area.

"Where did it go?" he cried.

"A bird that size would be strong. It might have walked some distance." The old man made his way down the slope to join the boy. "We will find it."

Nemesis glided onto the road. She balanced the butt of her rifle on her hip and made herself visible. "Or the bird has found you," the VI translated for her.

The boy cried in alarm, and the old man moved his rifle toward her.

"Ah, ah," said Nemesis, snapping her rifle out like a pistol. With her strength, the rifle didn't waver from the old man's chest. "Why are you shooting me?"

"What are you?" said Amit.

"News must move slowly out here. I am an Angel and here to assist you. The war isn't your fault, and you shouldn't pay the price." Nemesis pulled her sniper hood off, stuck it in a loop on her shoulder, and slicked back her flyaways into her low dark ponytail.

Amit slumped. "You're not a giant bird." Nemesis' hood continued to translate for the group.

"Do not worry, Amit. We will find food," said the old man as he lowered his rifle.

"You have no food?" said Nemesis. "I saw goats and crops on my way here."

"The army protects that area," said the old man. "Our village is ruled by a warlord from Leh. They take all the food and women and make the men fight for them."

"And the army does nothing?"

"The Indian army fled, leaving the area lawless. When the new soldiers arrived, they fought a battle with the warlord. The army took back some villages but refused to leave the safety of the cities. They don't come out here and have abandoned us to our fate."

"The army should put a stop to this. That is what they are for."

The old man gave her an unsure look.

"Listen," said Nemesis, "I know people who can help. I will get you food and protection. A warlord should not be allowed to run free in the Empire."

"What is an empire?" said Amit.

"For the last three years, the Republic of India has been a territory of the Empire of the United States. I thought Kimmy would have announced that to every corner of the world. Where is your village?"

"Follow the road east for two miles," said the old man.

"What's your name?"

"Raj. I am the elder for the village of Shuhul."

"I will go to the army and see what the problem is and bring food and protection to you in a few days."

Raj bowed deeply. "Thank you...Angel."

"Call me Nemesis. I'll be back soon." She floated above them, spread her wings, and flew to the southwest.

NEMESIS LANDED TO ONE SIDE OF A LONG LINE OF people at a military checkpoint. A cry of panic erupted around her as the Kashmiris fled in all directions.

"Wait!" Nemesis cried, "I mean you no harm." A rock hit her in the back. She spun around. "Hey! Don't do that."

Men holding large stones came at her from three sides.

Uh-oh. I really wish Kimmy had gotten that Angel PSA out. Nemesis held up her hands. "I'm not here to hurt you. I'm looking for the army."

"Stop! Get back!" yelled another voice. It didn't sound Kashmiri.

Two Chinese soldiers in full battle kit with AK-47s pointed at the people approached her. *Why are Chinese troops in India?*

"Your Highness, come with us," said a soldier with EUS Army sergeant stripes on his helmet.

Nemesis wasn't going to argue over the wrong honorific and glided between the soldiers. More soldiers joined them.

"Come with us, Your Highness," said the sergeant.

"Sure." Nemesis stayed in the center of her escort as they pushed people out of the way, moving toward two jeeps and a truck that blocked the road. Soldiers in the jeeps and truck pointed machine guns at the people. A man with an EUS Army second lieutenant tab got out of the jeep and gave her an American-style salute. She returned it without thinking.

"Are you ok, Your Highness?" said the lieutenant. His nametag said, Lui.

"Yes, I'm fine, Lieutenant. I didn't expect such a

hostile response to my presence. Why isn't the region aware of us?"

"Kashmir is very superstitious," said Lui with disdain.

Nemesis wasn't sure if the man's contempt was for the Kashmiri in general or for them being superstitious. As far as she knew, the Chinese were just as bad.

"Hey, LT, I'll take her," said a tall, broad-chested African-American sergeant coming up with a squad of Chinese soldiers. He wore an EUS Army Combat Uniform with a patch on the shoulder Nemesis didn't recognize. "Nemesis, right? I know you're a colonel in the Air Force. I apologize for not knowing your name. I'm Sergeant First Class Duncan." Lui walked down the road a few yards to his men, seeming fine with letting the sergeant handle her.

"I wouldn't expect you to know my name, Sergeant. Nemesis is fine. I need to talk to the commander of the area."

"That would be Lieutenant Colonel Zhao. He commands the Fifth of the Seven-Oh-First Infantry Regiment stationed here in Dras."

Nemesis never heard of an infantry regiment with such a high number. *I guess Kimmy has lots of regiments now.* "Can you give me directions to the HQ?"

"I'll take you there. It'll keep the locals off you. Hey, LT, I'm taking the command jeep. Colonel Nemesis needs to go to HQ. I'll hand in our report while I'm there."

"Very well, Sergeant," Lui said with a wave of the hand.

Nemesis chuckled to herself. She remembered being

a young lieutenant and having a senior sergeant lead her by the nose. Duncan led Nemesis around the truck to a pair of parked jeeps.

"Sorry, Ma'am, these Chinese jeeps aren't made for wings...or anybody else." Duncan was eight inches taller than Nemesis.

"It's ok. I'll sit in the back." She ended up sitting on the spare tire hanging off the back, putting her feet on the back seats.

Duncan cranked the ignition, stomped on the gas, and turned onto the road. The edge of the city was a few hundred yards away.

"So what brings you here, ma'am? We didn't get any notices you'd be coming."

He wants to know why I'm out here unescorted and ended up in his lap. "I originally came from Russia, through Afghanistan. I'm on a humanitarian mission to help people impacted by the war. I worked with the Russians until Imperial agencies moved in and took over. I was told India has problems, and I thought I might help."

"That's an understatement."

"I know India fell into unrest, but why are the Chinese here?"

"The Indian Army deserted. The Empress ordered the Chinese in to restore order. They're still working on it." Duncan wove his way through the streets, honking his horn while shouting at people and animals to get out of the way.

"What's wrong with the Chinese?"

"Nothing. They're disciplined, loyal, and follow orders—they just don't take initiative. Someone always has to tell them to do things. ICOM just doesn't have enough units to pacify one-point-three billion people. Some areas, like Kashmir, have been left lawless until India proper is secure."

That explains that. Still, they can take care of one more village. It's not that far.

Duncan pulled up to a rod-iron gate with two soldiers standing guard. A soldier approached. "Sorry, I don't have a plaque for you, Nemesis. They're not going to know who you are."

Nemesis hadn't been a full bird colonel long and wasn't used to all the perks that came with it—including people saluting her vehicle when the proper plaque was mounted. She had jumped straight to Angel perks instead.

"Hey, guys," said Duncan. "I've got Colonel Nemesis to see Colonel Zhao. She's a VIP from the Empress. Rabbit."

Rabbit?

"Rat," said the soldier. "Yes, Sergeant. Open the gate," he yelled at the other soldier.

Ah, sign and countersign. I guess the Chinese are that disciplined.

Duncan pulled into the dusty courtyard and parked the jeep next to several others. He hopped out, and Nemesis floated to the ground. She followed him past a pair of large rocks painted infantry blue with crossed rifles and 5th of the 701st above them. Duncan opened a metal gate and waved Nemesis inside.

Several Chinese soldiers sat at desks working on laptops. Nemesis guessed they managed the regiment's paperwork.

"Hey, Sergeant Walter, you got anything to drink in

this place? We got a VIP," called Duncan across the room to an office. "Oh yeah, Regiment, ATTENTION!"

The Chinese soldiers jumped to their feet as a middle-aged man carrying a bottle of water took a form of attention reserved for career soldiers who were high enough rank and too old for that shit.

"At ease," said Nemesis politely.

The older sergeant crossed the room and offered Nemesis the water. "Ah...Angel?"

"Call me Nemesis, Sergeant. Thank you."

"I'll let the colonels know you're here." He disappeared out a doorway. He returned with a short Chinese man with flinty eyes and a tall, lanky American with a weather-beaten face. They both had silver oak leaves on their collars.

"Colonel Adrestia. Lieutenant Colonel Tuff, and this is Lieutenant Colonel Zhao, commander of the Fifth of the Seven-Oh-First. Excuse us for being caught flat-footed. No one told us you were coming."

Fitting name. "Don't worry about it. I think only the Vicereine knows where I am." The mention of Kita's title made both men flinch. "I'm traveling the world helping those who need it. I've been in Russia, and I'm on my way to India in hopes that I can ease tensions. Earlier today, I came across some villagers from Shuhul. They shot me thinking I was some kind of bird." Tuff's jaw tightened. Nemesis could imagine the shit show he would catch if she'd been hurt. "I was able to get their story. They are starving and being terrorized by a warlord. I told them they are part of the Empire and are entitled to protection and food. I want to know why they're not getting it."

Tuff looked at Zhao. "Let's talk in your office. Follow us, Colonel."

Zhao led them down the hallway into an office at the end. Two Army issue metal desks with laptops and paperwork faced opposite walls. A map of the region hanging on the wall was marked with symbols.

Zhao went to the map, tracing his finger around the Dras area.

"I understand why the Chinese are here, but what are you doing here, Colonel?" Nemesis asked Tuff.

"Me and my men are liaisons and trainers for the regiment. The Fifth of the Seven-Oh-First hasn't been officially trained by the EUS Army. India's situation got so bad, so fast, DoD sent untrained Chinese units in to support the Regular Army units. We were supposed to rotate stateside last year for training, but the situation here hasn't allowed it. Until then, we show them how the Army does things."

"I've heard they're good."

"Yeah, we just have a different way of doing things. We're making it work."

"It's too far," announced Zhao.

"What is?" said Nemesis.

"Shuhul village. It's outside the security area."

Nemesis went to the map. Zhao had his finger next to the village name. A red line went between Dras and Shuhul.

"It's not that far beyond, just a few miles," said Nemesis.

"Orders from ICOM are to hold here," said Zhao.

"Shuhul is on the main road. It's minutes away by truck. It doesn't require much. A squad at the most."

"It would require reworking the entire security plan ICOM has approved."

Nemesis growled. "Listen, security is my specialty. One squad would be more than enough. We can take an initial delivery of food, and Supply can figure out how much they need after that."

Zhao frowned. "All changes must go through ICOM."

"You want me to go over your head? Fine. I'll call the Vicereine. I'm sure she'll be thrilled to come deal with some light colonel who can't secure a village."

Zhao pressed his lips together tightly.

"Ok, no need to get heated," said Tuff. "We can figure this out. Z, we can push the boundary out a few miles. We just move the outer patrol point to Shuhul. The squad that anchors the line currently at patrol point Delta can be moved to secure Shuhul and set up a patrol point there. It'll add a few minutes to the patrols and response times, but we can absorb it. We'll send the change to ICOM. In the meantime, we can go ahead and get started."

"If ICOM has a problem, they can talk to me," said Nemesis. Tuff looked relieved by her pronouncement. *I have no problem taking the heat for this. Kita and Kimmy wouldn't deny me.*

"How about it, Z?" said Tuff.

Zhao folded his arms and frowned. "This is what you call taking the initiative?"

"Yep. Sometimes as a commander, you have to change the game plan to fit the details on the ground. No one knows the ground better than us."

"Yes," said Zhao. "The squad and food will move out tomorrow. Is that satisfactory, Colonel Adrestia?"

"That works. I will accompany them to make sure the food and security get to the right people."

NEMESIS SAT ON THE BACK OF THE LEAD JEEP AS THEY made the short trip across the valley to Shuhul. Duncan sat next to her, and Lui sat in the passenger's seat. The area around the village was beautiful. High mountains framed a green valley dotted with forest and terraced fields. A wide glacier-fed stream ran next to the village.

The driver slowed as they entered a mix of square stone structures, yurts, and peaked roof corrugated metal buildings. An old woman sat on a stool working a crude spinning wheel at the first structure. She jumped up quick as a cat and ran into the village ahead of the convoy, yelling, "Soldiers!"

Duncan and Nemesis exchanged a look. "Is that a good sign?" said Nemesis.

"No idea. Hey, LT, we might get a hot welcome. Best to keep the soldiers in the trucks until we get a chance to work it out with the elders."

Lui picked up the radio hand mic and gave orders to the trucks. No one came out to greet them as the jeep and three trucks drove through the village—the convoy parked in the village center. Nemesis and Duncan dismounted, keeping their weapons on their backs. Nemesis didn't wear her hood, so she didn't scare the locals.

"Hello!" yelled Nemesis. "Raj? I'm looking for Elder

Raj! I spoke to him yesterday." Her VI's volume was only so loud. She doubted anyone heard her.

Lui stood up in the jeep and, using a bullhorn, repeated Nemesis' plea in broken Kashmiri.

"We might have to search the place," said Duncan. "Raj could be out hunting, and the rest are scared."

That sounds logical. Nemesis looked up at Lui. "Lieutenant, have the men search the village. Don't harm the locals. We're looking for—"

Three *whooshes* were followed by the trucks exploding.

"RPG," yelled Duncan as he and Nemesis dove to the ground. From doorways around the village, men with AK-47s fired on the convoy. Lui was cut down as the driver dove from the jeep and crawled to join them.

Duncan unslung his rifle and returned fire while yelling instructions to the driver. Nemesis pushed herself to a kneeling position and flipped the safety on her rifle. She spread her wings to give the soldiers cover as she engaged targets.

"Tight three-sixty on the jeep," yelled Duncan as he fired with one hand and motioned to the soldier where to go. "Private Chen, take the center. Colonel, I'll take the right. You get the left."

Nemesis scooted toward the jeep, firing at targets as they appeared. "How many bogies you got?"

"I'm trying to keep four doorways suppressed," said Duncan.

"Two," said Chen.

Nemesis wished for her hood and the extra sensory data it provided. "I've got eight—five firing from doorways and three moving up. No sign of the RPGs." A round thumped against her. *I bet I'm going to have lots of bruises later.*

A *whoosh* came from the other side of the jeep.

"Down!" screamed Nemesis as she threw herself to the ground.

The jeep exploded in a fireball, flipping into the air. Nemesis rolled away as the jeep landed between her and the others.

"Sergeant! Status?" yelled Nemesis as she got to her knees and shot an attacker in the head. He looked like a regular Kashmiri man, probably not older than twenty. The only difference between him and the men from yesterday was that he had an AK-47.

"The jeep landed on Chen. I took something in my back, but I'm still in."

The attackers pushed their attack, and the volume of fire increased.

"Col—"

Shit. "Duncan!" *Nothing. I have to get out of here and regroup.* She dropped two more attackers. Another *whoosh* came from behind her. Flapping her wings hard, she flew upward. The RPG rocket struck her in the leg, sending her tumbling back to the ground.

Nemesis's ears rang as she lay in the dirt. Her rifle was gone. Bullets struck her and the ground. She fought through the disorientation and pushed herself to her knees. *I'm not going down like this.* The first attacker reached her and smashed his rifle into her back. Nemesis lunged, grabbing him by the foot and yanking him off his feet. With both hands, she slammed her fists on his chest with a satisfying *crack*.

More bullets struck her, but her adrenaline masked

the pain. Nemesis got to her feet as an attacker ran up and shot her twice in the chest. She recoiled as three more rounds struck her across the back. She spun, smacking the first attacker with her wing. Nemesis charged the other attacker. He raised his rifle and fired. Two rounds hit Nemesis in the forehead, and the world went black.

NEMESIS GROANED AS THE GROGGY HAZE LIFTED. Weight pulled at her wrists and wings. Rough wood pressed against her skin. *Wh...what...*Pain radiated from her butt and vagina. She moved her leg, and something dry and crusty pulled at her skin down her legs. *NO, NO, NO...*

She smashed her cheek against the unfinished wood as tears filled her eyes. *Why? What did I do?* She wept as dark clouds of fear, anguish, and embarrassment swept through her mind like a savage storm. A pit of despair opened in her stomach, threatening to swallow her whole as the feeling of being so brutally violated crawled over her.

Loneliness crushed her. Nemesis had never cried for so long or hard in her life. *I want to die. If only to escape. No one can help me. I'm alone. And they're going to do it again.* She cried even harder. Waking up to such a violation was horrible enough. Doing it conscious? *I can't do it.*

Nemesis cried until she hyperventilated, choked, then cried some more. No amount of tears washed away the feelings that crawled over her like insects and coated her insides with black tar. The emotions, the thought of being violated, the isolation, made her hate herself.

She thrashed her arms, wings, and legs, trying to break free in a desperate rage, but discovered them chained firmly to the floor. She couldn't generate the strength to break free. She gave up after rubbing the skin under the chains so raw she bled.

I have no way out. They're going to keep doing this to me until I die. I can't even kill myself. What do I do?

Nemesis stared at the table. *I trusted Raj. He needed help. How could he do this? To Duncan, Lui, and those soldiers? We were going to help him. Did I trust too easily? Did my desire to help blind me to the danger? Am I wrong about the world? Is the world like Kita says it is? Is it just people doing what has to be done to survive? Is it really them or me, and there is no good or evil? Is evil like she said, in the eye of the beholder? If Kita is right, then what is right and wrong? She said what is right is what helps the right people. Who are the right people? Kita says she puts herself first, then those she cares about and are loyal to her...It works for her.*

Look how much she's done. No one would dare rape her. Is that my problem—I put others before me? Does it make me weak? Nemesis choked up as fresh tears fell. *I don't want to be raped again. I don't want anyone to ever touch me again. From now on, I'm first. I take care of myself before anyone else. Getting raped is what it took for me to see the truth. Kita's going to laugh at me—but she's also the only one who can help me. Can I take being told, 'I told you so?' I can take it...once. Then never again. No one will ever touch me again. Starting with these bastards.*

"Kita?" her voice came out a whimper over the biological communication suite each Angel had in her head. It allowed them to communicate silently and over long distances. Kita could reach anywhere in the world.

"*Nicole!*" Kita said in a happy tone. "*I didn't expect to hear from you. How was Russia? Reports say you're on the move.*"

"*They raped me...*" Nemesis said, gasping around sobs.

"*By the Crushing Depths! I have your location. Don't worry. I will come get you right now. I can be there in ten minutes.*"

No I-told-you-so? Not being ridiculed and Kita's genuine concern for her predicament calmed Nemesis. "*Wait...I want to be like you.*"

"*What do you mean?*"

"*No one would touch you.*"

"*Now, but that hasn't always been the case.*"

"*What? But, you're...*"

"*We all come from somewhere, even me. I was raped when I was sixteen by my father's best friend.*"

Nemesis burst into tears. *No...No...If they can touch her, they can touch me.*

"*Nicole.*"

"*There is no escape. I'm going to die here, and they're going to do it again.*"

"*NICOLE! Listen to me. Being like me won't make this go away. The first thing you have to understand is: this isn't your fault. Nothing you did or didn't do brought this on you. You are now on a painful journey of self-discovery. You're not alone. I've been raped, many Angels have been, both before and after getting wings. Getting through it is going to take time, strength, and you can't give up hope. I'm here for you. I will help you. I'll hold you while you cry and tell you what you feel isn't true. But you have to make a choice: Are you a victim or a survivor?*

Victims let the men who did this control them. They never get beyond the fear, the self-loathing, embarrassment, and guilt. Eventually, it destroys them. I've seen it happen to Nina, Nell, and Kylee. A survivor accepts that it happened, understands it wasn't their fault, does what they need to do to cope with the pain, and eventually come to terms with it. The pain never goes away, and the trust can never be put back together, but you can't let it define you. You are more than the assholes that did this. They are nothing. Worse than garbage, and I will slaughter them."

Nemesis cried. No one had ever shown her such caring, understanding, or loyalty. *How could I have been so blinded by beliefs that I failed to see who she is?* "What if I want to do it?"

"Whatever you think will let you heal. I will do whatever it takes."

"They took my rifle and suit. I'm chained to a table, and I can't break free. But I want to kill them all."

Kita chuckled. "I made you the best sniper in the world, but I gave you more than that. While raiding my great-grandmother's notes, I found something called quicksilver. After I made some improvements, I gave it to you."

"Why didn't you tell me?"

"You were so happy with being a sniper I thought I'd save it for when you got bored...or needed it. I sent the activation code."

Nemesis moved her head as silver liquid bubbled up through the skin on her shoulder and arm and covered her. In a few places, short tendrils rose into the air and danced.

"*Quicksilver,*" said Kita, "*is a bionanite that responds to your thoughts. It flows like a liquid, can make shapes like blades and shields—anything you can dream up as long as it isn't complex. It can stop bullets, increase your strength and agility, be resistant to fire and ice, camouflage you, or go invisible; it will heighten your senses and even mimic living things. You can shoot tendrils to grab, catch, or punch. It should get you out no problem. But I don't want you taking on Kashmir by yourself. It's a bigger problem than one person. The region is controlled by a brutal warlord that's taken most of the eastern region. He has a good size army that's armed with small arms and some heavy weapons. What makes them worse is they get high on a mixture of cocaine and gunpowder. It makes them feel no pain and think they're invincible. It's a headache Kimmy and I have ignored until we have more troops."*

"I want them to pay. All of them. I'll find the one in charge and rip him apart."

"I know you want to, but not yet. The Free Kashmir Army is entrenched. I want you to get free of Leh and return to the Srinagar airport. I'll bump Kashmir up the list and send you some Angel help and a few military units. Your goal will be to take Kargil."

"Send me Lizzy, and we'll destroy them."

"I'll send her and some others, but baby steps. I don't want you in over your head. A mobile hangar is being dispatched to Srinagar to give you some heavy airpower. You're going to need it to clear the city."

Nemesis took a deep breath. She pulled with her arm and ripped the anchor from the floor. *Wow.* *"Ok. I will meet Lizzy as soon as I'm free."*

"You have some time. It takes seventeen hours to fly there."

"Thank you, Kita. For being understanding."

"You're my friend. I take care of my friends. When we're done, we'll get you the counseling you'll need."

"Ok. I'm sorry."

"*No need to be sorry. I have the utmost respect for what you believe.*"

"*I don't think I believe it anymore.*"

"*Find your way. If you need anything, you know where to find me.*"

"*Ok. I'm going to show them a woman's wrath.*"

"*Have fun.*"

Nemesis could see the whole room at once. With a little practice, she learned to control it like an eyelid. She pulled her other arm, legs, and wings free. Stretching her limbs, she admired her shiny silver skin. *Aargh. I* am *not beautiful. I'm a hideous monster. The outside should match the inside.*

Her quicksilver became black with red streaks. Spikes jutted from her knuckles, arms, and shoulders. Her silver and blue feathers changed to black with red tips. The quicksilver on her face formed a demon mask with glowing red eyes, a large mouth full of teeth with a four-foot prehensile tongue covered in barbs—a long, thick tail with a spike on the tip formed from the back of her head. Tendrils slinked through the chains, giving her control of them.

Time to meet the monster you created. Nemesis smashed the table with her fists, throwing the pieces around the stone room.

A voice came through the door. Nemesis pressed against the wall next to the door and went invisible. A guard unlocked the door and opened it. He yelled, running into the room.

Nemesis unmasked herself and stepped behind him. She rattled the chains that bound her. "Looking for me?" she said in a low, demonic growl.

The man turned and screamed.

Nemesis grabbed him by the throat, the tips of her fingers becoming long needle-like claws. She wrapped her tongue around his head.

"You taste like the sample you left in me," said Nemesis, slithering her tongue around his head.

"What are you?" he gasped.

"Nemesis. And you will suffer for what you've done to me." She shoved him to his knees. A line appeared between her legs up to her stomach. A mouth formed and opened, revealing rows of sharp needle teeth.

"NO!" the man screamed as he tried to pull his head away.

Nemesis chuckled lowly. "Wrong head." She flipped him in the air and caught him by the leg. The man wailed as she lowered him into position. With a *snap,* she took a bite out from between his legs.

The chatter of an AK-47 and the rounds hitting her in the back caused Nemesis' head to whip around. She tossed the bleeding man into the wall as her second mouth disappeared. She flashed forward, hitting the shooter and pinning him to the far wall.

Spikes on her forearm pressed into his neck. A chain wrapped around the rifle and wrenched it from his hand, tossing it *clattering* down the hallway. Her tongue wrapped around his head and constricted. Nemesis growled, "Another donor."

NEMESIS LANDED NEXT TO THE LARGE, WHITE, inflatable, clam-shaped hangar at the end of Srinagar airport's runway. Pierced steel planking ran from the runway to the hangar to keep the aircraft from sinking in the turf. Two giant C-17s sat next to the hangar with their ramps down as crews went about performing maintenance. She fashioned her quicksilver into a set of EUS Air Force Airman Battle Uniforms with colonel tabs. Satisfied she looked official, she entered the hangar.

In the back were pallets loaded with parts, missiles, and ammunition. Workbenches, bomb carts, and other equipment to service fighter aircraft were around the perimeter. In a corner was a table with a handful of crew and pilots gathered around a group of coffee pots—essential non-essential pieces of equipment for cargo planes. Each plane had its own favorite blend.

Nemesis approached the group. There were several women, but it was the men that made the pit in Nemesis's stomach grow. She closed her eyes. *They can't touch me. I'm the highest rank here, and I'm not the only woman. I have my quicksilver, and I can kill them in an instant.*

"Group, attention," an EUS Navy lieutenant named Handel called when Nemesis was close enough to be identified.

"At...ease," said Nemesis. "Carry...on." She was surprised to see Navy personnel with the Air Force. Kita said she was sending air support, but this was a long way inland for the Navy.

"When—Did any Angels arrive with you?" said Nemesis, hoping Sapper was around.

"Not with us, ma'am," said a major named Vargas.

"We expect a flight of F-twenty-fives at any time," said Handel.

"What's an F-twenty-five? Sorry, I've been in the field for a long time," said Nemesis.

"It's the new top-secret fighter, Colonel. The Velociraptor. It just came into service, and only the One-Five-Four has them."

The 154th Strike Fighter Squadron was Kita's elite squadron. It made sense she would send them. It explained why the Navy was here.

"Are they double seaters?"

"No, ma'am."

Is Lizzy arriving via the Star Bridge? If that was the case, Sapper could show up at any time.

"Hey, coffee crew!" someone yelled from the hangar entrance. "News from the tower. Flight of four VRs inbound. Should be landing in the next five minutes."

"Thanks, Sergeant," called Vargas.

From what Kita said and with the hangar size, I thought we were getting two. There's no way they would leave two top-secret fighters exposed. Maybe they have to get another hangar.
"Are the C-17s leaving soon?"

"No, ma'am. We're here as long as the fighters are here. We go where they go."

How am I supposed to be in charge if I don't even know what assets I'm getting? Do I have to talk to the Army—again—about getting ground troops? I thought Kita was going to send some. I guess I'll wait and see who arrives from the One-Five-Four. Nemesis only knew one of the girls that flew for the fallen angels—Karen, Kita's Angel-in-training, who was waiting to get her wings.

Nemesis grabbed a cup of coffee and settled in to wait.

"So what's going on?" said Vargas.

"I don't know," said Nemesis. "I was just told to be here."

The other officers chuckled. Nemesis grumbled to herself. She was high enough rank that she was beyond these games. *Kita must have a plan. It would be nice if she shared it.* Nemesis sighed. *I'm sure she's busy and taking time out for me. But, but, dammit! Me first.*

"*Kita!*" Nemesis snapped over the comm.

"*Hey, Nicole. Did you make it to the airport?*"

"*Yes, but Lizzy's not here.*"

"*Ah, the flight should be landing any moment.*"

"*How is she getting here?*"

"*With the fighters.*"

"*Are you telling me she learned to fly?*"

"*Not unless Bombshell taught her.*"

"*Who?*"

"*All will be explained. I promise. I sent Alpha Company of the Third Ranger Battalion to help, too. They should be landing after Lizzy.*"

Nemesis huffed. "*Ok.*"

"*Don't worry. It's all taken care of. Once the Rangers arrive, you can meet up with Colonel Zhao—I understand you've met —and they'll give you trucks and some extra troops.*"

"*Zhao knows this?*"

"*I cut the orders twelve hours ago.*"

"*Ok, thanks.*"

"*Good luck. Call me if you need anything.*"

The fighter backing into the hangar surprised Nemesis. Normally, they were loud and needed help to park. This one was backing in like a car, and the main engines were off. She couldn't tell where it was getting its propulsion. A second fighter silently moved across the hangar's mouth, spun ninety degrees, and moved backward to park next to the first. The fighters' wide fuselage, diamond wings, and V tails were unlike any Nemesis had seen. One fighter said *CAPT Karen "Poison" McKnight* and the other *CDR Zhi "Venom" Shen*.

The canopies opened, but no crew came to put ladders in place. Instead, the pilots jumped from the cockpits and glided down next to Nemesis and her open mouth.

"Hey, Nicole," said Poison. Her voice a mixture of happy sympathy. She gave Nemesis a hug. "It's good to see you again. Kita said you were in trouble but didn't give us any details."

Nemesis rested her head on Poison's shoulder. "Thanks, Karen. Congratulations on getting wings. When did it happen?"

Poison's cheeks turned red. "Professionally, it's embarrassing."

"Hi, I'm Zhi," said Venom giving Nemesis a hug. "We were shot down over Iran and blew up a bunch of scud missiles using rocks."

Nemesis smiled for the first time in days. "Did you throw rocks at them?"

Venom laughed. "No. We put big rocks under the rocket nozzles."

Nemesis didn't know much about rocketry, so she nodded.

"The rocks kept the gas and heat from going the right way and made the missiles go out of control," said Poison.

"Oh," said Nemesis. "Sorry, I'm not doing well."

Poison put an arm around Nemesis. "What happened?"

Nemesis gulped. "When's Lizzy arriving? I don't want her to know."

Poison gave Nemesis a concerned look. "I can have Bombshell keep her flying as long as you want."

"Ok. Let's go outside."

"Why?" said Poison. "We're the full birds here. Zhi, you want to chase the younglings out?"

"No problem," said Venom as she turned to the officers gathered around the coffee pots. "Ok, everybody out. Back to your birds. The big girls need to talk."

Vargas and the others nodded, gathered their stuff, and exited the hangar.

"I can go to if you want," said Venom.

"No," said Nemesis. "You're an Angel. You need to know."

"But not Lizzy?" said Poison.

"She's too young."

"She's grown up a lot in the last two years. Kita assigned her to work with Special Forces in the Middle East. She was promoted to lieutenant a couple of months ago."

"That's a big jump. I'll tell her when the time is right."

Poison took Nemesis's hand. "So what happened? You look shook and not your usual confident self." She guided Nemesis to the table and sat her down. She and Venom pulled up chairs next to her. "What happened?" Poison said gently.

Nemesis stared at the ground as she explained about the village and the ambush. "When I woke, they'd raped me." She broke into tears. "Thirty-three of them. I feel awful. Like I have bugs crawling across my skin, and my stomach is just sick. I don't want anyone to look at me because they'll know." She buried her face in her hands.

Venom and Poison slid off their chairs and held Nemesis.

"I'm so sorry," said Poison.

"I promise we'll hunt every one of them down," said Venom. "Wait until Anna gets here."

Nemesis wiped her hands and eyes, trying to feel the others' emotional support, but she was so numb. "Who is Anna?"

"A new girl Kita picked up about a year ago," said Poison. "She's—"

"Sweet but a psycho," said Venom.

"She's not a psycho. Kita calls her a manufactured sociopath. She was trained by the Soviet's Cardinal School. If you want someone found and killed, next to Kita, she's the best. It's just that upstairs she can be a little unstable, especially around men. I guess the things the Soviets forced her to do left unhealable scars. When it's just us girls, she's fine, but she can get a little handsy and forward and has a thing for Kita."

Nemesis raised an eyebrow. "And Kimmy hasn't—"

"Killed her? Kita's been very good at turning her aside gently and redirects her energy. They and Leaf go on assassin missions together. Kita said you had some people needing to be tracked down?"

"The problem is I don't know who these men are... I...I only have their DNA."

Poison raised an eyebrow. "Uhm..."

"It's part of who I am now. I'm no longer just a

sniper."

"What happened?"

"I'm the demon they made." The quicksilver wrapped around Nemesis in a warm, safe embrace.

"Holy shit," said Venom.

"The outside matches the inside."

"No, it doesn't," said Poison. "I know this is how you feel, but it is not you. What they did to you doesn't define you."

Nemesis's mask retreated back to her neck. "What else do I have?"

"You have us. We'll help you," said Venom. She hugged Nemesis.

"What am I going to do? This is how I feel safest."

"That's fine," said Poison, "but you can't become it. If you do, they win."

"I want to use it to crush them."

"Ok, but you have to know where it stops, and you begin."

Nemesis lowered her head. "I'll try."

"You're not alone. If I have to, I'll get Kita here."

"No, and don't tell Lizzy. I don't want to distract her."

"If that's what you want. I'll call Bombshell and Knockout, so they can land. The Rangers should be landing any time."

Outside, a Velociraptor with a sparkling hot pink and turquoise paint job landed vertically. The canopy opened, and a blonde Angel with cardinal red wings glided out. On the far side, an identical Velociraptor landed, and Sapper glided out of the canopy. The two Velociraptors morphed into twin Angel Morphicons, or at least that's what Nemesis thought they were. They didn't look like any Morphicon she'd seen. These looked like human-shaped androids, and from the colors and sparkles, they were either teenagers or into drag. The twins shrank from twenty feet to six feet as they entered the hangar with Sapper and Cardinal.

Nemesis changed to her uniform and did her best to compose herself. Seeing Sapper made her smile. She missed her, but Sapper looked much older than the twenty-one she was supposed to be. The group of Angels met Nemesis' group.

Sapper saluted. "Reporting as ordered, ma'am."

"Hi...Lizzy," said Nemesis. She wasn't sure why Sapper was being formal.

"Ma'am."

Nemesis frowned and returned the salute. "I don't know the rest of you."

"Cardinal," said the new Angel with a sensual Russian accent and a smile to match, "but you can call me Anna or anything you want, later."

Nemesis gulped hard. *Karen wasn't kidding.*

"We're Bombshell and Knockout," said one of the twins. They didn't bother to tell who was who. The only difference between them was a sparkling diamond over a different eye. Their bodies were painted turquoise and hot pink and covered in sparkles.

"Did you come from Chellexon?" said Nemesis.

The twins giggled. "Mom won't tell us who we came from," said one of them.

"They're Velositi and Kita's girls," said Poison.

"Ah, how?"

"The magic of Kita. I think it was Kita's way of

escaping Chelsea. She and Velositi have spent a lot of time training them."

"How is baby Chelsea?"

"Imagine a toddler who can fly and the trouble she can get into."

Nemesis's eyes went wide. "Oh, god."

"Yeah. They have a quartet of full-time nannies keeping an eye on her. *The girl with the diamond on her left eye is Bombshell, and the other is Knockout,*" Poison said over a private channel on the Angels' biological communication system.

Nemesis wasn't sure what the twins' names referred to. From their looks, they fit the beauty connotation. But if they were children of Kita and Velositi, then they could probably deliver major punishment.

The roar of a C-17's engines filled the hangar as one parked in front.

"Who the hell is blocking us in?" snarled Poison.

The ramp of the C-17 lowered, and four platoons of soldiers wearing tan berets marched out. At the head was a large man with a rifle and rucksack. They marched to the mouth of the hangar. On the runway, another C-17 landed.

The commanding officer barked at his disembarking units, "First Platoon, drop your gear, find the Air Force pukes, and get those MRAPs off the plane when it finishes taxing. Second Platoon, clear out some of this junk so we can establish a rear base of operations. Third Platoon, get security setup. Obviously, the Air Force is letting anybody walk in here. Maintenance Squad, help Second Platoon and check over the trucks when they get them offloaded. Top, I'm going to go find out who's in charge of this rat-screw."

"Are those the Rangers?" said Venom.

"Gotta be," said Poison. "Only the Army marches in and pretends to own the place."

From around the corner of the hangar ran a Navy petty officer and an Air Force sergeant. They yelled at the Rangers moving the carts and supplies along the hangar walls.

Nemesis scowled. "Go help them, Zhi. Tell the Rangers if they didn't bring tents, they can sleep outside. I'll deal with whoever thinks they're in charge."

Venom went the long way around a Velociraptor to avoid the Ranger commander. Poison and Nemesis walked between the fighters to meet with the man with captain's bars on his beret.

"Who are you?" said Poison. "And why are you moving equipment that doesn't belong to you?"

"I'm Captain Rich Mallory, Commander of Alpha Company, Third Ranger Battalion. I'm in charge of this mess. The orders didn't say Angels would be in support, ma'am."

Nemesis and Poison exchanged a look.

"I was told you'd be supporting us, Captain," said Nemesis.

"The mission states we're to take Kargil. That's a mission for my boys."

"Boys?" snarled Nemesis. "I see plenty of girls among your ranks, Captain. I'll take them and leave you and your *boys* here to guard the planes." She stuck a finger in his chest. "Or do you want to see what a girl can do?" Her uniform exploded, and she became the demon, lashing her tongue angrily. "I'll rip you apart."

The confrontation brought Cardinal flying to them,

her eyes glowing green, fingertips hardened into claws, and fangs out. She landed next to Nemesis and hissed, "Save some for me."

"Onca uncia pardus!" said Poison as she drew a pattern in the air with her glowing fingers.

Nemesis and Cardinal froze mid-step.

"Unless you think you can defeat them, you're supporting the Angels," Poison told the Ranger.

"What kind of freaks are you?" demanded Mallory as his rifle wavered in his hand.

"Sir," said Sapper. "Angels are genetically engineered beings, each with her own abilities to accomplish individual or team missions. Our abilities are unconventional, but can assist regular units or, when working together, we can be combat multipliers."

"Who are you, Lieutenant?"

"Lieutenant Elizabeth Wallace, sir. Previously, I was assisting Bravo Company, First Battalion, First Special Forces Group in the Iranian mountains. I've been assigned to assist Colonel Adrestia and Captain McKnight by the Vicereine."

"Lizzy," said Poison, "why don't you help Captain Mallory? It seems the Army could use a liaison with the Angels."

"Yes, ma'am."

"Captain, this is Colonel Adrestia's mission, and she's backed by the Vicereine. Just because it says Navy and Air Force on our uniforms doesn't mean we're strangers to ground combat. Understood?"

Mallory stiffened. "Yes, ma'am."

"Good. The hangar is off-limits. If your Rangers need tents, we'll get you some. Our contact is Colonel Tuff and Colonel Zhao of the Fifth of the Seven-Oh-First. They're headquartered in Amamath. They'll be here tonight once they hand off their garrison duty. Their advanced party should be here in an hour. So, get your people settled in and vehicles ready. We'll have a leaders' meeting as soon as Tuff and Zhao arrive. We'll find you if we need you. Lizzy, keep me updated."

"Yes, ma'am. Sir, let's get your Rangers squared away."

"My Rangers do not need to be squared away, Lieutenant," snapped Mallory.

"Stop," commanded Poison. "Just because she wears a lieutenant's bar doesn't mean she is the rank of lieutenant. That just denotes her leadership experience level. Her combat experience exceeds yours, Captain. She is an Angel and will be treated like one. If you abuse her, once I'm done with you, I will turn you over to the Vicereine, and Lizzy is very special to her. Am I clear, Captain?"

"Yes, ma'am," he ground out between clenched teeth.

"Dismissed."

Mallory spun on his heel and went back to his company with Sapper trailing.

Poison put her hands on Cardinal and Nemesis's shoulders.

"*You ladies ready to behave?*"

"*I want to smash him into the ground,*" said Nemesis.

"*You have to give him a chance. He was not being sexist or demeaning. The fact that he considers the women in his command 'boys' means he sees them as equals to the men. I have no doubt they will perform exceptionally.*

"*I know you're hurting, and you have every right to be, but if you can't control it, I will have Kita send you home. We have time. If you want to talk or cry, we can do that. But I can't let your emotions run wild and have you threatening our side. Save it for the enemy."*

"Fine."

"Anna?"

"He steps out of line; I'll tear him apart."

"If he does, that's for me to handle. Not you. If you want to feed, you can wait until dark. Until then, behave yourself, or I'll leave you like this and ship you back to Kita."

"Send me hunting."

"You'll have to wait until we have a target."

"I won't wait long."

"You'll wait as long as I say."

"I hate you."

"Take it to Kita when we get back."

"Ugh. Fine. I'll be patient."

"Good. Onca uncia pardus!"

Nemesis' quicksilver changed into her uniform. With a sneer, Cardinal left to join the other Angels.

"The equipment is safe," said Venom, returning to the Angels.

"Thanks," said Poison. "Come on, Nicole. Let's go talk."

NEMESIS SAT AT THE TABLE IN THE BACK OF THE hangar, holding a cup of coffee, staring at the ground. Her mind was balancing on a precarious edge—part of her wanted to lash out, and the other wanted to crawl in a hole and escape. Talking to Poison didn't help. She was unable to let out her emotion and spoke of the event in a detached way—like it happened to somebody else she didn't know. A shroud of numbness enveloped her and kept her from feeling anything.

The officers and senior non-commissioned officers from the Navy and Air Force talked and drank coffee around her.

"Excuse me, Colonel?"

Nemesis looked at Mallory. "Yes, Captain? Is there a problem?"

"I'd like to talk to you in private, if that's ok, ma'am."

Nemesis shrugged, set down her coffee, and stood, knocking over the folding chair with her wings. Using a tendril, she righted it. "Lead the way."

She followed him out of the hangar around the back. The city came right up to the airport, leaving the generators within easy reach of a crumbling cinder block wall with broken glass on top. *Who put these here without a guard? I bet the ground crew didn't even think of security when they set up.* Site security was her specialty after spending years in the EUS Air Force Security Forces. "Captain, when we're done, I want guards on these generators until the Fifth of the Seven-Oh-First arrives to take over security."

"Sure thing, Colonel."

"What's the matter?"

"I, ah, wanted to apologize if I offended you earlier. I assure you the males and females in my company are treated equally and fairly. No one gets preferential treatment, and everybody carries their weight. I'm proud of my Rangers for their teamwork and unit cohesion. *Boys* was in no way meant to be a slight on the females in my command, you, or any female in the military. We're here to do a mission, and I don't care if my Rangers are male or female; we'll get the job done. I have overheard several of my female Rangers talking about Sapper. They want to know how to become an Angel."

"Thank you, Captain. I owe you an apology for overreacting. I've had a long couple of days and a lot on my mind. Becoming an Angel is up to the Vicereine. I got my wings on a Majestic-Twelve mission."

Mallory raised an eyebrow. "Never heard of Majestic-Twelve."

"They're a black group tasked with researching Neophormes and defeating them. Until the Angels arrived, they were the ultra-elite special forces of DoD."

"If you're looking for a place to get away and crash for a few hours, I can give you an MRAP. They're quiet and have room to stretch out."

"Thanks for the offer, but I can't sleep."

"I'm sure I can find you some chems to knock you out."

"I just slept ten days ago. I won't be tired for another ten and chems don't work on us. There are downsides to being an Angel. I can't sleep or get drunk to escape."

"That's incredible. I only know what I've seen on TV."

"Do—do you have a sniper? I lost my rifle, and shooting helps me clear my mind."

"Sure thing. We can set up a range if you want to fire a few rounds. I remember you had a rifle that day at the White House."

"I had it taken in Leh a few days ago."

"Say the word, and we'll help you get it back."

"Kargil first. If we take it fast, I'm sure the Vicereine will let us go after Leh."

THE YELLOW LIGHTS OF THE C-17 LEAKED OUT ONTO the temporary tarmac as Nemesis, Poison, and Venom glided up the ramp. They met Tuff, Zhao, Mallory, and the other Angels inside and sat around a table. Nemesis carried a rolled-up map and a laptop. The officers and Angels made way for the new arrivals.

Nemesis unrolled the map on the table and set the laptop so everyone could see. She hadn't planned a mission like this since her days of commanding a security forces company, but she felt she had a solid plan for their first steps to Kargil.

"Ok, everyone. This is the mission brief. Our goal is to take these three villages—villages one, two, and three —along the main road to Kargil." She pointed them out on the map. "CIA analysis shows activity in all three villages, the majority in village one. They count twenty people in village one; at least fifteen are armed. From a previous engagement, I know they have AK-47s and RPGs.

"The village lies in a valley with steep slopes and a creek running through it. I want two Ranger platoons to move up the sides of the valley and attack from the sides and rear as a vehicle convoy led by the MRAPs moves up the road. Trucks following the MRAPs can deploy troops and sweep the village. Angels will go in with the

MRAPs. Once the village is clear, we'll move on to village two."

"Why not use helicopters?" said Bombshell.

"And hit all three at once?" said Knockout.

"I don't have any helicopters," Nemesis growled.

The twins giggled.

Bombshell's blue-glowing eyes brightened. "We can do that. What do you want? Apache? Cobra? Comanche? Chinook? Black Hawk?"

"I suggest Chinook. We can move a platoon at once," said Knockout.

"I thought you could change into only one thing?" said Nemesis.

"That's our mom's generation of Vehlix. We can change into, like, a hundred different things—as long as we have the mass."

"That's how you went from the size of a Velociraptor to Angel-size?"

"Yep. Momma-K says it's basically the same way Kimmy controls the size of her dragon, but instead of carbon, our gravity wells hold tungsten and other metals."

Nemesis had no idea about Vehlix physiology or biology. She just knew they had metal cells that rearrange themselves. *Of course, Kita would figure out how to improve it.* "I guess instead of going up the valley, we could land behind the village."

"Why not hit all three at once?" said Knockout. "Village two and three are less defended. Land helicopters at those villages and secure them. At the same time, use the MRAPs and vehicles to assault village one. Assign an Angel to each team for extra support.

After we make a drop-off, we can offer air cover, come as heavy ground support, or ourselves depending on what the situation on the ground is."

"Thanks, but—"

"But what?" said Bombshell. "You don't sound sure of yourself. Your telemetry is all over the place. Mom trained us for covert missions, and we've been working with First Cav on combined forces operations. Momma-K said you'd need help."

"I don't need some goddamn teenager telling me how to do my job!" screamed Nemesis.

"Easy," said Poison, placing a hand on Nemesis's shoulder.

"I don't need to take crap from a teenage robot that was just constructed yesterday! I'm not about to divide my forces so they can be slaughtered. I want to hit them hard with everything we've got."

"But the terrain dictates differently," said Knockout. "We're being funneled into the village where we can't bring our firepower and numbers to bear. They can pick us off individually. Hitting all three at once maximizes our firepower and numbers. It gives them no place to run, and they have to defend three places instead of one."

"I will not risk my forces that way. I've fought here before. I know what kind of ambush they can pull off. What happens if one team gets ambushed? There's no one there to support them."

"It's a quick hop by helicopter. We're talking two minutes—"

"They could be dead in two minutes!"

"You're fortunetelling and catastrophizing," said

Bombshell.

"What!"

"You're afraid what happened to you last time will happen again. Even though the situation is different. You have a different mission. More soldiers. Better intel. Lots of Angels. Between three villages, it looks like forty enemy combatants. If you're so worried, send Knock and me, and we'll be back by sunrise."

Nemesis screamed, grabbed the laptop, and threw it against the side of the C-17. She turned invisible and stormed out of the plane, behind the hangar, and collapsed against a generator. She buried her head in her arms and cried.

"*Nicole?*" called Kita gently.

"*Goddamnit, what, Kita?*"

"*The others are worried, and they wanted me to check on you. What's the matter?*"

"*Those goddamn kids. I know how to do my job. I don't need some teenage sexbot telling me what to do.*"

"*First off, those teenagers are mine. There's no need to be insulting or insinuating about them. I understand they lack tact and military bearing, but they are very good at what they do. I know they can be frustrating and arrogant. They take after their moms. They've spent the last six months with First Cav learning combined arms warfare. I thought you could use a heavy punch. I'm putting Karen in charge of the mission.*"

"*It's my mission! You can't remove me.*"

"*I'm not removing you. I'm handing the planning and leadership duties to Karen. You're still going, but this frees you from the stress of command, and you can concentrate on healing.*"

"*I can do it!*"

"*If it was under normal circumstances, I know you can. But you're hurting. I've been there. There are plenty of times I've turned over command to someone else because I was incapable, but I went along to help. I'm trying to find a similar way for you to participate and accomplish the mission.*"

"*I don't need to be taken off the mission. I need your damn kids to shut up!*"

Kita sighed. "*Nicole, I know you're suffering, and there's a lot of pain. The others will gladly listen, hold you, and let you cry. You can pour your heart out to them or me. You can be upset, hit and break things, yell and scream, but you* cannot *take it out on those you command and your friends and family. If you continue, I will bring you home, and we'll get you the help you need here.*"

"*You're threatening me? You would take their side. No one cares about me. I'm an embarrassment to you. You just want to lock me away and forget about me. I won't go. I won't let you take me!*"

Nemesis changed into her demon, vaulted the airport wall, and landed on a corrugated roof. She bounded across the densely packed rooftops of the sprawling slum in a haze, her thoughts tumbling over and over each other as she ran while the moon climbing high into the sky. She stopped on the corner of a tall square building overlooking a market area.

The open-air market was shut down for the night. Tables were either covered or empty, and no one was around. From around the corner came a couple of young men holding hands. Nemesis snarled. *Teenagers.*

The teens walked among the stalls and stopped in front of a cold case wrapped in a blue tarp. The first teen looked around, then took his boyfriend's face in his hands and kissed him. When they came up for air, the first teen led the other by the hand around behind the cold case.

The sight of them filled Nemesis with seething rage, her tongue lashing like a whip. *If I can't get at the bitches who ruined my night, I'll ruin someone else's.* She leaped into the air and glided down, landing on the cold case. The boys were too busy to notice.

"Didn't your mother tell you not to put those in your mouth?" Nemesis growled.

The boys looked at her. The one on his knees screamed while the other tried to turn and run but tripped over his pants. Tendrils shot from Nemesis's hands and wrapped around their legs. She pulled them to her, dangling them in the air. She ran her tongue over each boy's head.

"Sex in a public place is illegal. Maybe you should learn a lesson." Nemesis stood, and her second mouth formed and opened. She moved the two boys closer as they screamed.

Something slammed into Nemesis and sliced through her tendrils, letting the boys fall. Nemesis hit the stone-paved ground and rolled to a stop. In an instant, she was on her feet, searching. "Who dares attack me?"

A mist gathered in front of her and formed into an Angel with glowing green eyes. The mist spoke with a Russian accent, "Kita says return to the hangar."

"She'll have to make me."

"If you won't come, I will drag you back."

"I'll tear you apart."

The mist changed into Cardinal. She bared her fangs

and raised a hand to show her claws. She rushed forward with blinding speed and struck Nemesis in the jaw hard enough to cause the quicksilver to ripple. She spun and slashed Nemesis across the chest, her claws slicing through the quicksilver, leaving bloody lines. Her spin turned into a roundhouse that sent Nemesis skidding across the ground.

Nemesis screeched, dug her claws into the stone, and charged Cardinal. She shot tendrils to wrap up the other Angel's arms, but Cardinal's speed and agility let her dance around them while slashing through them. Nemesis lunged to tackle Cardinal, but the vampire exploded in a cloud of bats and took off in every direction. She slammed her foot into the stone in frustration. "Stand and fight!" she roared.

A shove in the back knocked Nemesis down. Her tail shot back to grab the other Angel. Cardinal sidestepped, grabbed the tail, and yanked, pulling Nemesis into the air and slamming her against the ground. Cardinal smashed Nemesis back and forth until the quicksilver receded. Nemesis lay naked on the ground, tears streaming down her face.

Cardinal knelt next to Nemesis, brushing her hair out of her face. "Are you ready to go home now?"

"Just let me die," Nemesis sobbed.

Cardinal stood to make room for Poison and Venom.

"Good job, Anna," said Poison. She put a hand on Nemesis's shoulder. "You can't die. Not now, not from this. If you do, then you've become what they want—a subservient girl they can abuse anytime they want, who is too scared and scarred to fight back. What's worse is, because you won't fight, they'll do it to some other girl who can't fight back—who needs our protection."

"Don't send me back. Please," Nemesis blubbered.

"I think you need some serious help, Nicole."

"I know I do, but please. Don't do this to me. I can't be a failure and a rape victim—survivor."

"We haven't even begun yet. What are you going to do in combat?"

"I can do it. I promise. I need to do this. I have to prove I'm not weak. That they can never do it again. I'm sorry about what I did. It won't happen again. I promise. You can lead; just let me go. Don't send me away and make me fail twice."

"*What do you think, Kita?*" said Poison.

"*Brings back memories. It's your call.*"

"*Please, Kita,*" said Nemesis. "*I'm sorry about everything. I can do this. I'll do anything you want; just don't send me home.*"

"*Karen?*"

"*She needs a shrink. Someone she can talk to during downtime.*"

"*Will do,*" said Kita. "*I'll have someone lined up by the time this is over.*"

Poison turned to Nemesis. "Nicole, you have to get yourself under control. I've got some time, and you're going to talk to me. I want to know what you were thinking and what set you off, so we can avoid it in the future."

"Ok." Nemesis wiped her eyes, and Venom helped her up. Her quicksilver flowed over her skin and reformed her uniform.

"I also need you to tell Anna who we're after in

Kargil so she can find them."

"I...only have their DNA."

"That is enough," said Cardinal. "How many?"

"I have thirty-three donors. I found fifteen of them. Most of them are probably in Leh."

"We'll see if any have traveled. Do you have a file with this information?"

Nemesis shook her head. "I just have the samples they left in me." She opened her hand, and eighteen tendrils lifted from her hand, each containing a DNA sample.

"Perfect." Cardinal took a device from her pocket and touched it to each tendril to read the sample. "I have what I need. I will search Kargil and look for our rapists."

"Also, look for the leaders of the militia groups, too," said Poison.

"If they sneeze, we will know." Cardinal exploded into her cloud of bats and flew into the night.

Poison lifted off the ground. "Come on, Nicole. Let's get back to the hangar. I'll brief you on the plan, and you can tell me what happened."

Nemesis stared at the steel planking as she sat at the table in the back of the hangar.

"Here."

Nemesis looked at Poison and took the cup of coffee. "Thanks. Listen, I'm sorry for putting you through this. I know the last thing you want to do is babysit me."

Poison and Venom took a chair around the table.

"I find it interesting," said Poison. "I majored in military psychology. How to get into the head of enemy pilots. But other courses about learning to help others cope with stress and trauma have been helpful as a commander."

"What's with the hocus-pocus chanting?"

Poison laughed. "Not all missions require pilots. I wanted to be useful to the group in any situation. So, I asked Kita to make me a witch."

Nemesis snorted in her coffee. "A witch?"

"I know thirty spells."

"How? I mean, magic doesn't exist."

Poison and Venom chuckled.

"You have wings," said Venom, "and become a demon."

"That's because of DNA," said Nemesis.

"I have special programmable omni-bionanites that I can project or form into what I want. The chant and the finger waving are for show. I program them using special glands in my hands."

"What have you been doing the last two years?" asked Nemesis. She'd been out of touch with the Angels, ignoring Kita's attempts to contact her.

"Flying mostly. I took command of the One-Five-Four from Commander Frazer a year ago. Since then, we take every dangerous mission Kita can dream up."

"Just the two of you?"

"Even we have limitations," said Venom. "The entire One-Five-Four is made of Angel candidates—girls that have the basic Angel package—but not the wings. Kita runs a special school at Area Fifty-one looking for recruits."

"Wow, you girls must rule the skies."

"Fifty-four kills. Overachiever here has seventy-four." Venom pointed at Poison.

"Kills have been on the decline since the Europeans pulled out. Now, we do mostly ground support or targets Kita wants eliminated."

"Why would Kita get to choose?"

"The One-Five-Four's heart and soul belongs to her. It's part of the requirements for selection. The candidate has to give up her status as a citizen of the Empire and swear personal loyalty to Kita."

"Like she's a queen?"

"She's the Vicereine."

"And Kimmy allows this?"

"It's only led to one argument—that I know of. The Arab Alliance Army is augmented by partisan fighters— it's impossible to tell them from ordinary citizens. These guys can slip through lines and terrorize rear areas. They kidnapped soldiers and left the bodies crucified next to the roadways. They did this to a couple of female soldiers, and autopsies showed they'd been raped. Kita was furious. She ordered us to bomb every temple, schoolhouse, and market in the AA. When Kimmy found out, she was livid. She couldn't order Kita to stop, but she threatened to cut off our fuel and ammo. We flew until it was gone. I guess they kissed and made up because we were resupplied after a day."

"And you did that?" Nemesis's mind reeled. The old part of her was appalled, but that was a small part. The rest said the Arabs got what they deserved.

"Kita ordered it. I don't know if it was the smartest

move if we're trying to win over the populous, but the number of kidnappings decreased in certain areas. Though we did spend a week dropping leaflets over those areas explaining why. I guess it was the compromise."

"Are they—fighting often?"

"Oh no," said Poison. "I've never met a couple more in sync than Kita and Kimmy. Nothing seems to bother them. They rationally talk out their differences. Even when Kita gets in a mood, Kimmy just knows how to handle it and make the best out of it."

"What about Chelsea?"

"From talking with Kimmy, she spends most of the time with Chelsea, but Kita does spend a preset number of hours with her. I understand the deal is when Chelsea gets older, Kita will be a larger part of her life. I think Kimmy found the one thing that freaks Kita out—children." Mallory and Sapper walked up and waited to one side. "Yes, Captain?"

"Reporting in, Captain. My Rangers are bedded down for the night. Guards have been posted, and roving patrols are guarding the perimeter. We scouted an area for the Fifth of the Seven-Oh-First to set up when they arrive in the morning."

"Excellent. Thank you. Interested in some coffee? I think the pot on the left has decaf."

"Captain, I'm going to check on the guards," said Sapper.

"Lizzy, why don't you stay? I haven't even gotten to say *hi* to you," said Nemesis trying to sound warm and inviting.

"Sorry, Colonel. Security can't wait."

Nemesis huffed. "It can wait a few minutes. I just want to talk to you."

"Why now, ma'am?"

"Lizzy, what's wrong? This is an informal setting. You're an Angel; I'm an Angel. The rest doesn't matter."

Sapper looked at Poison. "Can I be dismissed, ma'am?"

"I'm not going to force you to stay, but you might want to tell Nicole why you don't want to talk to her."

"Permission to speak freely, ma'am."

Poison nodded.

"Colonel Adrestia can go to hell."

"Lizzy, why?" said Nemesis. She set her coffee on the table and jumped up to take Sapper's hand.

Sapper yanked her hand back. "Don't touch me," she snapped.

"Lizzy, please. What did I do wrong? I'm sorry for whatever it is."

"Sorry doesn't make it better, ma'am."

"Quit calling me that. I'm your friend, dammit. Whatever it is, I want to make it right."

"If she tells you, will you let her leave?" said Venom.

Nemesis huffed. "I at least want to apologize."

"Lizzy, just tell her what's on your mind, and you can go."

Tears dribbled down Sapper's cheeks. "You *left* me!" she yelled. "You used me and didn't even say goodbye. You were supposed to be there for me. Instead, you ripped my heart out worse than Kita. Now, suddenly two years later, you want to be my friend and act like nothing happened? To hell with you!" She spun on her heel and took flight.

"Lizzy, wait!" cried Nemesis. She took off after the younger Angel. "Lizzy! It's not like that. I promise. I'm sorry I didn't say goodbye. Please let me explain."

Sapper flapped her wings and exited the hangar, disappearing into the night.

Nemesis stopped at the mouth of the hangar and looked for Sapper. *"Lizzy? Please? I'm sorry for everything."* She hung in the air, but no answer came. Defeated, she flew back to the table and sat heavily in her chair. "Am I the reason she's been so rigid?" she asked no one in particular.

"I'll go track her down," said Venom. "No promises she'll talk to you, but I'll see if I can get her settled down." She downed her coffee and flew out of the hangar.

"I didn't mean—"

"I know," said Poison, "but that's how she sees it. There's not much you can do until she's ready."

"How did I mess up so badly?"

Poison glanced at Mallory. "I don't know why you left. So, I can't help you."

"I left because I disagreed with Kita's view on good and evil and how Kimmy seized power."

"As far as I know, Kita doesn't believe in good or evil. And Kimmy proved herself worthy of being Empress. She's done more than her father and grandfather combined. I think she'll surpass FDR by the times she's done."

"It doesn't bother you that she got rid of Congress and the Supreme Court?"

"They're still there. They suggest legislation all the time, and the Supreme Court still rules on laws. The only difference is Kimmy can decree without anyone else's approval. I know it's only been two years, but it seems to be working. I'm no economist, but the GDP is up twelve percent, poverty is down thirty-four percent, and wages, including government pay, went up twenty-one percent. You can't argue with success."

Mallory nodded. "I didn't like her as Princess, but as Empress, she led us to victory, and she's changed the Empire for the better."

"What if she becomes a tyrant?"

"I like to think I'm in a position to influence her. You, me, Zhi, and the other Angels."

"It's just not the principles this Empire was founded on."

"I had my reservations at the beginning," said Mallory, "but her declaring that all the states were to become independent after she dies really sold me that she's in it for the good of the Empire and not worrying about her legacy."

Nemesis shrugged. She knew The Legacy. Once Apocalypse and Kita were done here, they were moving on to new universes. This one would cease to be. She stared into her coffee at the wavy reflection. "When did my life become such a mess? I thought I was one of the best and had a firm grasp on where I stood and what I believed in. Now, I can't even fight."

"You shot perfect earlier," said Mallory.

Nemesis shook her head. "Hand-to-hand. I got tossed around like a doll."

"To be fair," said Poison, "Anna is one of the greatest. Not only her combat skills, but she's a master of her Angel abilities, too. I think that is part of your problem.

You haven't trained yours. You've been going on instinct."

Mallory rubbed his chin. "If you want, I can put together some hand-to-hand training. The stuff the Rangers are taught is far better than the stuff they teach at basic training."

"That would be good," said Poison. "It'll help with your confidence, Nicole."

"Ok. I'm sorry for earlier, Captain. My behavior is unbecoming. I know personal issues aren't supposed to get in the way. I'm trying."

"I don't know about the Air Force, but in the Army, if things aren't right at home, things won't be right in the fight. You have to solve those problems first. That's what I tell my Rangers. I don't care if it's financial, family, marital, or what. We'll get it solved so you can be the most effective on the battlefield."

"I wish it was solved that easily."

"It's up to you. But, one team, one fight. We support each other. I can't offer help unless I know what the problem is."

Nemesis bit her lip.

"*Nicole,*" said Poison. "*It's up to you if you want to tell him. He might have an answer or at the very least understand where you're coming from.*"

"*What if he laughs at me?*"

"*He wouldn't dare. At the worst, he can't offer anything and has an explanation for your behavior and can adjust fire accordingly.*"

What do I do? It's one thing to tell Karen and Zhi. They're Angels. I don't know Mallory. He seems nice enough. He's competent and professional. He seems to care about his Rangers.

My fate and the mission are in his hands. Is it fair to him not to know? Secrets destroy units, and so does having someone unfit to fight. Am I unfit to fight? I haven't proven that I am. I've been a mess. But this is my fight, my mission. I need to go. I need to do this. I just wish it wasn't a man. Admitting that I was raped is embarrassing. Is he going to think less of me? That I'm not capable? I wish I knew the answer...and there's only one way to know the answer...

Nemesis's uniform changed into the demon but left her head exposed. Poison raised an eyebrow, and Mallory set down his coffee.

"What's your name, Captain?" said Nemesis.

"Rich."

"Nicole. When I arrived in country, I was captured while on an aid mission with the Fifth of the Seven-Oh-First. While I was held captive, I was raped. Using a new ability, quicksilver," she held up a hand, and a tendril rose from her palm, "I was able to escape and meet you here. This mission is to get back at my rapists and those who attacked us. I'm still dealing with the emotions. They seem to change moment to moment."

Mallory nodded and picked up his coffee cup. "You have my sympathies, and promise we'll help you get them. I know a lot is happening emotionally, and it's tough and going to be hard on you. I had a Ranger raped seven months ago. We've been helping her ever since. She goes to counseling, and everyone in the unit supports her."

"She's still with you?"

"Of course. I gave her the option to leave, but she refused. I sure wasn't going to kick her out. It wasn't her fault. I've talked to her a few times to see how she's doing. In the first couple of months, she had some problems, but the rest of the unit was supportive and helped her through it, and proved she could still be a Ranger. She's recovered and is on the mission with us—if you want to talk to her. She might have some advice, or at least you'll have someone who understands."

You're a victim or a survivor...This Ranger is a survivor, just like Kita. If they can do it, so can I. "I would like to speak with her in the morning."

"Specialist Fortune's on roving patrol now. I'm sure she'd like someone to talk to."

"Why don't we go out and introduce ourselves," Poison offered.

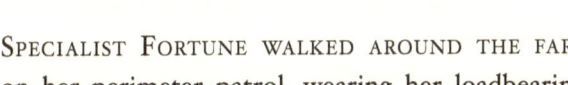

SPECIALIST FORTUNE WALKED AROUND THE FAR C-17 on her perimeter patrol, wearing her loadbearing vest and patrol cap with her name on the back. She carried the latest M-4 assault rifle with a reflexive sight, laser, foregrip, and light.

"Specialist Fortune," called Mallory.

Fortune stopped and turned. The moon was waning but still bright enough to see by. "Yes, sir?" She came to attention but didn't salute so as not to give away Mallory and the Angels' ranks.

"At ease. This is Captain McKnight, EUS Navy, and Colonel Adrestia, EUS Air Force."

Fortune stiffened. "Ma'ams."

"It's ok, Specialist. We just want to talk to you about a private matter," said Poison.

Fortune looked between the Angels and then at

Mallory. "Am—am I in trouble, sir?"

"No. no," said Nemesis. "I'm looking for help, and Captain Mallory said you might be able to help me."

"I'll do what I can, ma'am."

"Just call me Nicole." Nemesis extended her hand.

"Amy. How can I help?"

"When I arrived in country, I was on a mission with the Fifth of the Seven-Oh-First and were ambushed. I took two rounds to the head—"

"You took two to the head?" Fortune exclaimed.

"Angels have thick skulls, but it doesn't stop the force from scrambling our brains. But I was captured, and...and..." Nemesis swallowed hard. Saying it out loud was so hard. It was like waking up to it all over again.

"Oh... I'm so sorry," said Fortune, realization washed across her face. She slung her weapon on her shoulder and hugged Nemesis.

"I was hoping you could help me with ways to cope," Nemesis said, fighting tears in her eyes.

"You're doing better than I did. I was a mess for two weeks."

Nemesis shook her head. "I'm forcing myself to be normal, but inside I'm all over the place."

"Nicole, we're going to go," said Poison, "and let you talk privately."

"Ok. Thanks, Karen, Rich. I'll find you when I'm done." They walked around the C-17 back toward the hangar. "You don't have to if you don't want to," Nemesis said to Fortune.

"It'll be good to talk to someone else who's been through it. A lot of people care and are nice, but no one understands until it happens to you. Captain Mallory has been supportive and helped me a lot. My whole company has. After it happened, my squad leader, Sergeant Avery, gave me a hug and promised to help me any way he could. He took me to all my doctor, psych, and CID appointments and made sure they treated me right."

"The other Angels are helping me. Karen's counseling me. This mission is so I can get back at those who did it."

Fortune laughed. "I didn't get to go on that mission. I heard Sergeant Avery took a platoon's worth of Rangers to the tanker barracks where it happened and roughed them up. My best advice is, don't chase the rabbit."

"What's that mean?"

"It means don't give in to the feelings and emotion because it only takes you down a hole of misery, self-loathing, and pain. I used to get stuck there for days at a time. Now, it's a dark hole in my mind that I try and stay away from."

"My emotions are everywhere," said Nemesis.

"I know. It took me months to get them under control and look myself in the mirror. If it wasn't for being a Ranger, I might still be there. It gave me something to hold on to and the will to fight. You're going to have to fight. Every day. Or that hole gets bigger."

"How do I fight it when it's everywhere?"

"I used to watch the clock. One minute without thinking about it became two, and so on. The others motivated me to get back into training. That helped a lot. Once I got back into the rhythm of training, it gave me a safe space to breathe."

"I do need to train. I'm going to try and work with the Rangers tomorrow."

"I'm sure you have cool Angel stuff, too."

"I've been working in the devastation around Moscow, trying to help people rebuild. Nothing that's very cool."

"You're not a pilot like the others?" said Fortune.

"No. I was a sniper for the Air Force Security Forces when I was enlisted, and I commanded a company as captain. I was selected for Majestic-Twelve after that."

"Never heard of them."

"An Air Force black group that researched and fought Neophormes."

"Wow, nice."

Nemesis chuckled. "I was a glorified secretary until Kita came along."

"Vicereine Kita?"

"Yeah."

"I saw you on TV. It was amazing. What's it like to fly? I mean, I've jumped and ridden in Black Hawks, but to have wings would be incredible."

"Ah, you want to go?" said Nemesis.

"You—you're serious? You can lift me?"

"Sure. Put your arm around my neck, and I'll pick you up."

Fortune shifted her rifle into one hand and put her other arm around Nemesis. She lifted Fortune in her arms and spread her wings. With a strong flap, she lifted off the ground.

"Oh my god, this is amazing," exclaimed Fortune as they rose into the air.

Nemesis climbed several hundred feet and circled, letting them overlook the dark countryside.

"I should do this more often," said Nemesis. "I forget how quiet and relaxing it is." Already her turmoil of emotion was receding, and her troubled mind eased. There was something about being able to put physical distance between her and the world that eased her mind.

"It is peaceful. How high can you go?"

"Kita can go into space. I usually stay closer to the ground. I can go higher."

"I shouldn't leave my post unguarded."

"I'm watching it for you."

"Through me?"

"Through this." Tendrils sprang up across Nemesis's uniform and skin.

"What is that?" gasped Fortune.

"It's called quicksilver. It's a bionanite that lives in my skin. It can do all sorts of stuff—like let me see in panoramic vision and watch the ground."

"Did—did this come with being an Angel?"

"Yes. Each Angel is given certain abilities."

"What else can you do?"

"I can see in the dark. My body and mind are set up to make me the perfect sniper. When I had my rifle, I could hit targets five miles away."

"That's insane. Where's your rifle?" said Fortune as she looked down.

"My attackers took it. I plan on getting it back. Anna is out looking for those who have it."

"Is she another Angel?"

"Yes."

"Damn. I thought the Rangers were high speed."

Nemesis chuckled. "Kita's always recruiting."

"What do I have to do to get preselected?"

"I don't know. Karen mentioned an Angel school, but that was for pilots. I don't know if Kita has one for soldiers. I know Angels are selected on need, friend, potential, and reward."

"How were you selected?"

"We were on a mission to destroy an Illuminati base. The teams were down, and Kita went from being a regular, hardheaded twenty-one-year-old to an Angel god. She transformed us, and we went down and killed five Neophormes."

"That sounds so cool."

"If you're interested, I'll tell her."

"Hell ya. My life plan was Green Berets or Delta Force, but Angels would be unreal."

Nemesis smiled. Fortune's enthusiasm was like a bright light in the darkness, and it beckoned her onward. *There is hope. I can beat this.*

NEMESIS STEPPED INTO BOMBSHELL'S CARGO compartment on the night of the assault. As a Chinook helicopter, Bombshell easily fit the platoon of Rangers and the pair of Angels. The inside looked exactly like a military Chinook, except everything was hot pink, turquoise, and sparkled.

"All aboard, Bombshell. Let's go," called Venom.

"I got clearance from the tower. Going up!"

The deck pushed against Nemesis's legs as they lifted off. The Rangers were settled in for the flight. They would be attacking village three. It was considered to have the least resistance. Nemesis volunteered to go, not because the mission would be easier, but because Fortune's platoon would be doing the sweep. Fortune was near the front, having a conversation with another Ranger.

"New friend?" said Venom.

"Huh?" said Nemesis, surprised that her staring had been discovered.

"Hey, don't let me stop you. She's cute."

"I—I'm...no. She helped me, and it was nice to have someone to talk to who's been through it."

"Whatever makes you feel better. What's with the rifle?"

Nemesis raised the rifle she'd borrowed from the Rangers. "I don't plan on being a commander who leads from the rear."

"That's cool and all, but why use that when you can unleash the demon?"

Nemesis swallowed hard. "I don't want to be that."

"Why not?"

"Because it's not me."

"It is you or part of you."

"If I lose control of myself like I did in the market—"

"Then you learn to control it. It's a new power. It's going to take some time to master. Right now, you're running on instinct. I saw you practicing hand-to-hand with the Rangers yesterday. You must not have completely given up on it."

"I—I don't want to be embarrassed again. Anna threw me like a rag doll."

Venom chuckled. "To be fair, Anna is one of the best. I've seen her throw Kita across the room. Just because something bad happened to you doesn't mean you stop being who you are and give up on yourself. The demon came from something bad, but you can turn it into something good. What happened to you can push you forward. You know what a mudfish is?"

Nemesis shook her head.

"You're looking at her. Mudfish was my call sign when I flew in the Chinese Air Force. I didn't come from a privileged background like the rest of the pilots. My father was a poor fisherman who worked the Yangtze River his entire life. Most fishermen toss back the mudfish, but we were so poor my dad would sell the better fish, and we ate the mudfish. They're as appetizing as they sound.

"I showed a remarkable aptitude for flying, and The Party put me in flight school. My dad was so proud and happy that his daughter would live a better life than him. In flight school, the cadre didn't want me, and they told the rest of the class where I came from. I was bullied, tormented, and humiliated. Being called mudfish was a constant reminder I'd never be good enough for the rest. But I refused to go back to my dad. I worked to prove them wrong. I made them begrudgingly admit I was the best. Even as the best, I got shit assignments, bad planes, and useless crews. I used that to fuel me. When Kita came looking for pilots, I wasn't on the roster. But you know her, she dug around until she found the best. I outflew everybody, and I can get Karen fifty percent of the time.

"Don't let what happened steal your life. It's part of you now, but it doesn't define you. You're still a sniper, leader, Airman, and Angel. Rape survivor is way at the bottom of the list. You're the best sniper in the world, and you're going to be the best demon in the world."

"Were you given instructions like Karen?"

Venom smiled. "Karen is the ghost of Thanksgiving Present and was asked to keep you from falling apart. I'm the ghost of Thanksgiving Future. I was asked to make sure you remember why you're an Angel, and there is a way forward to a bright and happy place. It's just going to take work and perseverance to get there."

Nemesis sighed. *Everyone says it takes work. I wish there was an easy way forward.*

"One minute out," said Bombshell.

"Rangers, listen up," yelled Venom. "Change of plans. You won't be breaching the huts. Leave that to me. You're just to catch and detain. If anyone starts shooting, shoot back. Understand?"

"Yes, ma'am," they responded loudly.

Venom tapped Nemesis on the chest. "Get suited up."

"What good is that going to do?"

"Fear is a powerful force. We need to prove to these rebels we need to be feared. If we're feared, they won't fight back."

"How are you going to get them out of their huts?"

Venom held her hand out, a hole opened in her palm, and black widow spiders crawled out. They climbed up her arm. "No one likes spiders." She opened her mouth, and the spiders disappeared inside.

"Holy shit!" yelled a Ranger.

Venom grinned. "You should see my other party tricks."

Bombshell touched down with a *thump,* and the ramp came down. Venom led the way as Nemesis, now shrouded in the demon, followed.

"Spread out and be ready to catch them," said Venom. "We'll start on this end and work our way to the far side."

The platoon of Rangers spread out under the direction of their lieutenant and squad leaders. Bombshell morphed and joined Venom and Nemesis. They landed on the road and followed it into the village of stone, mud brick, and corrugated steel huts. Low stone walls sectioned off yards and empty livestock pens. The Rangers silently moved through the village taking up stations near doors and watching lines of approach from the far side.

"Here we go," said Venom. She knelt and placed her hands on the ground. Holes opened in the top of her hands, and thousands of black widow spiders streamed into the village, finding holes and cracks to enter the huts.

The first scream cut through the still mountain air as an old woman burst through a rickety hut door and ran while trying to shoo the spiders away. A pair of Rangers grabbed her, and the spiders receded and joined the stream going to the next hut.

"That was loud," said Bombshell. "She's going to wake up the entire village."

"Rangers, search that one." Venom pointed to a hut. "There's a sleeping man and an RPG."

The Angels moved through the village driving more people from their homes. Most were elderly, along with some children. Venom released them from the spiders when they were outside. The men they found were kept covered in spiders to keep them occupied.

Venom pointed out more huts that contained weapons or sleeping people. The Rangers herded everyone into the center of the village. The adults were quiet once the spiders were removed, but the children continued to cry.

The chatter of an AK-47 rang out. It was answered by an M-4.

"Almost got them all," muttered Venom. "Go deal with it," she motioned to Nemesis.

"Ok." *Beats walking around feeling useless on my own mission.* She took off and glided over the huts searching for the gunfire. Rangers pointed her toward the enemy. Turning invisible, she flew over a hut and found two men —one armed with an AK-47, the other was readying an RPG.

Nemesis landed and turned visible. "Don't you think that's overkill?" She flashed forward to grab the grenadier, but the RPG fired, blasting Nemesis with flame and smoke. She roared and grabbed the man. A tendril shot out and wrapped around the second man's neck. "You better hope you missed," she snarled at the grenadier, then licked him with her tongue.

"Bones! We got wounded," yelled a voice twenty yards away.

Nemesis leaped into the sky carrying her captives

and landed near two Rangers as they worked to pull the armor and load-bearing vest off a third. A helmet lay in the dirt. One of the Rangers turned and pulled a bag with a red cross from his pack. Nemesis's breath caught in her throat. The injured Ranger was Fortune. She lay against a stone wall, the RPG round in her lap and her M-4 still in her hand.

Nemesis's demon mask split open and retreated around her neck. "Amy!" She looked at the medic. "What's wrong?"

"I don't have the four-leaf clover tattooed on my ass that she's got. She caught that RPG round right in her front armor plate and knocked her into the wall." He opened Fortune's fatigue top and cut through her brown t-shirt, revealing a black sports bra.

"Oh, whoa. What happened?" said Fortune coming around.

"This," said the other Ranger holding up the unexploded RPG round.

"Damn. Check that box."

"Yeah, no shit."

"Can you feel everything?" said the medic.

Fortune moved her arms and legs. "Yeah. No sharp pains, just a dull ache. Like I landed hard on a jump."

"Let me check your eyes."

Nemesis's grim expression greeted two more Rangers. One was Sergeant Avery, and the other was a lieutenant.

"How she doing, Bones?" said the lieutenant.

"No sign of a concussion. She's going to have a hell of a bruise on her chest."

"Everything ok, Fortune? You're living up to your name," said Avery.

"I'm ok, Sergeant. I'll be on my feet in a second."

"No rush," said the lieutenant. "We swept the last huts and, uh..." the lieutenant glanced at the two terrified, forgotten men dangling in Nemesis' tendrils. "Angel Nemesis has the last of the combatants. Get some water. I'm going to call you Lucky from now on."

Nemesis wiped a tear with her free hand. She yanked the grenadier up to her as her demon head reformed. "You are mine." She shoved the other man at Avery. "Take him to the others."

"What are you going to do to him?" said Fortune.

"See if he can fly."

"Nicole, he's a captive. You can't kill him."

"He'll just wish he was dead."

"—Or torture him."

"You were a bad primer away from death. No one threatens my friends."

Fortune sat up. "I appreciate it, but the risk is part of the job. Hurting him won't help you. It doesn't help me. Let him go. You said you didn't want to be the demon. Now is your chance to prove it."

Nemesis stared into the fear-filled eyes of the grenadier. She squeezed her hand tight around his throat to watch his eyes bulge. With a snarl, she slammed him to the ground at Fortune's feet. "Others won't be so lucky."

"That's fine, but he's not one of the ones who assaulted you."

"He's protecting them."

"He's fighting for independence. There's nothing

wrong with that. Nicole, you're chasing the rabbit, and you need to stop."

Nemesis ground her teeth.

"Everything ok?" said Venom coming up with Bombshell.

"Minor injury when an RPG round didn't go off, ma'am," said the lieutenant.

"Going to be ok, Ranger?" said Bombshell.

"I'll be fine, ah, ma'am."

Bombshell snickered. "I'm younger than you are."

"How are you doing, Nicole?" said Venom.

Nemesis spun, her arm becoming an ax, and she cleaved the grenadier in two.

"Feel better?"

"No," she huffed, her anger and tension oozing downward into a leaden lump of fatigue in her stomach.

"Luckily, we're done for the night. We just have to wait for the Fifth of the Seven-Oh-First to arrive." A Ranger arrived holding a cell phone. "What do you have?"

"We were checking the villagers' phones, and this one made a call after we arrived."

Venom took the phone from him and flipped it open. It was a cheap Chinese brand with a simple interface. The call log was open, showing the call that went out. "Lucky for us, I know just who to call. *Hey, Kita.*"

"*Hi, Zhi and everyone else. How's it going?*"

"*Ok. We're finishing the first step to take Kargil,*" said Poison.

"*How are you, Nicole?*"

"*Grumpy.*"

"*I heard. I promise it'll get better. You can't do it all at once. So, did you all miss me or what?*"

The other Angels laughed.

"*I have a phone number I need traced,*" said Venom and gave it to Kita.

"*Found it in a section of Kargil. I'm hacking into it now. Bunch of names, numbers, and texts about controlling the region. Anna, I'll pass it on to you, and you can hunt them down.*"

"*With pleasure. And the pleasure we will have later.*"

Kita laughed. "*Only if I can bring Kimmy.*"

"*Why do you need two? I will be enough.*"

"*Because I want someone for you to talk to when I'm comatose. Keep me posted.*"

"Good find, Ranger," said Venom. "We'll get the information to the right people."

"Do you need a radio to call?" said the lieutenant.

Nemesis smiled slightly. "The call has already happened."

"Come on," said Venom. "Let's get this place cleaned up. Nicole, you made the mess; you get to clean it up."

Nemesis huffed but picked up both halves of the body and took off to throw it on top of the hillside. She landed on the crest of the steep valley walls next to a deep crevasse. Looking into the gash in the Earth was like looking at a physical manifestation of her mind. Staring down, she had the urge to jump and be swallowed by the darkness. *I might as well...I can't seem to do anything right.*

She collapsed to her knees, curled into a ball, and cried. *Why did this happen to me? I'm not strong enough. I'm not like Amy or Kita. I'm weak. I keep failing myself, my friends, the soldiers...I'm a menace. I should go home. Everyone will be safer that way. I can be what I am...a pathetic useless piece of shit that can't do anything. I don't want to go home. I want to die. Death will be a release. I don't care what the others say about* them *winning.*

Nemesis crawled to the edge of the crevasse and peered over the edge. She couldn't see the bottom. *How long will I have to wait to die?* A ringtone pierced her thoughts. Turning around, it was coming from the lower half of the man. Curious to who would be calling a corpse, she crawled over and retrieved the flip-phone from a pocket. She opened it.

"Veer?" said a woman's voice.

"Hello?" croaked Nemesis.

The woman said something in Kashmiri.

"I'm sorry. I don't understand."

"Where Veer?"

"Veer? His name is Veer?"

"Yes. Where Veer? Why on phone?"

"I'm sorry. Veer is dead."

"No. Where Veer? Put him on phone," the woman yelled.

"He's dead," Nemesis blubbered. "I killed him. I'm sorry."

"Who is this? Where is Veer!"

"I'm so sorry." Nemesis closed the phone and hung her head. *How many lives did I ruin tonight? Was that his sister? Mother? Girlfriend? Wife? Another victim of me and my inability to cope. I thought I was stronger than this. I was supposed to be. I'm an Angel. An officer. An Airman. Why can't I deal with this? Why do I have to suffer? It's not fair. I did my duty. I followed what was right. Where did I fail?*

"Don't chase the rabbit," said Fortune.

Nemesis's head popped up looking, but she was alone.

"Amy?" Nemesis called.

Only the silent mountain air answered.

"Don't chase the rabbit," whispered Nemesis. She shook her head at the crevasse. "No. I was wrong for killing him, but it's not my fault. It's theirs—those thirty-three. The blood is on their hands."

Nemesis stood up and picked up the body. She laid it out on the hillside and covered it with rocks. *Does he have a religion? Does it matter? I know god, and I doubt she would care...unless I make her.*

"Kita?"

"*Hey, Nicole. How was the attack on the villages?*"

"*I need a favor. I killed a prisoner, and I want to tell his family 'I'm sorry.'*"

"*I don't know if that's possible.*"

"*I have his phone. Someone just called.*" She gave Kita the phone number.

"*Ok. Searching. I've got the other number. It's in Kargil, and I have a building. Once Kargil is liberated, we'll send someone to them.*"

"*I want to do it.*"

"*Let's see how you're doing and then make a decision. Fair?*"

"*Fair.*"

"*Anything else?*"

"*I'm at the location of the grave, so we can give it to the family.*"

"*Ok. Got it. Good luck with the rest of the night.*"

Nemesis placed a hand on the grave. "Forgive me. Those responsible will pay." She spread her wings and took off to catch up with the others.

Tendrils from Nemesis's thigh, hand, shoulder, back, and chest shot out in different directions. Each found its target, wrapping up a spider or knocking it out of the air. With her tongue, she caught a large tarantula on the table. Her tail snapped, knocking a hissing cobra aside.

"Getting better," said Venom.

"I don't even have to think," said Nemesis.

"Good. You want to be able to do it instinctually, just like sniping. You don't think. You just do."

Nemesis nodded. She had tens of thousands of hours in as a sniper and only fourteen training to be the demon, but already her control and reaction were faster.

"Ready for your next test?"

"What's that?"

"Me." Venom grinned. She stepped away from the table and transformed into a black scorpion. She was as big as the table, her stinger above Nemesis's head.

"What the hell?" said Vargas. He and the others sitting around the table jumped up and scrambled to the far side.

Venom charged around the table and struck her stinger at their feet.

"She says you should be used to the unexpected by now," said Nemesis.

Venom jumped onto the table and struck at Nemesis.

Ducking out of the way, Nemesis shaped her arm into a blade and swung at Venom. Using a claw to block, she scurried off the table and rushed Nemesis. She thrust her blade at Venom's face, but a claw grasped the blade and pulled Nemesis off her feet. Tendrils shot downward, catching Nemesis and propelling her upright. A thick tendril flattened into a shield, blocking another stinger strike. A claw grabbed her calf. Even with her quicksilver, the pressure was immense. She tried to use tendrils to free herself, but she couldn't break Venom's grip. Concerned about her foot, Nemesis lost sight of the stinger. It found her, hitting her twice in the chest.

Nemesis's head floated drunkenly off her shoulders. Sound was distorted and slow. She turned to the others, but one side of their heads were huge, the other shrunken. Her vision swimming, she fell to the ground, but nothing stayed still. Grabbing her head, she shook it, trying to clear it. Venom came into view, her face contorting and shifting. The other Angel said something, but it sounded like she was underwater. Afraid she was losing her mind, everything suddenly snapped back to normal.

"You, ok?" said Venom, standing over Nemesis.

"What...was that?"

"Just a hallucinogenic drug. Nothing serious. Just something to remind you of the cost of losing."

"How am I supposed to be of any use on this mission if I can't beat you?"

"I don't expect you to beat me," said Venom. "I've been doing this way longer than you have. I want you to act and react smartly. Just because you're not the haymaker doesn't mean you can't land some jabs and help win the fight."

"But it's my fight."

"Sometimes, to win, we have to let others fight for us. We're your friends and want to get justice for you as much as you do. I promise you'll be there to deliver the final blow."

"I hate this," Nemesis yelled, anger exploding in her chest. "I used to be able to take care of myself. I didn't need others to fight for me. I've put in the work and paid my dues. Why did they have to do this to me?"

Venom seized Nemesis' hands. "It's not your fault. You did everything right. You *are* the greatest sniper. But that doesn't diminish the truth of what happened. We can't change the past, but we can change how you react to it. You're letting it hold you back. You need to use it to propel you forward. Use that emotion to make yourself better. Stop using it to tear yourself down. I know it's hard. There will be setbacks. You just spent fourteen hours getting better, don't let one thought throw all that away. Take a breath. You *will* be the best demon. I won't let you be anything else. Ok?"

Nemesis fought the tears in her eyes. "Ok."

"Everything ok?" Poison asked, flying up with Bombshell and Knockout.

"Two steps forward, one back," said Venom. "She's doing well and is fit to fight."

"Nicole?"

"I'll be ok. I'm still struggling to grasp it actually happened to me."

"Acceptance takes a while, but it will come. But that is still only a small part of the healing process."

Nemesis sighed. "I know."

"Damy, *the enemy is on the move*," said Cardinal.

"*What's happening?*" said Poison.

"*A convoy of tacticals and trucks just left Kargil, heading west toward you.*"

"*That must be their response to losing the villages. Ok, we're on it.*" Poison pointed to Mallory. "Tell Tuff and Zhao to prep for an attack. We've got a large force moving toward the villages. The Angels will try and stop them before they get here, but they're to be ready. Put your Rangers on alert in case the Fifth of the Seven-Oh-First needs support."

"Yes, ma'am."

"Zhi, let's get our birds in the air. Bombshell, Knockout, use the A-tens. There's some depleted uranium against the wall over there." Poison pointed to a crate with a radioactive symbol on it.

"Oh, hell ya!" they said together as they rushed to the crate, popped the latches, and took off the lead-lined lid.

Nemesis followed them over. "What are you doing?"

Each Morphicon had a hand on a stack of metal ingots.

"Absorbing the material so we can make it into shells to fire," said Knockout. "Normally, we fire only energy weapons, but if we have the right material, we can make kinetic rounds."

"Wow. Kita thought of everything."

"Our DNA sequence is a hundred times as long as mom's."

"You want to ride with me?" said Bombshell.

"Really?" Nemesis said excitedly.

"Sure. Unless you want to stay here."

"No. I'll come."

"Ok, then let's go."

The Morphicons absorbed half the crate of material before gliding out of the hangar onto the runway. They morphed into matching A-10 Thunderbolts. Bombshell opened her canopy, and Nemesis flew in and took a seat.

"Just don't touch anything, or you might cause us to crash," said Bombshell.

Nemesis put her hands in her lap. "I don't know how to fly, anyway."

"I'm kidding. It's just for show, but it all works. So, you'll be able to see the targets with the infrared camera. You've been in a fighter before, right?"

"I've sat in one. I've never flown. I wasn't in that part of the Air Force."

"I'll have to give you a ride. And, there's the tower. We're clear for takeoff."

The Morphicons taxied onto the runway, turned, and throttled their engines.

"Hang on," said Bombshell.

Nemesis was thrown back into her seat after Bombshell slipped her brake. They rocketed down the runway until Bombshell's nose tilted up, and they lifted off.

"Wow, what a ride." Nemesis turned her head to look at the quickly vanishing city. It was a different sensation than flying with her wings. Her wings were quiet, and she felt weightless. Here she could feel gravity and hear the engines roar.

"*Ok ladies, form up on me,*" said Poison. "*Venom and I will lead. On the first pass, we'll block them in with hellfire strikes. Bombshell, Knockout, you're to take out the vehicles. We'll form two wheels. Bombshell, you'll be with me, and we'll circle north. Knockout and Venom will circle south. Understood?*"

"*Roger,*" everyone answered.

"*We're nearly on station. I've got highway One-D below me. We should reach them momentarily.*"

That's one advantage over wings: speed. We covered that distance in no time. It was a short hop over a mountain range to link up with the highway. The camera showed minimal traffic at this time of night.

"*I've got a long line of vehicles ahead,*" said Poison. "*Identify as enemy vehicles. I've got tacticals and trucks with people in the back.*"

"*Identified,*" said Venom. "*I see mounted weapons.*"

"*Let's light 'em up!*" yelled Knockout.

The camera view shifted to the head of the convoy. A white dot streaked into view and exploded, blocking the convoy's path. The convoy's reaction showed they were partisan fighters. Instead of pulling off the road in an alternating wishbone to making strafing harder, they slammed on their brakes and stopped.

Bombshell lowered her nose and spit fire. The 30-millimeter shells tore into the lightly armored vehicles. Some burst into flames, others blasted apart. They flew down the line walking their fire between the nineteen vehicles. She pulled up and banked to the left, following Poison in a turn to make another pass.

"*Wahoo! Look at them go!*" yelled Knockout.

Even through the carnage, man and machine survived. Three vehicles pulled off the road, trying to take shelter in neighboring fields. Men were taking cover wherever they could find it.

"*Launch! Launch! Launch!*" announced Poison. "*Take evasive action Knockout!*"

"*Roger. Blowing shaft,*" Knockout responded.

"*Don't blow shaft, stupid!*" yelled Bombshell. "*MPADS*

are heat seekers!"

"*No, they—*"

A bright orange fireball lit the night sky reflecting off Bombshell's canopy.

"*Knock!*" Bombshell screamed.

"*She went down in a field next to the highway,*" said Poison. "*Bombshell, get on the ground and protect her. I'll get the Fifth of the Seven-Oh-First moving to support you. We'll keep attacking from the air.*"

"By the Crushing Depths, these slagbags are slagging dead!" snarled Bombshell.

"Where are we going to land?" said Nemesis.

"We're not."

"Huh?"

Bombshell's canopy opened, and Nemesis was tossed in the air. She spread her wings and caught herself as Bombshell transformed into a Bradley fighting vehicle and fell to the ground. Nemesis followed. Bombshell opened her commander's hatch, and Nemesis landed inside. She'd been in a Bradley before when training with the Army. While she got situated, Bombshell opened up with her 20-millimeter cannon. The sharp crack echoed in the night.

Bombshell raced forward toward her crashed sister. Her engine screaming as she climbed the highway embankment and smashed through several vehicles. In the neighboring field, Knockout was in two pieces; partisan fighters were gathered around her celebrating their kill.

"Die, slagbags!" Bombshell's turret moved back and forth as she engaged the fighters, the large-caliber rounds blowing many to pieces. She circled the wreckage chasing after them. A fleeing tactical was trying to climb the highway embankment but couldn't maintain traction. Bombshell didn't fire on it. Instead, she charged.

"What are we doing?" said Nemesis.

"Showing them why they don't mess with us."

Bombshell's front slammed into the rear of the tactical, crushing it like tin foil. Using her powerful tracks, she ground the vehicle into scrap.

"*That's the last of them, Bombshell,*" said Poison. "*Check on your sister. The Fifth of the Seven-Oh-First is in route. We'll continue to loiter.*"

Bombshell pulled up next to Knockout's wreckage. The cockpit and wings were tilted to one side as the left wing had dug into the ground. The tail and engines were twenty-five yards away. Nemesis floated out of Bombshell as she morphed back into her angelic form. The young Morphicon ran up to her sister and hugged the fuselage. "Knock? Knock!"

Nemesis saw raw fear in Bombshell's eyes when she looked back at her. Nemesis glided over and put her arms around the teenager.

"*Kita?*" Nemesis called over the comm.

"*How bad is it?*"

"*They blew Knockout in half.*"

Kita sighed. "*That is something we can attempt to fix. I'll send Sprokkit to collect the pieces.*"

"*I'm sorry, Kita.*"

"*It's the life of an Angel. Even I can't make us invincible. It's not your fault, Nicole.*"

"*She was here because of me...*"

"*We all know the risks. Death, injury are real possibilities.*

But I don't know any Angel that would have it any other way."

"I promise her sacrifice won't be in vain. We will get them."

"I know you will."

"Kita says she's going to try and fix her." Nemesis hugged Bombshell tight.

Bombshell broke into loud sobs as a blue fluid leaked from her eyes. Nemesis leaned her against Knockout's fuselage and held her.

A knot of guilt wove around the empty pit in Nemesis's stomach. *This is my fault. If it wasn't for me, this wouldn't have happened. What am I doing? This is supposed to be my revenge, and instead, I'm getting my friends injured and killed. Why can't I get it right? I didn't use to be this big a screw-up.*

Diesel engines and air brakes alerted her to traffic on the highway. Soldiers were dismounting trucks and jeeps.

Nemesis squeezed Bombshell. "Sweetheart, help is here. We have to figure out how to get your sister back to the hangar."

Bombshell lifted her head and wiped her eyes. "Ok." Nemesis helped her stand, and together they walked around Knockout, deciding on the best course of action.

"How's it look, Nicole?" said Poison.

"The Fifth of the Seven-Oh-First has arrived. Bombshell thinks her sister's tail can fit in the back of a truck, and she can airlift the rest back to the hangar."

"Ok, we'll continue to loiter in case more show up."

BOMBSHELL—AS A FORKLIFT—LIFTED KNOCKOUT'S tail out of the truck. A Ranger guided her across the tarmac, and she placed the tail next to the rest of the body. Nemesis wiped a tear from her eye as Poison put her hand on Nemesis's shoulder.

"Are you ok?"

"It's my fault," whispered Nemesis. "First Amy and now Knockout. My own selfishness is causing harm to those who don't deserve it. If anyone deserves to be blown in two, it should be me."

"No. This is part of combat. It's the risk of the mission."

"The mission is because of me," snarled Nemesis.

"Part of it is. This mission had to happen regardless of you. We're just doing it now, instead of later. What you're feeling is natural, but the blame isn't yours to take. Knockout made a rookie's mistake and fired the wrong countermeasure. She didn't know what kind of weapons' systems we would be facing, and that's my mistake. Kita and Velositi rushed their kids into a Special Forces mission before they were ready. Both are understandably upset. There's lots of blame to go around, but none of it is yours, Nicole. But if anyone can put Knockout back together, it will be Kita. A team will be coming via the Star Bridge to take her back to Area Fifty-one."

Nemesis' shoulders slumped. It didn't matter hearing it wasn't her fault; that didn't fill the pit in her stomach.

"Why don't you go talk to Specialist Fortune and see how she's doing?"

Nemesis nodded. It sounded like Poison had lots on her mind and didn't need her adding to the pile. "That sounds like a good idea." She glided into the air toward the Ranger compound.

After getting directions from a Ranger, Nemesis found Fortune in one of the large army tents full of cots sitting around with the rest of her squad.

"When we stack up, make sure there's something solid between us and—" Avery looked up at Nemesis. "Can I help you, Colonel?"

"I—I was hoping to talk to Specialist Fortune for a few minutes."

"We're in the middle of something, Colonel," snapped Fortune.

Nemesis kept her face neutral, even though it felt like Fortune had slapped her.

"It's ok, Fortune," said Avery. "We can take a break."

Fortune rolled her eyes, grabbed her fatigue top and shrugged it on, and sealed it as they exited the tent. "What do you want, Colonel?"

"Do—do you want to go flying?"

"No, ma'am."

"I just want to talk."

"I don't, ma'am."

"Amy, what's the matter? What did I do?"

Fortune stopped. "Permission to speak freely, ma'am?"

Nemesis gulped as the pit in her stomach grew. "Go ahead."

"Why the hell are you not in the stockade?"

Nemesis gasped. "Why would I be there?"

"You killed a POW in a brutal and savage attack. I don't care what happened to you. That's no excuse."

"I know, and it was a mistake. I've already promised reparations and will visit the family to apologize."

"That doesn't bring him back. We don't do that. We're taught to be better than that."

"Yes, I know." A wave of panic swept over Nemesis. She didn't know what to do or say to make it better. "I feel awful. I was just upset he hurt you. I protect my friends. That's all I was doing."

"I'm not your friend," hissed Fortune.

"No. Don't say that," whispered Nemesis.

"Little harsh, don't you think?" said Venom, turning visible. "You want to be an Angel; it comes with a lot of responsibility. One of those responsibilities is the power of life and death. Angels are above the law. We answer only to each other. The Vicereine and the Empress both regret the man's death. His family will be taken care of; that can't replace him, but it's the best we can do. They do deem his death reasonable under the circumstances. He was an enemy combatant and attacked the Empress' soldiers. She feels it will act as a warning to deter others."

"How is anyone above the law?" gasped Fortune.

"We are the guardians of the Empire. To do what we do, we can't be restricted by the code that restrains the masses. We're guided by our principles and our own moral code. Right and wrong is a matter of perspective. We do what is right for the Empire, even if it means breaking the law or working outside it. As a soldier, you should know what that's like. You gave up your rights and protections of the law when you enlisted. You're subject to the Uniform Code of Military Justice, which is different than civilian law. Angel law is similar."

"So she gets to get away with it?"

"No. Her punishment has been decided. She'll face

the family and deal with her own guilt—which isn't just punishment on her; it's on all of us because we will help her deal with it. Those men didn't rape Nicole; they raped every Angel. We failed to protect her, and her pain is our pain. We'll heal together, and it will make us stronger. Just as your unit came together to help you, the Angels will come together to help Nicole. We take care of our own." Venom put her arm around Nemesis and hugged her. "You ok?"

Nemesis shook her head.

"Come on. Let's get some coffee, and you can train to get your mind off things."

Nemesis nodded. That sounded like a good idea. Venom guided her back toward the hangar.

"You want to be an Angel, kid; you have to learn morality is flexible. There is only one absolute in this universe, and she leads the Angels," Venom said over her shoulder.

NEMESIS STARED INTO HER COFFEE, LOOKING FOR SOME great cosmic sign that her nightmare would end and life would return to normal.

"Ni—Nicole?" said Sapper.

Nemesis's head snapped up. "Lizzy. I—I...I didn't expect to see you. I'm sorry. I can't—"

"No, I'm sorry. I heard what happened with Specialist Fortune. I can't do anything about it, but I thought I'd come give you a hug and tell you that you didn't deserve that." Sapper knelt in front of Nemesis and hugged her.

"Thanks, Lizzy. I'm so sorry for everything. I should have come and talked to you. I want you to know you're important to me; you always have been. I'm sorry I screwed it up. I shouldn't have let my anger at Kita and Kimmy get between us. I'm sorry. You deserve so much better than a broken-down has-been like me."

"I understand why you left. But you should have told me. I would have come with you."

Nemesis grimaced. "I didn't want you to have to choose sides."

"I'm not a kid. I can make up my own mind."

"I know. I'm sorry. I screwed up. It's all I'm good at anymore."

Sapper took the coffee from Nemesis, set it on the table, and took the other Angel's hands. "That's not true. You're still my hero. You helped me with Kita. You showed me what officers are supposed to be. You made one mistake this entire time, and that was leaving me behind. But I'm giving you a second chance. I'm not saying I want to get back together, but I still want you as my mentor. I can't think of anyone I want to be like more than you."

Tears streamed down Nemesis's face. "Why? Look what happened to me. I'm broken. I can't do anything right."

"Just because a bad thing happens doesn't mean it's who we are. Who we are is defined by how we respond to bad things. I've been in some desperate fights throughout history. I refused to give up then, and I'm not going to give up on you. You helped me at my lowest point; I'm going to help you at yours."

"What are you going to do?"

"Forgive you for leaving me behind. I get you were going through stuff, and you were trying to protect me. Now, you get to make up for it. You're going to tell me everything."

"Lizzy, it's not something you want to hear."

"I've served in some pretty deplorable armies. I'm no stranger to rape, torture, or murder. I've got stories that'll make your toes curl."

"You haven't..."

"Been raped? For most of my lives, I've been male. It's the only way I could get into the army."

"Did you..."

"Rape anyone? I don't think so. I think I would remember. But I'm not Kita. I don't have a perfect memory of everything I've done. I just have dreams and memories. I know I've been around it. The Mongol horde was famous for it. The funny thing was, I was a girl for that lifetime. For all the horrific things they did, they guarded me jealously. Babies from a female warrior were highly prized."

"You had kids?"

"A few. I'm not repulsed by the idea like Kita is. When I was female, I was usually bi, if I could find a female partner."

"How does it work, living so many lives?"

Sapper shrugged. "Like I said, I don't remember much. I'm not me when I go in. It's like that person gets folded up into me, and I gain their memories when it's over. You should try it sometime."

An escape...I can be someone else that wasn't raped. I could feel whole again.

"Ok, I want to hear what happened to you."

Nemesis closed her eyes. It was nice that Sapper was talking to her, but she wasn't sure she could relive it one more time. "I'm sorry, Lizzy. It's not you. It's me. I don't want to go back there."

Sapper stood up and sat in Nemesis' lap. She pulled Nemesis's head to her chest and held her. "I'm sorry, Nicole. It's not fair that it happened to you. You're a good person who deserves better than to have her life upset by a bunch of thugs. I promise we'll get them."

"D—do you want to go flying? I found it helps me relax and take my mind off things."

"Of course. I haven't done much real flying lately."

Sapper slid off Nemesis's lap and took her hand. They exited the hangar and took off into the light of dawn.

Nemesis and Sapper circled the Srinagar airport after touring Dras and the neighboring cities.

"Looks like Sprokkit is here to take Knockout home." Sapper pointed to a large Morphicon working on Knockout's tail section. Bombshell was next to him.

"We should see if they need help," said Nemesis.

They hovered behind the Morphicons. Bombshell was busy cutting a small hole in her sister.

"Hi, Sprokkit," said Nemesis trying to muster all the cheerfulness she could.

He turned around and looked at the two Angels. "Nicole, good to see you again. My condolences on your attack. I understand it is a brutal transgression against highly evolved carbon-based lifeforms. Are you returning home?"

"Thanks. I'm trying to heal. I—I think I am."

"That is good. Bernoot misses you. He does not like his new handler. The officer does not talk much, and Bernoot misses having someone to talk to."

"I miss him. I'll gladly be his handler again if he wants."

"The sooner, the better. I am tired of listening to him talk about YouTube."

Nemesis laughed.

Bombshell stood up and turned around. *Maybe this isn't Bombshell?* This Morphicon had two diamonds over her eyes. "Hi," she said in a bubbly voice. "You must be Nicole. I'm so glad I get to finally meet you."

"Who...are...you?"

"I'm Stunner. I'm the odd girl out. My sisters like to play in the mud, and I'd rather be in the lab. I'm here to help get Knock home and take her place on the mission."

"What's Knockout's prognosis?"

"She's been blown in half, so...dead."

Nemesis's heart skipped a beat.

"I believe Stunner is playing with you." Sprokkit crossed his arms across his massive blocky chest as his eyes lit at the younger Morphicon. "Nicole is in a fragile state. She does not need her emotions being toyed with anymore."

"Yes, sir," said Stunner, her eyes dimmed.

"I believe we can fix Knockout using the same method Kita used to fix Bernoot. We are in the process of accessing her system cores so we can morph her back to her angelic form for ease of transport. If her body cannot be healed, we will extract the system cores and build her a new body."

Nemesis relaxed. At worst, Knockout would be out for a couple of months, but she wasn't permanently dead. "That's good news. I was worried."

"Kita has advanced us light-years in repair technology. Only the destruction of a system core can render one of us nonfunctional."

"She likes to make sure nothing happens to her friends."

"Yes. If you will excuse me, we are ready to manipulate this system core."

Nemesis and Sapper glided back, letting the Morphicons work.

"That's awesome news," said Sapper.

Nemesis nodded in agreement as they went into the hangar. "It's a weight off my mind."

Poison waved them over to the table in the back of the hangar.

"What's up, Captain?" said Sapper enthusiastically.

"Anna called. She's ready."

THE MRAP EASED UP TO THE BURNT-OUT PICKUP truck and pushed the wreck out of the way, clearing the highway for the convoy of Army trucks. Above them, Nemesis stood on Stunner's skid. The Morphicon was morphed into a Black Hawk helicopter. Not far away, Sapper sat in the doorway of Bombshell. Nemesis waved to her and smiled when Sapper gave her a thumbs up.

The mission was straightforward. The Rangers would secure the VIPs currently gathered at the Zomsa coffeehouse, while the 5th of the 701st Infantry Regiment secured Kargil, a stronghold of the Free Kashmir Army. The city was built along a river, and the challenge lay in securing several bridges to gain full access to the city's districts. The hope was the EUS forces had the element of surprise, and the FKA couldn't react with all their local leaders in custody.

"*This is Bulldog Six. Phase line lion, reached,*" said Mallory. "*Super Seven-six and Super Seven-seven, go.*"

"*Roger,*" said Stunner and Bombshell.

The two helicopters stopped pacing the convoy and flew into the city. In the growing twilight, an infrared strobe light on top of a two-story building signaled their destination.

"Target in sight," said Stunner. "Get ready back there." The crew chief extended the boom arms and readied the rappelling ropes.

As Stunner hovered behind the building, her sister hovered in front. The coffeehouse had two points of entry, and the Rangers were going to assault both. A pair of guards appeared from the doorway and fired into Stunner's underside.

"Hey, that tickles!"

Nemesis jumped from the skid and landed on one of the guards. She grabbed the body by the head and threw it into the second guard. Shaped her arm into a blade, she thrust it into the guard's face.

The Ranger squad—known as a *chalk*—fast rappelled down the ropes and took up defensive positions around the back of the coffeehouse. The familiar *pops* of M-4 rounds came from the other side of the building. Nemesis burst through the back door of the coffeehouse into a kitchen, surprising a pair of cooks. One cook brandished a meat cleaver at her. Nemesis's arm became a bigger version of the cooking knife. She took a swing, causing both men to jump back. Nemesis ensnared them with tendrils around their necks and swung them back to the Rangers to secure.

Nemesis waited by the back staircase for the Rangers. Cardinal had provided the layout of the coffeehouse from her previous visit. Once everyone was stacked, Nemesis charged up the stairs. Screened by a beaded curtain, she burst into a dining area with a long tall table and stools along the back wall and comfortable chairs and tables facing windows near the front. A dozen men sat at the table drinking coffee or tea. They turned and looked at Nemesis, but none reacted.

A mist gathered in the front of the room and turned into Cardinal. "Ok, my pretty little lambs, it's time to go. Finish your drink, stand up, and put your hands behind your back. My pretty demon, you'll be interested in the two at the end." She pointed to two men.

Nemesis's tongue lashed back and forth as she stalked toward them. Sapper and the other Ranger chalk arrived up the main stairs. Nemesis grabbed the first man by the jaw, digging her claws into his cheeks. Her tongue traced a path across his face. "Another donor."

Sapper appeared at Nemesis' shoulder. "Is this one of the guys that raped you?"

Nemesis's head turned to look at Sapper. "Yes. I still carry his DNA with me."

Sapper turned to Cardinal. "Release him from the hypnosis."

"Both?"

"Any who are responsible."

Cardinal looked into the eyes of the two men. "Your minds are your own."

The two men shook their heads; their confusion was replaced by terror at seeing the three angry Angels.

Sapper grabbed the second man by the throat. "You like to rape girls?" She shook him, causing his head to snap back and forth. "How about you try and rape me, big man?" Sapper slugged him in the gut. She dangled him by the neck. "How about you try it on a girl that can fight back. You hurt my friend and took from her something she'll never get back. Now I'm going to take something you can never get back." She drew her Ka-Bar knife and thrust it between his legs. The man's screams escalated when she twisted the blade and withdrew. "Oh, shut up and take it like a man. You're man enough to give it; you're man enough to take it." She thrust him to the ground and kicked him in the gut. She bent down and cleaned her knife off on the man's shirt. She looked at Nemesis. "Sorry, I know it's your revenge. But he hurt me by hurting you."

Nemesis's teeth formed a menacing smile. She tossed the man she held in the air and caught him by the ankle. Her second mouth emerged from between her legs and up her abdomen. She lowered the man into position and took a bite from between his legs. She dumped the whimpering man next to the other one.

"Lieutenant, we're all set," said a Ranger sergeant.

"Good," said Sapper. "Let's get them downstairs and

ready for the trucks. I'll contact Captain Mallory and tell him we're good to go."

"What should we do about these two?"

Sapper exchanged looks with Nemesis.

"Give them aid," said Nemesis. "They might be useful, or at least they can live with their punishment."

"Got what they deserve, ma'am. Bones! See what you can do for our asshole rapists."

The medics from the Ranger chalks went to work on the two men.

"No painkillers," said Cardinal. "Their pain will be a fraction of Nemesis'."

The medics nodded as they tore open gauze packs. The rest of the Rangers hustled the captives downstairs.

Sapper hugged Nemesis. "I know it's cold comfort, but it's two more who got what they deserved."

Nemesis's demon mask pulled back from her head. "I'll get them all, but seeing you care gives me hope. You too, Anna. Thank you for finding them."

"You are not alone. I hope you find a better path than I was forced to take."

"I'm so sorry, Anna."

"It makes us who we are. I was a weapon aimed by fools. But it is never too late to retake what was taken from us. All you need is the desire that no one is your master."

"I will be my own master. But I won't let them go unpunished."

"Nor should they be. I can't get at those who stole my life, but I can use their teachings to help others be free. There is no dignity in slavery, be it the chains real or imagined."

Nemesis held up an arm and shook the chain attached to her wrist. "The chains aren't so easily removed."

"You may not be able to shed them, but your arm can grow stronger to carry them."

"I like to think I'm growing stronger."

"You are. The longer you carry them, the lighter they will be."

"We're all set, Lieutenant," said a medic.

"Stay with them. When the convoy arrives, we'll send stretchers up to get them. We're going downstairs to make sure the Fifth of the Seven-Oh-First doesn't need any help."

The Angels took the front staircase down to the coffee bar and outside. Overhead, Bombshell and Stunner were flying around as Apache gunships.

"*How's it looking, girls?*" said Nemesis.

"*So far, it's quiet. The Fifth of the Seven-Oh-First are moving in with little to no resistance,*" said Stunner.

"*I ordered all the fighters to be on holiday,*" said Cardinal.

"*I've gotten reports from Colonel Zhao,*" said Poison. She and Venom were loitering above the city, ready to provide air support. "*They are rounding up the FKA fighters and weapons caches. Everything is proceeding on schedule, and they've met little resistance.*"

"*I'm still short sixteen donors,*" said Nemesis.

"*Kita said Kargil was as far as we're to go.*"

"*Then I'll go on my own.*"

"*Let's talk to Kita and finish up here first.*"

Nemesis grumbled. She'd been promised she could take her revenge. She would have it—even if she had to do it alone.

———————✕———————

NEMESIS SAT IN FRONT OF A CURTAIN LISTENING TO Cardinal interrogate the prisoners in a makeshift cell in a C-17. The process was slow. The captives knew English, sort of. But to get nuanced answers, a translator had been brought in. So far, the first three captives didn't know much beyond their sectors of Kargil.

"Hey, Colonel," said Sapper placing a hand on Nemesis' shoulder.

Nemesis turned to look at her. "Hey, Lizzy. How are the Rangers recovering?"

"Everyone's doing fine. The unit's in recovery. Not much for me to do. We've held the after-action review, and no one identified any critical errors. Speed is what Captain Mallory wants, but every commander wants it to happen faster."

Nemesis laughed. She was guilty of that.

"How's it going in here?"

"Nothing to link us to Leh or the other donors."

"I think these are pretty low-level peons. I bet the two donors will have more when it's their turn. You want to go flying? Anna will let us know when to come back."

Nemesis's heart pounded in her chest. She was excited for the first time since the attack. "Yeah, sure." She hopped out of her chair and followed Sapper out of the plane.

In the air, they glided above Srinagar. The cool mountain air filled Nemesis's lungs as she admired the Himalayan Mountains that surrounded the city.

"How are you feeling?" said Sapper.

Nemesis mulled the question over. She felt good now,

but it was only on the surface; underneath was in turmoil. "I'm happy here with you. I haven't felt happy in a long time. My mind is still...trying to reconcile. Everyone says it takes time, and for everyone, it's different."

"What are you trying to reconcile?"

Nemesis wasn't sure how to explain. "I...I'm not sure if I'm the person who murdered the man in the village or if I'm the person who repented for it."

"You were justified in killing him. It wasn't murder. We all agree on that. Who do you want to be?" said Sapper.

"I don't know. When it first happened, I was determined to be like Kita, but I'm finding that hard to live up to."

"Kita is unique. I don't think anyone can be like her. She is a god, after all. She's a fusion of emotion and logic."

"I know. I just wanted to put myself first instead of the greater good, but I'm finding that's hard to leave behind. Amy reinforced that maybe my choice wasn't the right one."

Sapper barrel-rolled under Nemesis so she could look in her eyes. "Specialist Fortune isn't wrong, but she's not right either. There's nothing wrong with putting yourself first. At this point, you need to. Your health requires it. I've come to understand Kita's ideas on morality over the last two years. I used to think there was a greater good, and I was on that side. I was a United States Soldier fighting for freedom, democracy, and the right to life. The Soviets were the Great Evil, but you know who others in the world called the Great Evil? Us. They called the Soviets the Lesser Evil.

"I never gave it much thought until I came here. I believe in what Kimmy's doing and what she wants to achieve. But fighting in the Middle East and talking to the people, I understand why they resist. Their fundamental ideas of what is right and wrong are so different from ours that we're not on the same page. For some of these people, killing a gay person is the absolute right thing to do. When I tell them I'm gay, they're shocked. I don't understand how they can want to kill me over who I sleep with. They don't understand how a gay has so much power.

"It's as Kita says, neither side is right. Right is in the eye of the beholder. What I have come to believe is might makes right. Kimmy and Kita's might will remake this world into a place you and I will be safer because of who we are. They may not be able to stop rape, but if they can stop another gay person being lynched for being gay, I'm all for it."

Nemesis's mind tried to relate Sapper's experience with her own. "I don't think I was raped because I was gay; there was no way they could have known that. I was raped because I trusted people, and they betrayed me and killed innocent people. My belief that people are inherently good is shattered. I still believe I'm good. If Kimmy and Kita can't stop rapes from happening, maybe I can."

"What do you think you can do?"

"Kimmy and Kita are too busy running the Empire, but after I'm done here, I'll have free time."

Sapper smiled wickedly. "There's a trial right now

about a seventeen-year-old boy who raped a fifteen-year-old girl at a party. His sentence came down yesterday. Three months suspended sentence. The judge said he didn't want to ruin the young man's life."

"That's disgusting. Did anyone ask how she felt? That he ruined her for the rest of her life? I'm a mess, and I was raped at thirty-six. I can't imagine what hell it would be like at fifteen."

"Maybe you should pay him a visit," suggested Sapper.

"Maybe I will. I'm sure I can think of a way to ruin his life. Damn. Now I'm angry. And focused."

"Life is easier when you have a goal."

"It was one thing when it was me. It's something else when it's a teenager. I bet she's not the only one either."

"Probably not. There are lots of men who think they can get away with it...and do."

"Maybe I'll give them something to fear. Make them think twice if a demon is lurking in the darkness."

"*Damy, I have uncovered an interesting piece of information,*" said Cardinal.

"*What is it?*" said Poison.

"*Dina Nath, leader of the FKA, will be holding a cabinet meeting in three days in a hotel in Leh.*"

"*How confident is this information?*"

"*It came from the two rapists. They are expected to be there.*"

"*Kita said the mission ended at Kargil,*" said Poison. "*The Fifth of the Seven-Oh-First is fully extended holding the city. And Leh is a day's drive. We just don't have the resources.*"

"*We have the Rangers and us,*" said Sapper. "*We don't have to take the city, just a quick raid. We could borrow some trucks from the Fifth of the Seven-Oh-First and air assault in to take the prisoners. A company of Rangers, five Angels, and Sprokkit should have no problem."*

"You forget we still have to convince Kita. She was adamant that we don't go to Leh."

"It doesn't hurt to ask. If you won't, I will. Kita? I know you've been listening."

"Yes. No. Leh is dangerous."

"It's a quick raid. We'll have the element of surprise."

"As soon as the trucks and girls are spotted, they're going to know you're coming. Leh is the Wild West. It's lawless and crawling with FKA fighters. The neighborhood where the hotel is located is hostile and firmly under Nath's control. It's too dangerous."

"Then I'll go by myself," said Nemesis. *"I'll kill him and drag his body back."*

"And I'll go with her," said Sapper.

"Me, too," said Cardinal. *"Svin'ya like this do not deserve to exist. Let them know what it is to suffer."*

Kita sighed.

"It makes strategic sense, angel," said Apocalypse. *"If we can remove the head of the FKA, we can find the troops to take Leh. Kashmir will be secure, and it'll give the Indians one less place to retreat to."*

"There isn't enough time to plan or get equipment in place."

"Sometimes we have to go with what we have. I think five Angels should be more than enough."

"Fine. But put the Star Bridge on standby in case you and I have to be reinforcements."

"The Star Bridge is currently moving the Seventh Infantry Division into Turkey. I'll override it if I have to, and I'll have two Anti-Neophorm Teams standing by ready to deploy. You

have my permission. Send your plan, so we know how to prepare in case you need our help," said Apocalypse.

Kita grumbled.

"Easy, angel. It'll be fine."

"Famous last words."

"OK," SAID POISON. "THIS IS A SIMPLE RAID. WE GET in and get out as fast as possible. Anna is already in Leh trying to track down as many of Nath's cabinet members as she can. She's already sent back data on the city. It's divided into neighborhoods; they're all under FKA control, but the northern neighborhoods are more heavily protected than those in the south. Regardless, it's lawless, and the FKA militia is the authority. This militia contains the real hardcore fighters. They get high on a drug called firepower—a mix of cocaine and gun powder. It makes them feel no pain and makes them think they're invincible. If we get into a fight with them, don't expect them to go down easy or run away.

"The good news is the Kashmiri Ambassador Hotel is on the east side of the city in the Deepak Market. The convoy will take a southern route through the city, so we only have to pass through a mile of hostile neighborhood. But it's going to be a long mile. Two Ranger chalks and the Angels will fly to the hotel and secure the prisoners and the building. The convoy will arrive, we load the prisoners, and our soldiers then follow this road east out of the city. We'll follow a series of roads around the city back to the highway and return to Kargil, where we'll handoff the prisoners to ICOM. Any questions?"

"Air cover, Captain?" said Mallory.

"Bombshell and Stunner will provide close air support after the Ranger chalks are on the ground. Venom and my birds will be in drone mode flown by remote here at the airport. They'll provide a bigger punch if we need it."

"What about Nicole's revenge?" said Sapper.

Poison grimaced. "Anna's looking for as many as she can find. We'll try and get them all."

"I'll stay behind and find them if I have to," said Nemesis.

"I know, but let's get this much done first and see how much of a hornet's nest we kick over."

"You sound worried," Sapper said with a grin.

Poison frowned. "We won't have the element of surprise. The meeting is late afternoon when the militia will be wired. I'm not worried, but I want everyone on their A-game. No mistakes—no one gets out of control. We're all professional military. We need to act like it. We do our jobs, get our targets, and we bring everyone home."

"My Rangers will do their jobs, Captain," said Mallory.

"It's not your Rangers I'm worried about. I'm looking at the Angels. Stick to the plan, ladies. We're not Kita. We get into trouble here, and there's no one to bail us out, except each other, and we can't do that if we off running around not doing what we're supposed to. Understand?"

Nemesis understood that warning was for her. She

would do her part and be a team player. Afterward, if her revenge wasn't met, she'd decide how best to complete it. Sapper and Cardinal had offered to go with her, and she was considering taking them up on it. Not because she needed help, but they would expedite the finding and getting to the men.

"No problem," said Stunner.

The teenager sounded nervous to Nemesis. *How many combat missions has she been on?*

The other Angels readily agreed.

"Nicole?" said Poison.

"I'll do my part. I'll decide what to do after we're out of the city."

That seemed to take a weight off Poison's shoulders. "Ok. We move to the Kargil staging area in two hours. We'll link up with the Fifth of the Seven-Oh-First to refuel and grab the latest intel there. Make sure you're ready. I want this to go as smoothly as Kargil. Dismissed."

Nemesis drifted over to the computer showing a 3D rendering of the city and the convoy route. The streets were narrow, lined by two- and three-story buildings. What the rendering couldn't tell was what the buildings were made of. Most had peaked roofs, so there would be no one attacking from the roofs. It also didn't say anything about the people. *The great unknown. How sympathetic to the FKA are they? Will they help them? Scatter? I doubt they'll help us.*

"I'm glad we don't have to go through the streets," said Sapper.

"You think it'll be bad?"

"If it's like the Middle East, we'll attract attention.

I'm going to make sure the Rangers have their coax and fifty-cals ready. I have a feeling we'll be shooting on the move."

"I'm glad we have the MRAPs."

"Yeah, they're nice bunkers on wheels. Are you going to take an M-4?"

"No. I'm going straight demon. I don't want anything in my hands."

"Good. I'm glad to see you embrace your new abilities."

"I'm not a master yet, but I will be."

"Want to make the rounds with me?"

"Sure. It'll be interesting to see the Rangers up close."

Leh looks like it's seen better days. The city was rundown and damaged. Nemesis didn't know the city's recent history, but years of fighting had left little intact, just shells of buildings. Piles of rubble lined the streets, and many roofs had gaping holes. People moved in the streets, going about their lives doing their best to make do. There were few vehicles. Those she did see were militia tacticals.

"Why are they burning tires?" said Nemesis to Sapper in the other door of Stunner.

"In the Middle East, it was the signal that EUS forces were coming. They also did it to obscure the vision of the pilots."

"Not a problem for me," said Stunner. *"But it is harmful to the environment."*

"There are a lot of them all over the city," said Nemesis.

"The air above the city is going to be black."

"This is Bulldog Six. We're entering the Deepak Market. The drone shows the route is clear," said Mallory. *"Super Seven-four, Super Seven-five, proceed to target."*

"Roger, Bulldog Six. Super Seven-four moving to target," said Bombshell.

"Super Seven-five moving," said Stunner.

The wind pushed harder against Nemesis as Stunner picked up speed. As they moved deeper into the Deepak Market, they attracted more gunfire. A round went through Nemesis' feathers.

"Careful, Stunner, they're taking potshots. I've got some damaged feathers."

"Yeah, I had a round hit my tail. Luckily it's just random and light."

Stunner arrived over the hotel first and hovered above the northwest corner. As the crew chief extended the repelling lines, the volume of fire increased dramatically.

"We've got to hurry," yelled Sapper as she jumped from Stunner and glided toward the ground.

Nemesis did the same, hoping to draw fire away from the Rangers. The shooters were running through the streets and shooting from windows. She landed on one and plunged a blade through his chest.

A fighter ran up to her, firing his AK-47 wildly in her general direction. She shot a tendril out and wrapped around the weapon, and yanked it from his hands. A spear from her shoulder skewered the fighter through the head.

Nemesis followed the sound of gunfire around the corner of the hotel. Halfway down the block, a fighter had an RPG aimed at Stunner. *"Stunner! RPG on your six! Firing!"*

The rocket leaped off the end of the launcher and streaked toward the Morphicon.

Stunner juked to the left, twisting, causing her cabin to tilt. A Ranger on the rappelling rope lost his grip and fell from Nemesis' view.

"They ok?" said Nemesis.

"This is Bulldog Two-Three. Reporting one wounded. We're going to need evac."

"Bulldog Six. Where's he wounded?"

"It's not a gunshot. Redbourn fell."

"He fell? How the hell did that happen? Get him stabilized, and we'll pick him up when we get there."

"Wilco."

"It's getting hot down here," said Sapper as she came upon Nemesis.

Nemesis agreed as more fighters entered the streets. Poison and Venom appeared from the other corner of the hotel.

"We need to get inside and secure the targets," said Poison.

"Should we all go? The Rangers are taking fire."

"I'll give the FKA something else to shoot at." Poison raised her hands and drew a symbol in the air while chanting, "Onca uncia pardus!" Two one-story tall stone golems grew from the street. "Protect the Rangers."

The golems moved out; one went left, the other right.

"Come on," said Poison as she led everyone into the hotel. They rushed past an empty fountain and some shabby furniture in the lobby, up a flight of stairs, through a set of double doors, to a large room with a long table surrounded by chairs. At the head of the table was a man wearing a set of Chinese military fatigues and a yellow beret.

"Everyone down on the table," yelled Venom. She jumped onto the table and transformed into a scorpion. She struck two of the men in rapid succession with her stinger, paralyzing them.

Sapper went around the table's right side shoving her M-4 into the men forcing them onto the table. Nemesis went down the left side, wrapping tendrils around the men's necks and pushed them down.

Cardinal materialized in a corner next to the man in the yellow beret. "I have verified this is Dina Nath, the leader of the Free Kashmir Army."

"You're now a guest of the Empire of the United States," said Poison. "We—"

"*I got a problem. I got a problem!*" screamed Bombshell.

"*What's going on?*" said Poison.

"*I'm hit. I'm hit. My tail's gone. I've got six Rangers and my crew chief. Super Seven-four is going down. Say again. Super Seven-four is going—*"

"*Bomb!*" yelled Stunner.

"*Where did she go down?*" said Poison.

"*I've got her on the drone. She went down twelve blocks northwest of the target. I have large numbers of indigenous people moving on the crash site.*"

"*What's that mean?*" said Nemesis.

"*Crowds of people are headed to the crash site. I'm not sure of their intentions.*"

"*I doubt it's to help.*"

"*Poison. Bulldog Two-Three. The rest of my chalk wants permission to secure the crash site.*"

"*How many Rangers do you have?*"

"*Six, including me.*"

"*You do know we don't know how long it'll be before we can get reinforcements to you? You could be out there a while.*"

"*Roger, Poison. We understand.*"

"*Permission granted. Stunner, when all the Rangers are on the deck, you're to give close air support. Your choice.*"

"*Roger. Wilco. I'm going to vaporize them.*"

Nemesis reached Nath first. She dragged her tongue across his face. Air escaped between her teeth. "The first donor." Jumping onto the table, she squatted in front of him and grabbed his collar. Her demon mask split, revealing her face. "Do you remember me?"

Nath glared. "I don't remember dogs."

"Maybe if I showed you my ass, you'd remember. I know you remember these." Her feathers changed from black and red to silver and blue.

"Foul abomination sent to defile us."

"Yet not foul enough to stick your dick in."

"Women abominations must be taught who their masters are."

Nemesis grabbed him by the face and dug her claws in. "No one is my master, especially not a cowardly pathetic male who didn't have the balls to try to rape me when I was awake."

"The next time I rape you, you will beg for more."

Sapper smashed the butt of her M-4 into the side of Nath's head. She drew her Ka-bar. "I should cut off your balls and shove them in your mouth, but I know what's coming."

"Later," said Poison. "We need him alive and conscious."

Nemesis stood up, and her second mouth formed. She grabbed Nath by the head and placed his ear against the teeth of her mouth. With a *snap*, she took off his ear. She lifted him up and turned him so she could whisper in his other ear, "The next bite I take will be your manhood." She shoved him back into the chair.

Nath didn't say a word as he sat stone-faced.

"*Poison. Bulldog Six. A truck just took an RPG. We're loading the wounded—Lay down some covering fire! Get the bodies loaded!*"

"*Bulldog Six. Bulldog Two-Two. We're taking heavy fire from all sides. What's your ETA?*"

"*Bulldog Two-Two, we're taking fire, and we've got to get this wreck out of the way. We'll be there as soon as we can.*"

"Ok, ladies, we need to get these men secured and downstairs so we can support the Rangers," said Poison.

Sapper produced a stack of cable ties, and the Angels bound the dozen men's hands behind their back then lined them up in front of the door.

"Everyone out the door and downstairs," said Poison. "Line up by the front door of the hotel. If you stop, you get the scorpion's sting. Now move." She pushed the lead man forward and moved alongside the others, guiding them where to go.

Nemesis was last, and she pushed Nath along. Venom moved back and forth, brandishing her deadly stinger. Sapper pushed the middle of the group along. She mounted her Ka-bar on her M-4 to be more persuasive.

"*Bulldog Six. Bulldog Two-Two. I've got one KIA and two wounded, plus Blackburn.*"

"You're going to have to hold on, Bulldog Two-Two. They've set up roadblocks we have to find our way around."

"Nicole, Lizzy, go out and help the Rangers," ordered Poison.

Nemesis nodded and pushed through the heavy hotel door. Outside, the cacophony of gunfire came from everywhere. A trio of Rangers were holding the near corner, and two more had the far corner. A golem moved up the street, throwing debris at fighters in the windows. Nemesis hurried up to the near group as Sapper went to the far group.

The Rangers armed with M-4s and a machine gun were taking cover in a rubble pile firing at windows and doors.

"How are you doing?" said Nemesis. She extended her arms and formed her quicksilver into shields. "Take some time to regroup and reload." Her shields attracted attention from the fighters, but they missed much more often than they hit.

"It's hot out here, ma'am, but they can't shoot for shit," said a specialist.

The Rangers swapped out magazines and drank some water from their water bags.

"Keep firing and keep your heads up and theirs down. It only takes one lucky shot to be going home in a box."

"Roger that, ma'am. We're ready when you are."

Nemesis lowered her shields and jumped down the street to a second-story window containing a fighter. Her tail divided into three parts, each with a spike on the end. She slammed the spikes into the wall next to a window, reached in, and grabbed the fighter. She yanked him out and slashed his throat with her claws. Dropping the body, she flew down the street, searching out fighters and dispatching them with ruthless efficiency.

"*Bulldog Six. Bulldog Two-Two. My corner is collapsing. It's just—*"

"*Bulldog Two-Two, say again, over.*"

"*They're gone,*" said Sapper. "*They were overrun. All Bulldog Two-Two and Two-Three elements fallback to the front of the hotel and secure the entrance. Nicole, meet me at the northwest corner, and we'll see if we can retrieve the bodies.*"

Nemesis flew over the three-story hotel and landed on the northwest corner rooftop. Below her, fighters celebrated their victory and were stripping the dead Rangers of their gear. Sapper landed next to her.

"Assholes. What is it about prims that they can't respect the dead?"

"I don't know, but let's teach them about celebrating early."

They stepped off the roof and landed among the fighters. Nemesis shot quicksilver spears out in five directions at once. Sapper attacked with her Ka-bar bayonet, disemboweling a fighter, smashing a second in the face, and plunging the knife into the chest of a third. The remaining fighters fled, only to be shot by Sapper.

Nemesis knelt among the Rangers, checking for signs of life. She found two alive. Three more, including two sergeants, were dead. "Get the dead. I'll get the wounded." She lifted the wounded Rangers and took off for the front of the hotel.

Pushing through the hotel door, Nemesis laid the wounded Rangers on the colorful rug. She opened the first Ranger's fatigue top and found a bullet wound in her gut. Pulling the Ranger's bandage from her gear, Nemesis pushed the pad against the injury. "You with me, Ranger?"

The wounded Ranger's head moved. "Yes, ma'am," she said through gritted teeth.

"You're going to need to hold this bandage against your wound, ok? Keep pressure on it."

"Yes, ma'am."

Nemesis turned to help the other Ranger, but Sapper was already bandaging his shoulder. "Karen, where's the convoy?"

"Coming. They have to take the long way. The FKA keeps blocking the streets."

"*This is Bulldog Two-Three at the crash site. I've got three wounded. We're doing our best to stabilize them. Doc says we can't move them, or we'll kill them. Everyone else, including the Angel, is KIA. We have a large crowd surrounding us, and the situation is deteriorating fast.*"

"*Roger, Two-Three. The convoy is almost to the target. We'll be at your location ASAP.*"

"*We'll hold as long as we can. Bulldog Two-Three, out.*"

"This keeps getting better and better," said Sapper.

"We knew this would be rough," said Poison.

The building shook as an RPG exploded against a far wall.

"Come on, Lizzy. Back outside. The Rangers need our help." Nemesis opened the door. Bullets snapped by her, one striking a VIP, and a second round hit her thigh. She looked down at the VIP. "I bet you wish you were me right now." Nemesis ran across the street and crashed through a door. She slammed into a fighter, wrapping her tongue around his neck and nearly pulling his head off. Up the stairs, she transformed her arms into blades and cut down two fighters firing from windows.

As she stepped back onto the street, the lead MRAP turned the corner. Its tan paint was marred with bullet and RPG strikes. The convoy pulled up to the front of the hotel. Rangers riding with the convoy jumped from their vehicles to help defend the area. The last MRAP morphed into Sprokkit. He moved around the corner, firing, giving the Rangers a diversion. Mallory exited the lead MRAP and walked over to some of his Rangers taking cover. Nemesis noted he walked erect, ignoring the bullets that went past him. When he was done, he came over to Nemesis.

"Colonel, are the VIPs ready to go?"

"Yes. Let's get them loaded and get out of here." She opened the door to the hotel. "Karen, the convoy's here!"

"Roger. Ok, you scum, everyone outside and on the trucks!"

With prodding from Venom, the group of VIPs was pushed out onto the street. Mallory and the Rangers shoved them into the back of the military 5-ton trucks. The trucks had no armor and only canvas sides to shield the occupants. Mallory detailed several Rangers to ride with the VIPs.

"Ok, let's go," yelled Sapper. "Keep firing as you board the trucks. Drivers! Get them cranked up. Angels, let's keep them busy."

Nemesis flew to the head of the convoy. In the street, several fighters fired at Rangers boarding the MRAP. She landed in front of them. Her tail whipped around and divided into three, spearing two of the fighters. The third fighter jumped back. Nemesis jumped at him, landing on his chest. She plunged her tail sections into him.

More bullets hit her from the left. She turned, but the shooters ran away. Behind her, the lead MRAP blew its horn and rolled down the street. Nemesis took flight and was joined by the other Angels. Sprokkit had joined the convoy as well as the two golems.

"Bulldog Two-Three, Bulldog Six. VIPs are loaded. We're headed to your location. What is your status?"

"Bulldog Six, I've got three KIA, and the rest are wounded. We're holding on, but they're coming from all sides."

"Roger, Bulldog Two-Three. We'll be there quick as we can."

Nemesis wasn't sure where the crash site was. Any sign was obscured by the oily black smoke that filled the skies. To make matters worse, the convoy came upon another roadblock made up of rubble and junk. The lead MRAP eased up to it and pushed the debris aside with its massive bumper as it climbed the mound of rubble. If it was slow for the MRAPs, it was slower for the 5-ton trucks. She could see why it had taken the convoy so long to reach them. It was going to take even longer to get to the crash site.

"We've got to speed this up," Nemesis said to Poison.

"I can put the golems in front. They can clear the rubble and junk faster. *Bulldog Six.*"

"This is Six."

"I'm going to move my golems to the front of the convoy to clear any more roadblocks. They should speed us up."

"Roger. Anything to get us moving."

"Onca uncia pardus!" The two golems at the rear of the convoy dissolved and two more formed at the lead.

They ran ahead down the street toward a pair of burned-out cars that blocked an intersection. They slammed into the first car and lifted it. From the cross street, a man stepped out with an RPG and fired. The projectile slammed into the side of a golem blowing it to pieces.

"*Dammit!*" snarled Poison. "*Those RPGs are going to be the death of us.*"

"*How did they get so many?*" said Sapper.

"*You can get a launcher for the price of three chickens and five warheads for a handful of rice,*" said Cardinal. "*An AK-47 is even cheaper. The city has more weapons than food.*"

"*And an Angel looks like a big chicken to them,*" said Nemesis.

"*I wonder how many RPGs one of us is worth?*" said Sapper.

The Angels giggled.

"*Roadway is clear,*" said Poison.

The convoy picked up speed as bullets peppered the sides of the vehicles.

"*WE NEED HELP!*" screamed Stunner.

"*What's the matter?*" said Poison.

"*The sergeant is dead! I'm on the ground! I've got a wounded soldier! They're coming from all sides! I'm doing my best, but I'm taking fire!*"

"*Keep calm. We're coming. I'm sending Nicole and Zhi to you.*"

"*Ok, hurry. I'm beginning to glow red.*"

Poison motioned Nemesis and Venom forward.

"*Nemesis. Bulldog Six. The crash site is five blocks down. Take a right, and go two blocks.*"

"*Roger. We're moving.*"

Nemesis flapped her wings, and the two Angels took off over the rooftops into the oily black sky.

"*Flying through this shit is going to ruin my feathers,*" said Venom.

They crossed over a building into a large square where Bombshell crashed into the cobblestones. The locals surrounded the young Morphicon and pelted her with rocks. Armed men fired wildly at Stunner, often hitting more locals than their target. Stunner guarded Bombshell's right door and a Ranger leaning against the opposite door. Several bodies were inside Bombshell with a medic working on them.

"*What a damn mess. The whole damn city is coming down on them,*" said Venom. "*Nicole, you help Stunner. I'll defend the other side. Push them back.*"

"*Ok. I...What the shit is that? That's Amy!*" Nemesis pointed to the back of the crowd. They were carrying several naked EUS soldiers above their hands, dancing and celebrating. A woman grabbed Fortune's hair and cut it off with a knife. She held the hair up and yelled something in Kashmiri. "*I'm going to kill them all!*"

"*Help Stunner. Amy's dead. We'll get the body back later.*"

"*To think I tried to help these people. They're barbarians.*"

"*Don't forget. In their eyes, their fighters are heroes. We're the bad guys.*"

Nemesis dove for Stunner. The teenager was covered in red spots where bullets had struck her. She looked like she had measles. Nemesis landed and extended her wings to shield Stunner.

"Hey, I'm here. I'm going to push them back."

"Thanks. Luckily they can't shoot for shit."

"Your case of the measles says differently."

"For the amount of lead their firing, I should be Swiss cheese."

Nemesis turned and leaped at the crowd sending tendrils out and grabbing six men by their necks. She yanked them into each other, turned her arms into blades, and slashed them across their abdomens. A man ran at her, firing wildly. She lunged, grabbed the rifle in one hand and his head in the other. She drove her claws into his face, crushed his skull, and flung the body into the crowd. It seemed to enrage them further.

"*Don't these guys have any fear?*"

"*They're hopped up on that firepower. They think they're invincible,*" said Venom.

"*I guess I'll just have to kill them all.*"

Two bullets struck Nemesis in the chest. She roared, baring her teeth and lashing her tongue. Her arms became blades, and she swung at the crowd, slicing through several. An explosion threw her into the air. She landed among the masses. A second explosion rocked the square. The crowd fell upon Nemesis. Some shot her, but two men attacked with kukri knives. One sliced the tendons running through her left wing; the other stabbed her in the gut. *Shit.* Nemesis shot tendrils out around the necks of those attacking her. She squeezed her tendrils until the heads came off. She jumped backward toward Stunner, but the teenager wasn't there, and Bombshell was blown to pieces. Beyond the crash site, Venom—as a giant scorpion—was lying on the ground, her tail down, not moving, her front smoking. On the far side, an MRAP was pushing into the square.

"*ZHI! NICOLE! STUNNER!*" yelled Poison.

"*I'm here, but I'm wounded, and they're coming from all*

sides," said Nemesis. *"Don't bring the trucks in. It's too dangerous."*

To punctuate her words, an M-2 machine gun on the lead MRAP fired into the crowd.

"We've got to get the dead out of here. What do we do?"

"Call Kita. She's going to be pissed she was right."

"Damn right I am. Nicole, clear us some space."

Nemesis sent out a series of tendrils and fashioned them into blades. She spun, slashing through the crowd around her. An electrical crackle signaled a rift gate's appearance—an interdimensional portal known at the Star Bridge. Nemesis turned to see who was coming through when a man plunged a knife into her lower back. She gasped and shot out a tendril through her attacker's chest. A flash and the man's head hit the ground. Kita and Velositi stood in front of her. "Kita, Velositi, I'm sorry."

Kita grimaced and shook her head.

Velositi didn't say a word; instead, she morphed into a giant mecha-dragon. She roared, lowered her head, and released a ball of flame that vaporized a section of the crowd. The jubilant crowd panicked as Velositi smashed them with her feet and tail. The crowd tried to escape, but many were engulfed in flames.

"Nothing like a mother's vengeance," said Poison.

Kita grunted. "I'm going to burn this city to the ground. Find Stunner and Bombshell's pieces, and move them and Zhi through the gate. Tell the Rangers to take up position around this square. Anyone wounded, move them through the gate. Nicole, how are you?"

"I've taken a couple of stab wounds, but I can help."

"No. Go through the gate and get patched up. Karen,

Anna, and Sprokkit can handle the cleanup."

"What about my revenge?"

"You'll have it. Now go."

Nemesis's demon mask split, revealing her head. "Can you find Amy's body?"

"I won't leave anyone behind."

Nemesis nodded. She gulped hard and stepped through the rift gate into the cave under Shiveluch volcano. A medical team met her.

"Do you need help, Colonel?" said a doctor.

"Just a place to lay and recover. Maybe clean out a few wounds."

"No problem. Follow me."

Nemesis let out a long sigh after the doctor left. She settled into the comfortable bed as medical equipment monitored her status in the room on level four of the bunker at Area 51. Not that there was much to observe. Her blood pressure and pulse were perfect. Still, she hurt. Her attackers had sliced her kidney, while her wing was suspended in a cribbing of wires to hold it until the tendon healed. The pain medication the doctor gave her only took the edge off. He said she should be healed in forty-eight hours.

It didn't seem fair. She was on her back while the others cleaned up her mess. The events that were supposed to make her feel better left her depressed. Amy was dead. The triplets were inoperable. Bombshell might be permadead. Venom was down the hall in a recovery tank.

The door opened, and Kita entered.

She looked stoic and serious like a person proven right and was now dealing with the aftermath.

"Kita..." Nemesis hung her head. She didn't know how to tell Kita how sorry she was. Instead, she said, "How is everything? Did you find the Rangers' bodies? What about the triplets? I—"

Kita held up a hand. "We're still recovering. Anna's tracking down the bodies. The Lehians dropped most of them but ran off with a few. We have Amy. Sprokkit has the triplets. Stunner and Bombshell are going to need new bodies and a few system cores. It'll be a couple of weeks before they're back."

"If you're still in recovery, why are you here wasting time with me?"

"I'm god. I better be able to be in two places at once," Kita said with a chuckle. "But, there's no trick involved. Just a solid hologram generator on an anti-grav pad connected to me through the computer. You've been gone for three years and have missed all the technology I've introduced to make this place livable."

Nemesis laughed tiredly. "You did grow up here."

"I grew up in lots of places. I call the White House home, but to me, Roost will forever be home."

"Roost?"

"A tiny space station orbiting around my homeworld. But I didn't come here to tell you about my past. We can do that some other time. I felt I needed to lift you up and tell you what happened wasn't your fault."

"It is my fault. Me and my stupid revenge got lots of people I cared about killed."

"There are days that are going to be like this. You

should know that as a commander. If you haven't experienced one up until now, you've been lucky."

"I've never lost a person."

"Those lost today aren't on your head. The buck stops with Kimmy."

"It was because of me."

"No. Kashmir was a problem before you got there. You just got tangled up in it. Your revenge is important, but it's not the reason Amy, Stunner, Bombshell, and the other Rangers died. They died trying to make Kimmy's vision a reality. That's the bottom line. We have the rest of the men who raped you. They're yours to do with as you please."

Nemesis wrinkled her nose. "I feel silly. It seems so petty and small in comparison to Amy's and the others' deaths."

"You don't need to take a bite out of them. If you won't think of something, I will."

Nemesis nodded. "I have some time to think about it."

"Yes, you do. There's no rush. They'll rot in Guantanamo until you're ready."

"How are you doing?" Nemesis asked. It just came to her that Kita was probably hurting, too.

Kita wiped her eye. "Losing your kids never gets any easier, even when you can put them back together. I'll be fine. I want to make sure you'll be fine."

"When I started, I wanted to be like you. Put myself first. See the world as you do. I realize I can't be like you. I understand your point of view, but I can't get over the fact that there is no good in the world. I'm good. Others need help. But I'm not interested in helping for helping's sake. It's too easy to be taken advantage of. I will help on my own terms. Starting with girls like us who have had our worlds destroyed by greedy, hedonistic males. I know too often they go unpunished by the criminal justice system. Now, they'll need to look over their shoulder because I will be coming for them."

"I won't stand in your way. They deserve to die screaming."

"I also want to start some kind of institution to help girls piece their lives back together. I thank you for all the support you gave me. They need that kind of help, too."

Kita nodded. "We can make that happen. If you want to be the face of it, I'll support you."

"During the day, I'll help the survivors. At night the hunters will become the hunted."

Nemesis saluted the flag the pallbearer held. She stood at the head of Amy's coffin in the committal shelter of Bay Pines National Cemetery. She took the flag between her hands, holding it waist-high, she marched around the coffin to the elder Fortunes. She faced Amy's mother and father and knelt.

She offered the flag and said, "On behalf of the Empress of the Empire of the United States, the Empire of the United States, and a grateful Nation, please accept this flag as a symbol of our appreciation of Amy's honorable and faithful service."

Mistress Fortune took the flag with tears streaming from her eyes. "Thank you," she whispered.

"Mistress and Mister Fortune, I would like to pass along my personal condolences. Amy helped me through a tough time in my life, and without her, I don't think I would have become whole. I will never forget her, and with your permission, I would like to name the new national rape crisis center after her."

The couple traded looks.

"Of course," said Mister Fortune.

"I promise her legacy will live on helping girls just like she helped me." Nemesis stood and saluted. She marched out of the shelter and joined the rest of the Angels and Rangers watching.

NEMESIS OPENED THE HEAVY METAL DOOR AND stepped inside the bare cinder block room. She was trailed by two men. The first wore military fatigues with a doctor's coat over them. His name tag read MAJ DAN BOWER, DDS. The second man had long hair, numerous facial piercings, and his visible skin was covered in tattoos.

Nemesis's tongue lashed back and forth as she saw the sixteen men bound to chairs, including Dina Nath. She ran her tongue over each one to make sure she had the correct men. When she was satisfied, she went to Nath.

"I bet you remember me now."

"Dog."

Nemesis's smile showed all of her teeth as she leaned into him. "You can call me a dog all you want, but you are going to be someone's bitch." She ran her tongue over his face and snapped her teeth at him, making him jump. She moved to the center of the room. "Now, I could punish you like all the others, but that doesn't seem appropriate. Most of those boys died of their injuries. I want you to suffer like I have and will. You took a part of me that I can never get back. I think it's only fair you get the same. These two gentlemen, Doctor Bower and Nitro, are here to help prepare you for where you're going. I'm sure you'll all be happy to learn you're leaving Guantanamo. The bad news is, you will all get homes in the worst jails and prisons in the Empire's criminal justice system.

"I'm sure you all think you're hard enough to survive. That's where Doctor Bower and Nitro come in. Doctor Bower is going to remove your top and lower front teeth and fit you for dentures. I don't want to ruin that smile of yours. Nitro is one of the top tattooers in Miami. He's going to tattoo *child rapist* across your forehead and on the back of your hands. You'll then be put it in with each prison's general population to let you fend for yourself. I hope you find it a pleasant place to retire." She pointed at Nath. "Let's start with him."

Apocalypse sat at her desk in the Oval Office. It was just after eight, and the morning briefings were arriving in her inbox. She flipped through the reports from around her empire. One about an unusual attack the previous night caught her attention. It happened just after ten. Something large landed on the car, smashed out the rear window, and pulled an eighteen-year-old boy from the backseat. The teenager was found in the early morning hanging from a light post by his hands, his genitals ripped off. The report said the teenager was still alive at a local hospital. "*Angel, you want to come here for a second?*"

Kita entered the Oval Office and walked around the couch to lean on Apocalypse's desk. "What's up?"

"Have you seen this story?" Apocalypse turned her laptop around so Kita could read it.

"That's the Brownstone kid, isn't it?"

"I'm not familiar with it."

"He raped a fifteen-year-old girl at a party, and the judge gave him a three-month deferred sentence stating he didn't want to ruin the young man's life."

Apocalypse turned her nose up. "My father's judicial appointments at work. I'll find the judge and have him removed." She sighed. "I might have to go through all of my father's appointments."

"Do you want me to tell Nicole not to be so public?"

"She did this?"

"That's my guess."

"No, tell her she's doing fine. I'll tell the police to drop the case into a shredder."

DEDICATED TO MY HEROES: THE BRAVE SOLDIERS, Rangers, and Operators that fought, died, and served at the Battle of Mogadishu and to all those sexual trauma survivors, you are not alone. If you need help contact me or 1.800.656.HOPE. For my fellow vets, contact me or 1.800.273.8255.

CHAPTER FOUR
KIMMY

THE DOOR OPENED WITH A *CLACK* AS THE DENVER Convention Center director pushed against the metal bar. "This way, Empress." He waved an associate toward the main platform.

The giant room was full of tables lined up in twenty rows with space for fifty players per row. Players sat across from each other playing *Magic: The Gathering*. Other players gathered along the walls talking, adjusting decks, and trading cards.

"Can—can I have everyone kneel?" said a hesitant voice over the loudspeaker from the main platform.

The room was slow to react as most players tried to figure out why.

"*Mom, did you have to? It's so embarrassing...*" said Chelsea over the Angel's bionanite communications.

"*Sorry, sweet pea. I had nothing to do with it this time,*" Apocalypse told her daughter.

Apocalypse waited for everyone to find their knee before giving the command, "Rise. Please, continue."

The convention center associate returned with a man and a woman wearing *Magic: The Gathering* polo shirts.

"Empress, I'm Mark Gardner, Grand Prix Director for Wizards of the Coast. I'm in charge of today's event. This is Frankie Saxx, Director of Player Engagement. I'm sorry, I didn't know you were coming." He looked pale.

"No need to apologize. We decided to take this trip this morning. My daughter Chelsea has taken an interest in the game after seeing it at school. Her mom bought her a starter deck and some other cards, but we couldn't figure out how to play after following the directions. My staff found this event, and I thought, what better way to learn than from the best." *I do hope you pass on to whoever writes your instructions that if the Empress couldn't figure it out, how do they expect an eight-year-old to do so...then again, maybe that's the point.*

Mark looked to relax. "We have some of the best players in the world here today. The premier league hasn't started yet. I'm sure a few of them would love to help your daughter learn. Frankie, can you see who's available?"

"My name's Chelsea, and I'm right here."

Apocalypse smiled from under her hood. Chelsea took after Kita in lots of ways.

"Sorry, Chelsea. Here, have today's collectible. It's a Grand Prix foil card." Mark took one from his breast pocket and handed it to the young Angel.

Chelsea took it. "Cool. What's it do?"

"It's a Garefort Rat. Tap it to get black or green mana. The more you have, the more mana they produce."

"Ok. Here Wendy, put it in the binder."

Chelsea's personal assistant took the card, removed a binder from a backpack, and slipped the card into an empty clear pocket.

The cards had cost Apocalypse a small fortune. She thought Chelsea should start small, but Kita was adamant that Chelsea should have the best. Her wife argued it was so Chelsea could master her ability to control the random number generator, part of the computer that governed all of Reality. To everyone else, it was simply called luck.

Saxx returned with a man in his early forties wearing a shirt with a blue raindrop on it. "Empress, may I introduce Jason Saunders. He's ranked fourth in the world."

"Hello, Empress, Princess," he said in a melancholy tone.

I wonder what she had to do to twist your arm to do this? "Hello, Jason. My daughter Chelsea is interested in learning *Magic*. I was hoping you could teach her."

"Ah, sure. No problem."

"You can use the head table, Jason," said Gardner. "The premier league isn't going to start for another hour."

"Ok."

"Please follow me, Empress, Princess," said Saxx.

Apocalypse followed her to a table on the main platform.

"Ok," said Jason, "Let's see what you got." He said with an impatient sigh.

Wendy set the backpack on the table and took out several binders as well as several boxes.

"The dealer said the cards in the binders were rare, and these in the boxes were common and uncommon," said Apocalypse.

Saunders took one of the binders and flipped it open. His eyebrows went up. "You have an Alpha set of the Power Nine?" He looked through the other binders, his eyes getting wider and wider.

"Chelsea's other mom felt she should have the best."

"She's got the best, that's for sure, at least if you're playing original series."

"Original series?"

"The Prix is divided up into series, so players are playing with the same generation of cards to keep it fair. You drop a Power Nine versus someone playing with today's cards, and you'd smoke them in a few turns..."

A tap on Apocalypse's shoulder took her attention away from the players. "Empress, the CIA is on a secure line."

Apocalypse took the phone and stuck it under her hood. "Yes?"

"Empress, we have a situation with the Vicereine," said Charlie Rosenstein, her CIA Director.

Apocalypse sighed. "What has Kita done now?"

"You'd best see it."

"Ok. I'm at the Denver Convention Center. It'll take me a few hours to get to Air Force One."

"Understood, Empress. We'll do our best to find out where they took her."

A sinking feeling hit Apocalypse's stomach. "What? Explain."

"We believe the West German military or state police have her."

"What was she doing in West Germany?" Apocalypse hissed.

"We were hoping you could tell us. Hopefully, the video will shed light on the reason."

"I'm leaving now. I will call you from Air Force One."

"Yes, Empress."

Apocalypse hung up the phone and growled. She was worried about Kita. Few things in the world should stop her, but why had she gone to West Germany? She leaned in to whisper into Chelsea's ear, "Sweet pea, I have to go."

Chelsea's head snapped up from paying attention to Saunders. "What's wrong?"

Apocalypse sighed. Giving the girl a cloud had been a blessing and a curse. "Something happened to Momma-K. I need to go help her."

"Are you taking the other Angels?"

"I don't know what's happened yet, other than she's been taken."

"Ok. Can I stay here?"

"Yes, of course you can. Right now, I'm going back to the plane. If I have to go home, I'll send a plane to pick you up."

"Cool."

"Just remember to practice. This isn't the same as the coin. You have more than three possibilities."

"I know." Chelsea put her hand on her deck, then drew a card. She held it up to Saunders. "Is this a good card?"

"That's a *Black Lotus*. That was on top?"

Chelsea shrugged. "Sure."

Apocalypse smiled. Chelsea was a fast learner. *But*

can she learn to call the card she needs when she needs it?
Chelsea had an unusual ability. Kita had plugged her into
the random number generator that governed reality. So
far, they'd practiced with flipping coins making the coin
land whatever Chelsea called. With *Magic: The Gathering,*
there were countless possibilities. Soon, she'd learn to do
it in the real world. Apocalypse wasn't sure she was
ready for that. "Dan, make sure she stays safe."

"Yes, Empress," said O'Brien.

Apocalypse motioned for her staff and security to
follow her as she returned to Air Force One.

APOCALYPSE TOOK OFF HER GLOVES AND PLACED THEM
on the edge of her desk. She swept off her hood and
hung up her calf-length Victorian coat. Pulling her
tomahawks from her belt, she stacked them next to her
gloves. *Being larger than life requires more pageantry than I
ever realized.*

She sat in her chair, specially designed for wings,
flipped open her laptop, and stuck her finger in the
biometric scanner. The scanner was an ingenious piece
of security technology that came from Kita. It scanned
the user's DNA and matched it against authorized users.
Those scanners provided by Kita were far more secure
than their predecessors. The new ones required a living
cell to provide the DNA.

The computer booted up, and Apocalypse checked
her inboxes. She had over a dozen—ruling the world
wasn't easy and required constant attention. She clicked
her domestic inbox and found a message with a FLASH

OVERRIDE header from the CIA. She opened the message and read the quick note saying the video provided happened during a Fat Sunny concert at Bonn's soccer stadium at nine thirty-eight local time. A YouTube link was included.

Oh hell. She didn't. Two weeks ago, the rapper Fat Sunny released a new album with a track entitled *Vicereine's My Bitch*. The song was profane and misogynistic. It included lyrics that she personally considered to be a threat of sexual assault.

She hit play, and the rapper filled the screen wearing a white tracksuit and a Starter cap with a bandana underneath. It was mid-song, apparently filmed by a fan in the crowd. *Thank god I don't have to listen to all of it.*

"I'LL LICK THAT SNATCH UP LIKE ICE CREAM,"
"I'll be balls deep in the Vicereine,"
"Make that bitch scream out my name,"

THERE WAS A SERIES OF FLASHES AROUND THE STAGE that filled the area with smoke. A harsh laugh filled the stadium as the air cleared. Kita, dressed in the Vicereine's black dress and hood, had Fat Sunny by the throat and was dangling him off the stage. Nemesis and Cardinal were flanking her. Apocalypse sighed. *This idiot picked on the wrong three Angels.* Each was a victim of rape, and none took it lightly. Nemesis made it her mission to seek out rapists and carry out her own vigilante justice. Apocalypse sanctioned her activities, but there were still too many rapists on the streets and too many weak judges leftover from her father.

Four security men in various thug/rapper attire rushed the stage with pistols drawn. Nemesis jumped in front of them, her black and red quicksilver tendrils waving in the air. Four tendrils shot forward and wrapped around the men's necks. Two took shots at the Angel, but the quicksilver covering her skin was bulletproof. Blades shot out from Nemesis's arms and plunged into the men's chests.

"You should have paid more than a million for security," Kita said in an eerily calm voice. "I understand you're a *Stan* of mine. Well, here I am. Make me your bitch."

"I—I'm s-sorry...I didn't...write the...song," Fat Sunny gasped.

Smoke grenades landed on the stage. The camera panned around wildly, trying to follow the action as the reality of the events on stage sank in, and most of the audience panicked and attempted to flee the venue. Dozens of men in paramilitary law enforcement uniforms wearing protective masks and armed with strange-looking weapons rushed up the stage's stairs from backstage. The Angels were on their knees coughing. The men fired into the Angels or stuck them with syringes. The Angels collapsed, and the men bound them as the video ended.

Apocalypse sat back, a pit the size of Air Force One in her stomach. *What do they have that can bring down Angels?* This was a problem she couldn't solve, but she knew others who could. She brought up her government messenger app and called three people.

"What?" said Sprokkit, a Vehlixen scientist who worked at Area 51.

"Hey, Kimmy. What's up?" said Ryan. A good friend of Apocalypse and Kita, he was a captain in the EUS Air Force and led the Majestic Twelve anti-Neophorm research team at Area 51. Ryan had bionanites like the Angels, but instead of wings, he transformed into a giant armored Panda. He refused to change for the Angels, but it was rumored he did it for his fiancée Sarah.

"Hey, Momma-Kim. How is Denver?" said Stunner, one of the Vehlixen triplets created and raised by Kita and Velositi. She was an up-and-coming scientist learning under Ryan and Sprokkit's supervision.

"Hi, everyone. Denver is fine. I'm afraid I won't get to see much of it. Chelsea's having a good time learning to play *Magic: The Gathering*. I have a video I need you to see. I don't know what or who has created, but we need to figure out a solution, fast." Apocalypse sent them the video.

"Momma-K! She's going to be ok, right, Momma-Kim?" said Stunner. "Does Mom know?"

"I don't know what Kita or the other Angels' status is. Right now, you know as much as I do. I haven't contacted Velositi yet. I will. What I need is a defense against whatever is in that gas and whatever they injected them with."

"Do you have a sample? We can't make an effective antidote or vaccine without something to work from," grumbled Sprokkit.

"Hello?" said Velositi. She led the Vehlixen on Earth and was one of Kita's partners.

"Mom!" cried Stunner. "They took Momma-K and threatened to rape her."

"What? Who?"

"Velositi, it's Kimmy. I'll send you a video that will explain what's going on." Apocalypse wished the teenager had more restraint. She understood being upset about her mother, but she was handling it. Apocalypse had included Stunner because she was a brilliant scientist, forgetting that she had a teenager's emotions.

"This does not look good," said Velositi after viewing the video. "Did you know she was going to West Germany, Kimmy?"

"No. When I spoke to her two days ago, she was going to Area Fifty-one to train with her Commandos."

"We should talk to them before they go looking for her."

Apocalypse grunted. There was a drawback to having people personally loyal to someone other than the country. Though she did pay for their toys, and it wouldn't be the first time she'd cut off their funding to bring them to heel.

"I'll take care of Kita's units. Leaf, are you here?"

"Yes. What's the matter?"

Kimmy sent her the video. Aspen was an assassin Angel and former student of Kita's, though she was a high angel and shared a different philosophy than Kita on how an assassin's skills should be used. *I should have just called everybody in the first place. So much for trying to keep it quiet.*

"Damn. I've heard of people gassing Angels before. I wonder what they were injecting them with."

"I was hoping you could find out what they used and where they took Kita," said Apocalypse.

"I guess I'm not too busy on the Farm to pick up the Grandmaster when she stumbles." She chuckled playfully.

"Tell me when you're ready, and I'll have the rift gate take you to the soccer stadium."

"Cool, no problem."

"I'm going to contact the West German delegation and demand an explanation. Maybe I can get Kita back through diplomatic channels. Velositi, why don't you come to the White House. I might need you."

"Yes, of course."

"Everyone else, do your best to figure out what this crap is, so maybe we can make a defense against it." She received a round of affirmatives and closed the app. Picking up the phone, she called Daisy, her personal assistant, and told her to get the plane moving back to D.C. and send Air Force Three for Chelsea. She didn't want to ruin her daughter's day of fun.

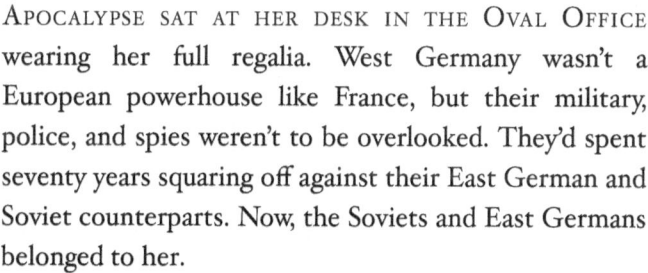

APOCALYPSE SAT AT HER DESK IN THE OVAL OFFICE wearing her full regalia. West Germany wasn't a European powerhouse like France, but their military, police, and spies weren't to be overlooked. They'd spent seventy years squaring off against their East German and Soviet counterparts. Now, the Soviets and East Germans belonged to her.

She pushed aside her laptop when the knock at the

door came. She steepled her gloved fingers and said, "Come."

Daisy led in the West German Representative, Alwin Schulz. He was a squat man having played rugby in his youth, and his physique still looked like it. Though, Apocalypse thought he could do better than a gray, pinstriped suit.

Apocalypse didn't get up, instead waving to one of the uncomfortable high-backed chairs across from her. "Representative, please take a seat."

"Ambassador, if you please, *Herrin* Apocalypse."

Obviously, the West Germans still don't recognize their new mistress. "I *am* your Empress. I've annexed all of Europe, *Herr* Schulz. You still have eighteen months to ratify the treaty. I'm willing to be patient. It would be a shame to raze Europe for the third time in a hundred years."

"West Germany will never submit to your tyranny and your betrayal of us."

"I didn't betray anyone. I got rid of your biggest adversary."

"And replaced it with a bigger one."

"All I'm doing is making the world a better, safer place. Unlike you, who kidnap my citizens and people under my protection."

The ambassador frowned. "We have done nothing."

Apocalypse turned around the laptop and hit play. "Where are my Angels?" she demanded when the video finished.

"They were not kidnapped but arrested for causing a public disturbance and threatening a German national. The Angel Nemesis is being charged with four counts of murder."

"It looks like self-defense to me. They charged her with pistols drawn. She has a right to self-defense. It was justifiable homicide if she felt her life was threatened. And the Vicereine also felt threatened. Fat Sonny made it quite clear he wished to sexually assault her and rape her."

"Musicians are covered by free speech."

"That's not free speech. Free speech would have him say he wants to lick some girl's vagina and be balls deep in some random girl. It becomes sexual assault when he directs it at someone personally."

Schultz rolled his eyes. "That is for the courts to decide."

Apocalypse slammed her fist on the table. "I am the law, *Herr* Schultz. It's whatever I decide it is, and I know this has bothered her since its release. Did you know the Vicereine is a survivor of rape and sexual assault? She doesn't take this lightly, and neither do I. But you're a man, and it's not something you worry about. How about we change the lyric to say: Be balls deep in *Herr* Schultz? How's that thought grab you?"

"That is preposterous."

"You wanna bet? I'm sure I can find some men who would be happy to be balls deep in you. This is a fact that women live with every day, as much as I'm trying to stamp it out, but men who think like you make it impossible until you take women's sexuality as something more than a way to gratify yourself.

"Now, where is the Vicereine. I demand her immediate release."

"She will face trial for her crimes and is being held in a proper facility."

"That wasn't a request. It was an order. The Vicereine answers to me. I will determine if any crime has occurred."

"West Germany doesn't answer to you."

Apocalypse jumped out of her chair, whipped a tomahawk to her hand, and threw it across the desk into Shultz's forehead. "Everyone answers to me," she hissed. She stabbed a button on the desk phone. "Daisy, I need a cleaning crew and a body delivered to the West Germans with a note saying they have four hours to release the Vicereine, or I'm going to start adding more."

APOCALYPSE'S PHONE BUZZED. SHE PULLED IT FROM her pocket and hit Aspen's icon. "Hello, Leaf. What have you found?"

"That soccer stadiums are big—a lot of territory to investigate. I found the stage they used last night and was able to pull a residue sample from a grenade burn mark. It contains a substance I've never seen before. During my search of the field, I discovered this." She held up a two-inch metal dart with three fletchings. "I found it in the area of the stage. It doesn't look like regular issue for police and might have come from the strange weapons they carried."

"Awesome work, Leaf. Get those to Ryan and Sprokkit so they can analyze them."

"Ok. I've got a lead on the vehicle they loaded Kita and the others into. I'm going to follow it up."

"Excellent. Don't go charging the fences when you get there. Wait for the rest of us."

"It might be better if I slip in and look around. If Kita's conscious, the four of us can get out."

"I don't want you running into those gas and darts, then you're in trouble too."

"I'll see what the situation dictates."

Apocalypse rolled her eyes. "Be careful."

"Will do. I'll keep you updated."

Apocalypse closed the app. *This sounds like I'm going to have a fourth Angel in trouble.*

APOCALYPSE SAT CROSS-LEGGED ON THE COUCH IN THE living area of the White House. Her laptop was balanced in her lap as she read emails and ate her favorite mint chocolate cookies. The door opened, causing her to look up and see her daughter entering. "Hi, sweet pea. How was the Prix?"

Chelsea shrugged with a smile. "It was good. I learned a lot. Jason made me a pair of decks to use at school. He says one is if I want to win all the time, the other is if I want to give them a chance."

"That was nice of him. I'm glad you had a good time. I'm sorry I couldn't stay."

"How's Momma-K?"

"I don't know yet. I think she's in West Germany."

"What's she doing there?"

"Settling a score."

Chelsea made a dubious face. "Who's dumb enough to piss off Momma-K?"

"I don't know. That's what we're trying to figure out. Are you hungry?"

"I ate on the plane and did my homework."

Apocalypse smiled. Chelsea didn't need regular homework like normal eight-year-olds. She already had what information she needed loaded onto the computer in her head. Instead, they were trying to teach the girl how to sort, manipulate, and comprehend the data she had. Chelsea was also learning to search the internet when she needed information that wasn't already on hand. Learning how to ask the right question to get the answer you sought was just as important. Chelsea called it Google-fu.

"And what did you learn?"

"Hitler shouldn't have attacked the USSR when he did and instead attacked the British. Defeating the British would have kept Great-Grandfather out of the war, and he could have put all his forces into taking on the USSR. It would have also given the Japanese a chance to solidify their foothold in the Far East and opened a second front on the USSR."

"And what do you think great-grandfather would have done?"

"Try to bolster the British to prevent an invasion and intensify the war in the Pacific. And hope for more luck like the Battle of Midway."

"Interesting. I'll be interested in seeing your report."

Chelsea rolled her eyes.

Reading an eight-year-old's report wasn't riveting reading, but Chelsea often offered unique insight.

The door opened again, causing Apocalypse to cock her head curiously.

"Hello? Dan said you are here."

"Hi, Velositi. Come on in." The Morphicon

squeezed her lithe eight-foot frame through the human-sized door. "I was just talking to Chelsea about her day."

"How are you, Chelsea?" said Velositi.

"Ok. I spent the day in Denver."

"Denver is a nice city."

"Sweet pea, why don't you go down and practice your sword," said Apocalypse.

"Ok, but Velositi has to come show me something cool."

"I'm sure she'll be happy to."

Chelsea gathered up her backpack and went to her room.

"You're here sooner than I expected," said Apocalypse to Velositi.

"I commandeered a MAC flight from Area Fifty-one. I am worried about Kita. I was hoping you had heard something."

"Not yet. I'm waiting on a call from Ryan. Leaf found a sample of the gas and a dart she thinks was used against the Angels."

"Good for Leaf."

"I'm worried she's going to get herself caught trying to free the others."

"Why would she do that?"

"Because that's what Kita would do. The student emulates the master. No matter how hardheaded the master is."

Velositi giggled. "Kita is that."

Apocalypse's phone rang. "That must be Ryan." She answered the phone, turned on the TV, and moved the call to it. "Hi, Ryan."

"Oh, hey Kimmy, Velositi. We checked out the sample and dart Leaf dropped off."

"Did you find out what incapacitated the others?" said Velositi.

"We did. It's basic anatomy. The gas was laced with a protein that sends Angels into anaphylactic shock. I got a whiff and was coughing for fifteen minutes. It's some nasty stuff that comes from a sea anemone. According to Leaf, they don't have them on the planet she and Kita came from."

"But it affects those of us born here?" said Apocalypse.

"The sea anemone protein is similar to one our bionanites use. It's so similar the bionanites mistakenly use it. When the body rejects the protein, it sends us into anaphylactic shock."

"Great. And the only person who can fix this is captured."

"It's simple enough to filter out with a respirator."

"Will it affect me?" said Velositi.

"It didn't affect Sprokkit, and your bionanites are different than the other Angels. You should be safe."

"What about other types of contact, like skin and eyes?" said Apocalypse.

"It can irritate your eyes and cause a rash. I haven't tested if it can be absorbed through the skin."

"Who was the Guinea pig?"

Ryan smiled sheepishly. "I was."

"I'll put you in for a decoration."

"It's no big deal."

Apocalypse shook her head. "It will be when we go get Kita. It'll keep us from ending up like the others."

"So, you are going to get them?"

Drumming her nails on the table, Apocalypse said, "I haven't made up my mind yet. I certainly want to go and hug and kiss Kita, then give her a lecture. What about the dart?"

Ryan tapped on his phone. "Ah, the dart was full of melatonin."

"The hormone? Why would that knock us out?"

"We don't make much of the hormone because our pineal gland works differently than a normal human. It's what lets us stay awake for weeks straight. Instead of generating a dose every night, it generates a big dose every two or three weeks. These darts could contain fifty milligrams, which is large even for us, more than enough to knock us out."

"I am surprised Kita has not broken out on her own," said Velositi.

"Keep a regular supply of melatonin in her system, and she won't wake up."

Apocalypse leaned back against the couch, rubbing her bare arms. Knowing Kita was trapped sent a cold chill through her. What scared her further was the thought of having to go rescue her. This wasn't the kind of thing she did. She could send others, but where? "Do we know where this stuff comes from?"

Ryan shook his head. "No idea. It's all stuff that if you have a pharmacy, you can make yourself. Except for the dart. It looks custom, but it could come from any weapons manufacturer."

"Turn the dart over to the CIA and see if they can figure out where it came from."

"Sure, no problem."

"Thanks, Ryan. We at least know what we're facing now and won't make the same mistakes."

"Sprokkit says he'll go on the rescue mission if you need him."

"That sounds like a good idea. Bring Stunner, too."

"How about Sarah? I kind of promised her a tour of the White House someday."

Apocalypse laughed. "Sure. I'd love to see her again."

"AND THIS IS THE WHITE HOUSE ROSE GARDEN," SAID Apocalypse.

"It's beautiful," said Sarah.

"It's been here since nineteen thirteen, established by First Lady Ellen Wilson, wife of President Woodrow Wilson. My cousin First Lady Edith Roosevelt established the original colonial garden in Nineteen-Oh-Two. My great-grandfather commissioned Frederick Olmsted Junior in nineteen thirty-five to redesign the gardens. It's been the same ever since."

"You must know all sorts of trivia about the White House."

Apocalypse laughed. "My mother trained me in all the duties of being the First Lady; only much later did I learn to govern."

"So, which of you is the First Lady?" said Ryan.

Apocalypse gave him a dirty look. "Kita is far too busy to do it, as am I. I don't think Velositi is interested."

"I would not know what to do. The house has a staff and no need for someone to oversee it. I much prefer training the new Vehlixen. Maybe Ryan should do it."

Ryan rubbed the back of his head. "I much prefer the lab. It's more interesting."

"Then why do you think Kita or I would enjoy doing it?"

"Ah..." The girls laughed at him as Ryan blushed.

"That's what I thought. The house runs itself. The way Kita and I like it." A siren went off in Apocalypse's pocket. She pulled out her phone, silenced the alarm, and opened the app. A second later, Ryan's phone also went off.

"I am receiving an alarm," said Velositi.

"As am I," said Sprokkit.

"Leaf hasn't checked in," said Apocalypse.

"What does that mean?" said Velositi.

"The app has a heartbeat function. If you don't use the phone, it sends out an alarm to the rest of us."

"Is that why it keeps bugging me to hit OK?" said Ryan.

"Yes. Kita didn't explain it to you?"

"No. She just said install it and said it will let us talk to each other using the military communications satellites."

"It's in case one of us gets in trouble." Apocalypse flipped through the screen and found Aspen's last position. "The phone, at least, is in Hamburg. Google says the GPS coordinates are a police station."

"The question is, is Leaf still there?" said Velositi.

"I don't know. We'll have to go and ask."

"Hey, what happened to Leaf?" said Sapper, appearing on-screen joined by Poison and Venom.

Apocalypse sighed. She'd purposefully left these three Angels out because of their unflinching loyalty to Kita. Sapper led the Commandos, and Poison and Venom led the 154th Tactical Squadron. "Kita has gone missing, and Leaf went to find her."

"How long has she been gone?" demanded Venom.

"A couple of days."

"Who has her? We'll tear them apart."

"I know you will; that's why I haven't told you," said Apocalypse.

"Tell us where to go, and we'll get her out," said Sapper.

"We'll bomb them back to the stone age if we have to," said Poison.

"You will do nothing," said Apocalypse, "...yet. I'm still investigating what happened. I don't know who has her or why. Leaf was supposed to find out. I'm not about to send warplanes or special forces into West Germany. Lizzy, you can come with me to find out what happened to Leaf. The rest of you are to wait until I give you orders."

"You have forty-eight hours," snarled Venom.

"Do not make demands of me," hissed Apocalypse. "You will do as I say. I *am* the Empress. I will ground you if I have to. If something happens to us, it'll be up to you to get us out. So stand down. I'll update you when we know more."

"That'll be fine," said Poison. "The squadron will be ready to fly."

"Lizzy, make sure your commandoes are ready to go. I'll meet you in an hour."

"Yes, ma'am."

Apocalypse looked up at Velositi and Sprokkit, "You want to go to West Germany?"

THE RIFT GATE SPARKLED WITH ENERGY AS A FOREST-lined, two-track road appeared. Apocalypse stepped through the gate into the West German forest.

"I can see why it inspires fairy tales," said Velositi as she stepped through and looked around.

"The Black Forest that inspired those tales is in southwestern West Germany," said Apocalypse. "We're forty miles east of Hamburg on a road going to a secluded CIA safe house. No one should see us."

"How far to the autobahn?"

"Not far."

"I understand it's the best highway system in the world."

"I don't know about the best, but it is the fastest. It has no speed limit." Velositi's eyes lit up eagerly. "Just remember, just because we're hard to kill doesn't mean whoever we hit is."

"I would never hit anyone," said Velositi sounding appalled. Her blue eyes glowed brightly.

"It's not you I'm worried about. It's the other driver. But don't do anything to get us noticed. We're just out for an afternoon drive."

"Ok." Velositi morphed into a black and pink Kawasaki H2R Ninja. Apocalypse climbed aboard and tied her hair back. Sprokkit morphed into a hi-vis green off-road firefighting vehicle behind them, and Sapper glided into his cab. At a moderate pace, they pulled onto a paved road and followed it for several miles.

Velositi turned onto the autobahn on-ramp. "Does it cost money to use the autobahn? Those sensors look like toll collectors."

"I don't think so," said Apocalypse.

"The internet says no tolls. I wonder what they are for?"

"Counting blue cars? No idea. I've never had to worry about it. I hope we don't attract a cop."

"I have studied international road signs, and we will go with the flow of traffic. It should not be a problem."

APOCALYPSE SHOULD HAVE ASKED VELOSITI WHAT SHE meant by "go with the flow of traffic." To Apocalypse, that didn't mean weaving around cars at one-hundred and seventy miles an hour. Fortunately, Sprokkit had no problem keeping up. Becoming separated concerned Apocalypse the most, besides an accident.

Her mind kept going back to Kita. She was worried what might be happening to her and if she would rescue her girl. Apocalypse wasn't trained for this. She fought from behind a desk, the rest was for show, or so she thought. Kita had always helped her win as a leader of a nation, not a small team. She hadn't led a small team since officer candidate school. *It's not a matter of* can *but a matter of* will. *I must free Kita and the others.* She thought about sending in the Commandos to do it, and they were still an option if she failed, but she didn't want to use military force while wrangling diplomatically with the Europeans. As much as Apocolypse feared she would fail, she knew it would prove to the Europeans that she was personally a force to be reckoned with. *And maybe that's what I'm missing from my persona.*

Ahead, on a median crossover were two black Porsche 911 GT2 RSs. *Are they cops? Could they catch Velositi?*

Velositi sped past the pair. After Sprokkit passed them, they pulled into traffic. Velositi left them far behind. *I wonder what their zero to one-hundred seventy miles per hour speed is? What's their top speed?*

"Velositi, Kimberly, those two Porsches we passed are moving up fast," said Sprokkit.

"Are they police?" said Velositi.

"They have given no outward indication nor have any identification markings."

"They seem too expensive for immigration services," said Apocalypse, trying to make a joke.

"I bet they're just looking to race," said Sapper.

"Then they will lose," said Velositi.

The Porsches pulled up beside Sprokkit and morphed into ten-foot Morphicons aiming energy cannons at the Vehlixen.

"Shit. Are those ours?" said Sapper.

"We have none working in Europe," said Apocalypse.

"These can't be ours, too ugly," said Sapper as she jumped from Sprokkit's cab at the attacking Morphicon. She slammed into its arm, making the shot go wide.

Sprokkit morphed, but not before absorbing a shot from the other Morphicon. He dug his feet in as he slid on the concrete. Grappling with the Morphicon, he twisted and slammed the enemy into the ground. He fired two shots into its back.

Velositi hit her brakes, causing her to rise onto her front wheel. She spun 180 degrees, brought her rear wheel down, and sprang toward the Morphicon battling Sapper.

Apocalypse jumped into the air. Opening her wings, she aimed her fists and eyes at the Morphicon and fired her energy blasts, punching a hole through its shoulder. The damage distracted the Morphicon, and Sapper caught him in a magnetic field. She slammed him back and forth as Velositi shot him.

Sprokkit grabbed the other Morphicon by the shoulders and slammed it down, driving its face into the concrete. The Morphicon kicked back, knocking Sprokkit backward. He grabbed the Morphicon's leg, spun, and slammed it back into the roadbed. Sprokkit stood upholding it by the foot when Velositi and Apocalypse fired simultaneously, blasting the Morphicon apart.

Velositi picked up the head of the destroyed Morphicon. "It looks like a Neophorm, but I thought they were all gone." She tossed the head to Sprokkit.

Different scanning instruments extended from Sprokkit's fingertips. "It's not very old. It was built after we defeated Savacron."

"Someone's still building Neophormes?" exclaimed Apocalypse.

"Yes," said Velositi. "It appears that way. Who and why we will have to discover."

"Great. Just what we need. No wonder Europe is so defiant."

"We do not know they are working with the Europeans, just that they are here."

"It's not that hard to connect the dots. Let's get out of here before the police show up."

Velositi turned the corner down Davidstraße street next to the Polizeikommissariat 15 Davidwache. The four-story brick building with white windows and a massive wooden door towered over Saint Pauli quarter. She hopped onto the sidewalk giving Sprokkit room to park. Apocalypse hopped off and helped Sapper out of Sprokkit.

"We'll go check out the station and see if we can find Leaf," said Apocalypse.

"*Be careful,*" said Velositi.

They walked down the street filled with lights and music coming from bars and clubs.

"This is a happening place," said Sapper.

"Yeah, we've attracted some attention." Apocalypse leaned into Sapper's ear. "Behind us. A group of guys. Come on. Let's get off the street." She ducked down an alley, and the Angels vanished.

As they invisibly exited the alley the way they came in, the Angels let the group of guys go by.

"*They're in for a surprise,*" said Sapper.

"*They'd be in for a surprise in more ways than one when they learn we're not interested in them.*"

They crossed Davidstraße street and waited for someone to open the precinct door. A police officer exited, and Sapper caught the door, holding it open just long enough for them to get inside. They glided up the flight of steps into an open area. A pair of wooden benches lined the walls, and an officer sat behind a glass barrier working on a computer. Next to him was a door.

"*It needs a keycard,*" said Sapper.

"*I bet our friend in there has one.*" They pushed up against the glass and looked the officer over.

"*I see it on his belt.*"

"*I can copy the magnetic tape; I just need to read it. How do we get at him?*"

"*Be girls. I'll come in and make a scene saying I had my money and passport stolen. When someone comes out to help me, you can grab their keycard. After I'm calm and fill out the report, I'll come outside, and we can slip in again.*"

They made their way down the stairs. In the landing, Apocalypse turned visible except for her wings. She opened the door and let it close with a *thwack* to sound like someone was coming in. *I can do this, just like on TV. I just have to tap into my inner damsel.* It wasn't hard; thinking of Kita in danger was enough to bring tears to her eyes. She let the emotion flow from there. In a few seconds, she was bawling. She ran up the stairs into the waiting area.

"Someone, please help me. They robbed me!" She cried out around her tears.

The officer behind the desk looked up, surprised. "Miss?"

"Help me! Please! They...they took my...my money and my...my passport." Apocalypse sank to the floor, crying. Her loud sobs echoed in the room.

The door opened, and two officers exited, but not the officer behind the desk.

Apocalypse grabbed onto one of the officer's arms. "They robbed me. He...he seemed so...so nice."

"Easy, Miss. Please calm down. We can help you," said the officer while trying gently to pry Apocalypse loose.

"He took everything and threatened me with a knife."

"*Ok, got it,*" said Sapper.

"*Good, let's get out of here.*"

Apocalypse let go of the officer's arm and wiped her eyes. "What do I have to do?"

"We will fill out an incident report and have you work with an artist to make a sketch of your assailant. Then we will escort you back to your hotel and help you contact your consulate for help."

"*Ah, shit, Lizzy. We've got to think of another way out.*"

"*I'm on it.*"

Sapper ran out of the room and glided back down the stairs. The door banged, and Sapper ran up the stairs. "Kimmy! There you are! I've been looking all over for you! I got your stuff back. The nice guy at the bar said you dropped it."

"I dropped it?"

"He said he bumped into you, knocking your passport out of your hand. When he reached down to pick it up, you were gone."

Apocalypse looked down at the ground. "Oops. I thought he was robbing me."

"He just wanted to buy us a drink." Sapper turned to the officers. "I'm sorry, officers. She gets hysterical easily. I have her stuff. I'll take her back to the hotel."

"*How long have you waited to get a dig on me like that?*" said Apocalypse with a laugh.

"*Ever since you took Kita from me.*"

"It's no problem," said one of the officers.

"As long as everything is ok," said the other.

"Everything is fine. She just needs to sleep off the excitement and booze. Come on, Kimmy." Sapper took Apocalypse by the arm and led her down the stairs. She opened the door and let it close.

The Angels turned invisible again and went upstairs, across the reception area to the security door. Sapper pushed her palm against the electronic key reader. The door opened with a soft *click*. Together they silently passed through the door and closed it.

Beyond them was a hallway that had doors leading off both sides.

"*Where's Leaf?*" said Sapper.

Apocalypse pulled out her phone. Aspen's phone was pinging, sending out a short-range electronic signal that the other Angels' phones could track. "She's below us."

They followed the hallway to the back of the building, where they found a metal staircase. Gliding to the bottom, they found another electronic key lock. Sapper opened the door. An officer behind a desk looked up. Across from her was a stout jail cell door.

The Angels moved aside and let the officer investigate the open door. They scooted along the wall to the jail cell door. Sapper bypassed the electric lock, and she pulled the door open with a *clank*. Apocalypse shut the door as quickly as she could, and they hurried down the hallway lined with jail cell doors.

Each jail cell door had a small window. They peaked inside a few cells, but they were all empty.

"The phone says she's in the back," said Apocalypse.

"Would this really be enough to hold Leaf?"

"Maybe if she does not want to upset the situation further. I'm sure she could get out if she wanted to." Apocalypse pulled out her phone, locked the program onto Aspen's signal, and followed the compass to the last door on the left. "Uh-oh. These don't use keycards, just regular keys."

"I can rip it from the wall."

"That would be noisy, and we've already stirred up enough suspicion. Let me see if I can melt it." Apocalypse aimed her fist at the lock and fired a bright ruby red beam that emanated from between her fingers. The lock melted and fell away.

Sapper grabbed the door in a magnetic field and pushed it open. "Hey, Leaf, I thought it was Kita's thing to sit in prison. Oh...oh...shit."

"What?" Apocalypse pushed her way inside the cell. She gasped and covered her mouth. "Oh, Kita, where are you!"

On the wall was Aspen, her limbs nailed in a crucifix position, dry blood from her slashed throat covering her naked body.

"Is...is she dead?" said Sapper.

Apocalypse swallowed hard. Her medical training told her the answer, but she climbed on the bed and checked for a pulse. She shook her head. "She's been dead a while."

Sapper picked up Aspen's phone. "What do you make of this?" She showed the phone to Apocalypse. A text message on the screen read CALL +92 0355 5552435. "It's a phone number, right?"

"Yes. Do you think it's a clue she left us?"

"Or it belongs to whoever did this. We'll call it later. Right now, we need to get Leaf home."

APOCALYPSE SAT ON THE OVERSIZED BEANBAG CHAIR IN the apartment she shared with Kita and Chelsea on level four of the bunker at Area 51. She read through Aspen's autopsy report as the rest of the Angels and Morphicons listened. Fighting tears, she shut the tablet off. *This is my fault. Kita's going to be furious. Will the others even trust me?* "I'm so sorry," she whispered.

"This is not your fault," said Velositi.

"I told her not to go. But I didn't stop her."

"It was her choice," said Sprokkit. "She knew the risks and deemed them acceptable. She was more qualified to go than anyone here."

"Kita wouldn't have let her go, or she would have had some plan or something..." Apocalypse broke into tears. "I'm so worried the next one we find will be her."

Velositi put an arm around Apocalypse.

"What's to worry about?" said Venom. "Won't Leaf just go back outside of the universe and wait? I'm surprised she's not back yet."

"It doesn't work like that," said Sapper. "To get into this equation, Leaf and I moved our entire selves here. Normally I copy myself and go in, but Kita wasn't available to copy us, so we just moved in."

"Then they killed the original Leaf?" said Stunner.

Sapper nodded.

"What about Kita?" said Velositi.

"Ah, from what I understand, she's different because she exists outside of reality. If she's killed, she just goes back to her giant glowing computer ball and comes out again. To kill her would require someone deleting her from the ball. If they'd killed her, I'm pretty sure she would just show up. But I'm no expert; that's just what I remember her telling me."

"That's good for Kita, but not the rest of us," said Poison. "What killed Leaf?"

Apocalypse took a deep breath. "Massive blood loss. There's evidence her bionanites tried to stop the flow of blood, but it was too much, too fast. Tests were positive for the sea anemone protein in her lungs and melatonin in her blood. Damn. If only she had waited." She wiped at her tears.

"You could not have known," said Velositi.

"But I'm supposed to know. I'm supposed to see all the risks and possibilities. It's what a leader is supposed to do."

"You make the best choice possible with the information you have available. That is the best you can do."

"Leaf should have waited," said Venom. "From now on, we should all go."

"But we're not leaving until we can protect ourselves from this gas and the darts," said Poison.

"We're working on it," said Ryan. "We found respirators and armor off the shelf that'll block the gas and darts. The armor doesn't cover everywhere, but it'll make hitting you harder, and if they do, without the gas to incapacitate you, the melatonin won't take immediate effect."

"Is there an antidote?" said Venom.

"No, but you can fight it long enough to get to safety."

"What about our animal forms? Will it affect those?"

"No idea. I don't know the physiology of a scorpion or a dragon. We can test."

"It might be better if the Morphicons lead," said Velositi.

"We don't know where we're going yet," said Venom. "It might be a hole too small for you to get into."

"Not for us," said Knockout, Stunner's sister.

"We should call the number Apocalypse retrieved and see who picks up," said Sprokkit. "That will help us decide our next move."

"Agreed," said Velositi.

Apocalypse pulled out her phone and Leaf's and entered the phone number from Leaf's phone message into hers. It rang several times before being answered.

"*Guten Tag, Engel.*"

"*Mit wem sprechen ich?*" Apocalypse put the phone on speaker.

"Call me Doctor Unixilite."

"Where are our friends?" demanded Venom.

"Ah, more than one of you. *Gut.*"

Apocalypse waved at Venom to be quiet. "What do you want?"

"I want to play a game—"

"You have three of my friends and have killed another. I'm not playing games."

"The death of the little Angel was unfortunate. It

was a test to see how well she healed. Not as well as I'd hoped."

"Bullshit," snarled Snapper. "You don't slice someone ear-to-ear to see how well they heal. You do that to make sure they don't heal."

"Maybe Angels aren't the vanguard you claim to be. You have weaknesses, and I've made it my mission to seek them out. If you want to see your friends alive, you'll play my game."

"What is your game?" said Apocalypse.

"Hickory, dickory, dock.

"The mouse ran up the clock.

"I have left for you a series of puzzles at three famous clocks. Find the puzzle and the answers to get your friends back. Now, all the Angels have to play; no one sits out, even the little one. To start, I suggest you take a trip to *Schwarzwald*. They have wonderful mineral baths there. Have a good day." The line went dead.

"There is no way I'm playing his game," said Venom.

"Agreed," said Poison.

If we don't play, I could lose Kita forever. I have to be a team leader and make them see reason. "If we don't play, then we just condemn Kita, Nicole, and Anna to death. I know it sounds stupid, but it's our only move right now. And he said only the Angels, not the Morphicons. Ryan and Sprokkit can help the CIA and NSA trace that call. Once we find where it came from, we can raid it."

"What about Angel Morphicons?" said Stunner.

"Velositi and Knockout will come with us. I'm willing to bet they don't know there are three of you. We can keep you in reserve until we find them. Does that sound like a plan?" Apocalypse looked at Poison and

Venom. She tried to make it sound like it wasn't a question but a statement. She summoned the look she'd seen Kita use when she wanted something from the Angels. A look that was between mother and commander.

Venom and Poison exchanged a look.

"Ok," said Venom. "We'll go."

"Where is the place he said?" said Knockout.

"The Black Forest of West Germany," said Apocalypse.

"What's there?"

"A house that looks like a clock," said Chelsea. She opened her hand, and a holographic image of a house that looked like a cuckoo clock appeared.

"How'd you find that so fast?" said Poison.

Chelsea made a fist, placed her other hand over it, and bowed. "Google-fu is strong with this one."

Apocalypse cracked a smile.

"He wants us to go there?" scoffed Venom.

"He said famous clocks. Cuckoo clocks are famous in the region, and they can't get any bigger than this," said Apocalypse.

"So, what, we just show up and say we're here to look at your clock?"

"That's exactly what I'm going to do. Whoever this Unixilite is, he's certain to have people watching. Dan, Chelsea's coming, so are you."

"Yes, Empress."

"Between all of us, we need to make sure she stays safe."

"Ah, Mom, I can take care of myself." Chelsea drew her sword and flourished it. It was a Masamune, created by the master smith himself in 1320. Kita considered it adequate until she could have something properly forged.

"Sweet pea, you're still an apprentice. I expect you to exercise caution and restraint. Let Dan and the rest of us handle the dangerous ones."

"You're still an apprentice, too."

A pearly white bubble encased Apocalypse. "Like you, I have one of these. I expect you to use it. Leave the dangerous enemies to the bigger Angels. Soon enough, you'll get your chance."

"Don't worry, Chelsea. We'll save you some," said Venom.

"Leaf says I was doing awesome in the simulator," said Chelsea.

"The simulator is not real life," said Apocalypse firmly. "If you keep arguing, I'll take your sword."

Chelsea made a face, crossed her arms, and huffed.

"Ok, everyone, let's get ready to go."

Velositi pulled to a stop in front of a three-story Bavarian house decorated to look like a cuckoo clock. On the first story was a giant clock face. On the second were the wooden cuckoo figurines. At the peak of the third-story roof was a door for a cuckoo. Out front were several planters and large rocks.

Apocalypse removed her arms from around Chelsea and got off Velositi. Behind them, the other Angels exited Knockout, who was traveling as a large SUV.

"What is this place?" said Knockout.

"It's pretty," said Poison.

"It's *Weltgrosste Kuckucksuhr*," said Chelsea. "The world's biggest cuckoo clock."

"Who turns their house into a cuckoo clock?" said Venom.

"*Das wäre mein Urgroßvater,*" said a man with a long beard sitting on a bench in front of the house wearing a corded sweater.

"Your grandfather did this?" said Apocalypse. "It's spectacular."

"Thank you. You can come inside and take a tour and see how it works."

"We're here to solve a puzzle," said Poison.

"Then this must belong to you. West German *Polizei* left it this morning." He took a piece of paper from his pocket and handed it to Apocalypse.

She read the note. "We must make the cuckoo appear."

"So...wait for the hour?" said Sapper.

Apocalypse shook her head. "Only the correct time will cause the cuckoo to come out. The correct time is when three or more of the same digits show up on the clock face."

"What's the answer," demanded Venom of the man.

"I don't know. I repair and sell clocks only."

The Angels turned and stared at the clock face on the side of the house.

"One eleven, two twenty-two, three-thirty-three," said Apocalypse.

"Seventeen combinations," said Chelsea.

"How do you know?" exclaimed Venom.

Chelsea balled her fist and wrapped her other hand over it. She bowed. "Google-fu," she whispered.

"How do we know that's correct?" said Poison.

"You want to argue with a girl with a computer in her head?" said Apocalypse.

"Count it out," said Chelsea. "I bet you'll miss one."

"What time do we set the clock to?" said Knockout.

"We'll just have to try them all and see," said Apocalypse.

Sapper and Knockout glided over a small fence and stood before the clock.

"What's the first time?" said Sapper.

"One eleven," said Chelsea.

Sapper moved the hour hand as Knockout moved the minute hand. The minute and hour hand moved to the twelve o'clock position. The minute hand started ticking off the seconds.

"That can't be good," said Knockout. "Next?"

"Two twenty-two."

The Angels set the clock, but no cuckoo. The minute hand returned to its prior position and started ticking off the seconds.

"We need to hurry," said Knockout.

"We'll never get through them all in thirty-six seconds!" exclaimed Poison.

"Then pick one."

"Eleven twelve," said Chelsea.

The other Angels set the hands.

"Nothing," said Knockout.

"Twenty-four seconds!" announced Venom.

"Twelve Twenty-two!"

"No good," said Sapper after moving the minute

hand in place.

"Eleven eighteen!"

"Nope!" said Knockout when the cuckoo failed to appear.

"Ten seconds!" cried Poison.

"Eleven sixteen!" yelled Chelsea.

"Try again!"

"Three seconds!" yelled Venom.

Chelsea flashed forward, grabbed the hour and minute hand, and set them to eleven seventeen. Above the Angels, a large cuckoo sprang from behind a pair of wooden doors followed by a deafening *cuckoo*.

"Are you trying to get us killed, old man?" Venom snarled at the proprietor.

"I know nothing about the new clock."

"New clock?" said Apocalypse.

He backed away before turning and fleeing into the house.

That's not a good sign. Apocalypse waved O'Brien to Chelsea. "Get your shield up. I—"

A pair of arms wrapped around Apocalypse.

A planter morphed into a Morphicon and grabbed Venom. "Let go of me," she snarled.

Apocalypse guessed that's what had her. From the house, the clock dial climbed down and sprouted squat arms, legs, and a head. It swung at Sapper and Knockout. The cuckoo flew down and attacked Poison. The two figurines jumped off the second-story balcony, morphed, and attacked Velositi.

Apocalypse looked down and blasted the Morphicon's hands with a beam from her eyes, partially melting the metal appendage. She thrust her arms down to break the Morphicon's grip, pushed its arms back with her wings, twisted, and fired a blast from her fist into the Morphicon's middle.

Venom grew into a giant scorpion, becoming too big for the Morphicon holding her to maintain its grip. The scorpion landed on the ground and struck with its tail, hitting her Morphicon in the leg knocking it down. Apocalypse wasn't sure if Venom had any toxins that would affect the Morphicons, but she was big enough to knock these around.

Velositi and the two figurine Morphicons were engaged in a deadly dance of flips and twists, exchanging cannon blasts. One figurine's chest glowed brightly, but Velositi's left arm was red.

"Onca uncia pardus!" cried Poison. A shimmering blue bubble appeared around her, absorbing the cannon blasts from the beak of the cuckoo Morphicon. Poison threw open her arms, and the bubble fired the energy back at the Morphicon, causing it to crash into the ground.

Sapper fired her rifle at the clock Morphicon to little effect. The Morphicon punched her out of the air and jumped on top of her, smashing her with its feet. Knockout's arms transformed into cannons and fired rapidly at the clock Morphicon, but her blasts refused to draw attention.

The cuckoo Morphicon let out a deafening *cuckoo* that stunned the Angels and Vehlixen. The cuckoo clock Morphicons backed toward the house. The clock Morphicon drew in its extremities and hovered off the ground. The two planter Morphicons morphed into a pair of legs and connected to the clock, while the two figurine Morphicons formed arms and connected. The cuckoo Morphicon drew in its wings and legs and slid into the top of the clock Morphicon. The large bonded cuckoo Morphicon jumped on Sapper and ground her under its feet.

Apocalypse shook the ringing from her sensitive ears. "Ever seen a six-way Morphicon?" she shouted to Velositi.

"I thought I was a unique bonded-pair. Our cores struggled to balance each of us. I cannot imagine what goes on inside its cores."

"Let's get it off, Lizzy!" Apocalypse fired her three beams at the Morphicon, drawing its attention and leaving a furrow across the clock face body.

"Onca uncia pardus!" yelled Poison. A large fist of earth reached up and punched the cuckoo Morphicon away from Sapper.

A trio of arrows from Chelsea struck the cuckoo Morphicon's chest and both shoulders, then exploded. It stumbled back into the house, collapsing a section of the roof. The cuckoo Morphicon's eyes lit, and it let out another deafening *cuckoo*. It jumped and landed on Venom, crushing her right legs, arm, and pincer.

"Dan, keep Chelsea back!" ordered Apocalypse when she recovered.

Velositi and Knockout charged the Morphicon, pushing it off Venom. Knockout fired a long burst into the cuckoo Morphicon's leg, but she did little damage. The cuckoo Morphicon jumped into the air at Poison.

"Onca uncia pardus!" A pearly white bubble appeared around the Angel as the cuckoo Morphicon landed on top, lost its balance, and fell to one side.

Apocalypse jumped into the air and fired another tri-beam blast into the chest of the cuckoo Morphicon, searing off the hour hand. Velositi joined her and fired her cannons, blasting a way through the cuckoo Morphicon's chest to a pair of its system cores. The glass cubes exploded like a shower of diamonds when she hit them.

The cuckoo Morphicon let out another stunning *cuckoo,* knocking the two Angels back. It climbed to its feet and grabbed Velositi, smashing her into the ground. Its arm morphed into a giant cannon and fired, turning the Morphicon Angel's entire torso, head, and arms red.

"Velositi!" cried Apocalypse. Enraged, she channeled her emotion into her energy ability. She fired all three beams at maximum, blasting pieces of liquefied metal off the cuckoo Morphicon and through its chest. Apocalypse moved the beams up, slicing through its chest until she separated the left arm from the body.

The cuckoo Morphicon stumbled as Knockout transformed into an Abrams tank. The teenage Morphicon fired a blast into the head of the cuckoo Morphicon as it opened its mouth to *cuckoo* again.

Two arrows from Chelsea landed in the center of the cuckoo Morphicon's damaged chest. Attached to the arrows were purplish-black balls. When they detonated, they blew the Morphicon in half.

"Watch it!" cried Apocalypse. "The other parts might get back up."

The Angels hovered around the two parts of the cuckoo Morphicon, waiting.

"I don't think it's getting up," said Poison.

"Can you bury it to make sure?" said Apocalypse.

"Onca uncia pardus!" the Angel witch chanted as the ground opened up and swallowed the Morphicon.

Apocalypse hurried to check on the wounded Angels. Sapper was unconscious, her body and wings a wreck. Running her hand over the Angel, Apocalypse could see the damaged organs and dislocated bones. She took a pulse and made sure Sapper was breathing. The injured Angel was going to be out for a while. Venom was still in her scorpion form; her exoskeleton was cracked, but the eyes showed movement. "Dan! Call Area Fifty-one and tell them we have casualties. And tell someone to call UNLV. We might need an arachnid expert."

"Yes, Your Highness."

"Velositi, how are you?"

"I will be ok. I just need time to heal."

Apocalypse turned and faced Chelsea. "I thought I told you to stay back."

"You did. But you needed me."

"Where did the purplish-black balls come from?"

"It's the crystal in the ring Momma-K gave me. She showed me how to do it and said the crystal comes from dead aliens. I'm only supposed to use it if we're in trouble. I thought we were in trouble."

Apocalypse sighed. She didn't want to scold Chelsea, but at the same time as her mother, she needed to be obeyed. She remembered the ring appearing on Chelsea's finger one day but figured it was something she found. If she'd known Chelsea had such weapons, she might very well have called on her for them. She couldn't blame Chelsea for that. That was Kita's fault for not telling her. She wasn't going to punish Chelsea for a gift

Kita gave her. "We were in trouble. You used good judgment in employing it like you did."

A rift gate opened, and teams emerged to collect the wounded Angels.

"What do we do now?" said Poison. "This can't be all to the game."

"I don't think so either," said Apocalypse. "We should search the area for clues."

As the others searched around the house, along the gravel road, and the garden, Apocalypse huddled with Velositi.

"How are you doing?"

"In a great deal of pain. It seems Kita made lots of changes, but she did not remove my ability to feel it."

"Pain is good. It lets you know something is wrong and helps you avoid repeating such activities. I'm curious to know where such a Morphicon came from."

"I do not know. Not from Chellexon. I am beginning to think maybe there is another group of Neophormes, but unlike any I have encountered before."

"How could they have made this in less than a decade?"

"You assume they started after Savacron was killed. They may have been here much longer."

"I thought Savacron ruled over all the Neophormes."

"He did or liked to pretend he did. This might be a group more powerful than he could rein in."

"Hey, Kimmy! I found something," yelled Knockout. She stood next to a wooden waterwheel in the garden holding a briefcase.

The Angels clustered around the teenager. Apocalypse took the case and examined the standard four-digit locking mechanism. She shook the case to see if it made a noise.

"Careful!" cried Chelsea. "We don't know what's in there!"

"What do you suppose is the code?" said Poison.

"Try the answer to the puzzle," said Chelsea.

Apocalypse turned the dials to eleven seventeen. She pushed the latches, and the case opened.

"What were you going to suggest if that didn't work?" said Apocalypse to her triumphant-looking daughter.

"Have you burn through the latches."

"Just like Momma-K, you have a plan for everything."

"She keeps telling me to be prepared."

Apocalypse opened the case. A voice recorder sat tucked in a foam encasement. She took the recorder, set down the case, and hit the play button.

"Congratulations on defeating Clockwork." Doctor Unixilite spoke with a German accent but was distinctly Morphicon. "Not to worry, I can heal him."

"He must not know what we did to him," said Apocalypse.

"Or he's overconfident," said Poison.

"But like many games, this one is not over yet," Unixilite continued.

"Humpty Dumpty sat on a wall,

"Humpty Dumpty had a great fall.

"Like most medieval cities, this one has walls and built into them is the *glocke*. I know there are many walled cities in Europe, but there is only one where German is not German. Good luck and maybe find a watchmaker to fix Clockwork, *ya*? You have four hours to get there and no taking the rift gate. Take a drive and see the countryside."

The recording ended. Apocalypse looked at the other Angels. "Does that mean anything to you?"

"I'm working on it," said Chelsea. "*Glocke* is German for bell. I think we're looking for a German medieval bell tower that's not German."

"I don't know, sweet pea. Keep searching. Knockout, see if you can find the owner of this place and see if he'll offer his assistance."

"Right."

There was a yell from the recovery team trying to help Venom.

"I'll be right back," Apocalypse told Chelsea. "Karen, can you help with Zhi?" She went over to talk with the head of the medical recovery team that was loading Sapper and Venom. Sapper was still unconscious, but Venom didn't seem interested in help; she kept snapping at the recovery team with her good claw and striking with her tail. "Do you need some help, Major?"

"Your Highness, Venom won't settle down."

"We'll see if Karen can tame her. I'm sure she's just upset and scared."

Poison walked around to the front of Venom and kept her hands visible. "Zhi, it's me, Karen. It's ok. They're here to take you back to Area Fifty-one and heal you. They mean you no harm." Poison placed a hand on Venom's head and stroked the hard surface.

"Why doesn't she change back?" said Knockout coming back with the man in the corded sweater. He looked to be sweating.

"She may be too injured to turn back, and from the look of things, it's going to take her nanites a while to heal all the damage. Unlike you, we revert to more animal instincts when we transform. Our mind is still in there, but there's a level of separation." Apocalypse turned to the man Knockout had brought. "So, *Herr* owner, are you here to be helpful?"

The man straightened up. "I know nothing of what is going on, just what the police told me."

"You must know they changed the clock."

"They said that was for the protection of the country."

"And now it's a scrap heap that has cost me three Angels. I am not happy. Make me happy by helping my daughter figure out this next clue."

"I will do what I can, under duress."

"Noted. Sweet pea, what do you have?"

"A bunch of clock towers. Some in Germany, most outside of it, but I don't know."

"We have less than four hours. How can you not know?" said Knockout.

"I'm still a kid, ok?"

"Enough," said Apocalypse. "*Herr* owner, where is German spoken outside of Germany?"

The man stroked his beard. "Bernese German is spoken not far from here, mostly in Switzerland."

"Does that help?" Apocalypse said to Chelsea.

"There is one in Bern: The Zytglogge. It's famous, and I'm finding it on all kinds of tourist sites."

"How far is Bern from here?"

"According to Google, three hours by car."

"Then that's where we're going. Knockout, we'll go by helicopter."

APOCALYPSE SAT IN THE BACK OF KNOCKOUT. THE teenager had morphed into a chinook helicopter to take the group to Bern, Switzerland. Apocalypse was staring at the floor as a knot of guilt and uncertainty ate at her stomach. Her first outing as the leader of the Angels hadn't gone very well. *What is Kita going to say? What would the injured Angels say?*

She thought she was better than this, but she had done nothing but react in reviewing the fight in her mind. No command and control, no leadership, she'd done none of the things she'd been taught in officer candidate school. Kita made it look so easy. She told the others what to do, and they did them—and the battle was won. *What am I missing?*

Chelsea came and leaned against her. She pulled her mother's hood back. "What's wrong, Mom?"

Apocalypse put her arm around Chelsea. Her daughter had saved the day. Her grasp of her abilities was already excellent, and Kita barely spent any time with her. Kita claimed she would when she was older— for now, she was busy training the triplets. Apocalypse knew it was more than that. Kita didn't know how to handle children, and Chelsea was just now becoming old enough to attract Kita's interest.

The purplish-black balls were new. She'd never heard of them from Kita or Chelsea, and Chelsea loved to show her all the things she learned. *Did Kita give this power to her knowing something might happen? Kita always has a plan for everything.* "I'm just trying to see how we could have done better, that's all."

"We won, didn't we?"

That's a Kita answer. "Yes, but it cost us three of our friends. I'm trying to avoid any more injuries."

"Momma-K says injuries are part of being an Angel. Everyone has to spend their time in the ward."

"I would prefer if they didn't...especially you."

"I have Dan and my shield. What more do I need?"

What more do you need? Do you really need me to protect you? "I just want you safe, sweet pea. You did a good job today. I'm proud of you. Without you, it would have been much worse."

"I know."

I wonder if Kita realizes how much she's rubbed off on her daughter? "Good. Keep it up."

"Hey, Kimmy?" said Knockout.

"Yeah?"

"I'm getting a radio call from a Swiss air traffic controller wanting to know who we are, and I'm picking up two inbounds squawking Swiss Air Force."

"Put it through."

Apocalypse connected to the helicopter's communications using the biological communications package she had in her head. "*This is Empress Apocalypse aboard Army One on my way to Bern. If you want to know why contact the West Germans.*"

"This is Swiss Air Traffic Control. You do not have permission to operate in Swiss airspace, nor have you filed a flight plan. Two fighters will escort you to Emmen airbase."

"I don't have time for that. Mine and your citizens' lives are at stake if we fail."

"If you have evidence of a credible threat against the Swiss people, present it to the authorities that meet you at the airbase."

Apocalypse snarled and disconnected. "Knockout, how far are we from Bern?"

"Twenty-five minutes."

"How far by car?"

"An hour. I'm following the highway."

Apocalypse tapped her daughter's knee, causing her to pop an earbud out. "How long do we have left?"

"An hour and twenty minutes."

"Good. Knockout, put us down. We'll go by SUV. Something non-descript."

"I'll scan a license plate; that should make us harder to track."

KNOCKOUT STOPPED HARD AT AN INTERSECTION IN the old city of Bern. The Angels had taken Highway 1 into the city unmolested. Now a red tram blocked the way.

"This is as close as I can get," said Knockout.

"If we hurry, we can catch the tram," said Chelsea. "Zytglogge Tower is only two blocks away."

The Angels climbed out of Knockout and flittered to the tram. They smiled at the other passengers as they boarded. The tram operator gave them a wary look. Apocalypse pulled out her credit card. *Money speaks in any language.*

The tram operator shook his head. "It free. Don't hit others." He pointed at the Angels' wings.

Apocalypse nodded in understanding and pulled her wings in around her as the tram lurched forward. "Girls, watch your wings."

They rode the tram past large four-story buildings, all made from a yellowish-gray sandstone with white windows and iron railings, the tops adorned with red tile roofs. They looked impressive and heavy, like medieval fort walls. The bottoms of each building had impressive arches that led to shops and restaurants. Everything was done in a Baroque style, but if you looked closely, you could see the Gothic and Burgundian style remnants.

The tram stopped.

"*Zeitglockenlaube! Marktgasse!*" cried the operator. He looked at the Angels and, with a wink, said, "Zytglogge!"

"That's us," said Poison.

"Thank you," Apocalypse said to the operator.

The man nodded and tipped his hat as the Angels filed off the tram.

"Wow, that's impressive," said Knockout as she looked up at the tower. When she looked back, she found a pair of tourists waiting with their phones out. "You want a picture? With me?" The tourists nodded. "Ok, sure."

Knockout wasn't the only one being set upon by tourists. All the Angels were surrounded by tourists asking for pictures and autographs. *I didn't know we had this big a fan base outside the empire. We don't have time for this.*

"*Girls, we need to find the puzzle.*"

"*Last time it came to us,*" said Poison. "*Let's look around, but someone stay in the area.*"

Apocalypse grumbled at being told what to do, but it made sense. She took a breath and remembered Poison had been leading small teams for a long time. She shouldn't take it personally. She walked around the tower and looked up at the ornate astronomical clock built in the form of an astrolabe. The stereographically projected planisphere was divided into three zones: the dark night sky, the deep blue of dawn, and the light blue day sky.

"It is most impressive, don't you think, Empress?" said a man coming up next to Apocalypse. She turned her head and found he wore blue workman overalls with a City of Bern logo stitched over the heart.

"It is. The tower and city are impressive."

"Have you seen the bears?"

"Bears?"

"Follow the street east over the *Nydeggbrücke,* and you will find the *Bärengraben.* You might find your answers there."

Apocalypse nodded slowly. "Thank you. We will take a look." She switched to her internal comm. "*Did you hear that, Chelsea?*"

"*I got it. He's talking about a bear exhibit at the end of the street over the bridge.*"

"*Good. Girls, let's go.*"

The Angels left their admirers and took flight following the street east, across the river to the bear pit. They flew low enough to wave to the people and slow enough for photos. They landed on the north side of the pit and looked in on the bears.

"There really are bears," said Knockout.

"The bear is the symbol of Bern," said Chelsea.

"They're so cute."

"Ladies, spread out and look for a clue," said Apocalypse. She guided Chelsea around the east side of the pit, looking for anything unusual. As they walked around the south end, they passed the Tourist Information window for the *BärenPark* and *Altes Tramdepot* that contained a restaurant with tables outside.

A woman sat at a table texting on her phone. She glanced around, saw the Angels, and put her phone away. She got up and approached Apocalypse at a rapid pace.

"*Fräulein* Apocalypse?"

"Yes?" Apocalypse put a guarded hand on Chelsea's shoulder.

"Doctor Unixilite sends his regards. The Zytglogge has two hands. How many times do they meet? You have twelve minutes to set the west clock face to the correct answer. Good Luck."

"Thank you," said Apocalypse to the woman. "Girls, back to the clock as fast as we can."

"Touch me," said Chelsea. All the other Angels put a hand on her wings, and Chelsea phased—moving via the fifth dimension—the group back to the clock tower.

"The west side," said Apocalypse. "How many times do the hand meet? Chelsea? Anybody?"

"Twenty-two," said Chelsea. "Starting at twelve."

Poison and Knockout glided up to the clock face.

"Twelve what?" said Knockout.

"She means twelve midnight," said Poison.

They moved the hands to the correct position, and

nothing happened.

"What's next?"

"One-oh-five," replied Chelsea.

The hands were moved, but still nothing happened.

"How much time do we have?" said Apocalypse.

"Ten minutes twenty-four seconds, Mom. Try two-ten. We have enough time we can brute force our way through this. I don't think our game master counted on me phasing us half a mile."

They tried the next four combinations, but none worked.

"Try seven-thirty-five," said Chelsea. "Six minutes left."

Knockout and Poison set the clock. In the top of the tower, the bell sounded, and the hands spun around the clock several times before stopping in the midnight position.

"Everybody, get back," cried Apocalypse.

The Angels drifted backward, waiting. The clock face swung open, and millions of tiny insects flew out.

"I didn't bring any bug spray," said Knockout.

The swarm of insects flew around the large intersection, landing on the Zytglogge and neighboring buildings. Bright lights flashed from the insects as they crawled around on the stone.

"What are they doing?" said Poison.

"I don't think I want to know," said Apocalypse as portions of the swarm left the buildings, carrying away large chunks of the yellowish-gray sandstone. The swarm coalesced in the center of the intersection on the west side of the clock tower. The insects formed the rocks into a stout humanoid-shaped golem.

A tram stopped so as not to hit the golem and disgorged its startled, chattering occupants. The Angels waved the people away from the area.

I've got to get in front of this. We need to make it react to us. I have to take the lead. "Don't you have those?" Apocalypse asked Poison.

"I do, but not so big."

"Get them ready. We might need them."

Poison waved her glowing fingers and cried, "Onca uncia pardus!"

In a flash of bright light, two stone golems rose from the cobblestone street. Even though they were only half the size of the insect golem, they banged their fists together and charged it.

"Karen, use your golems to keep that thing off the rest of us. Knockout, morph into something you can hit it with from range. Chelsea, try to blow him apart." *Now, what do I do?*

Apocalypse floated up behind Poison's golems. She fired her tri-beams into the center of the insect golem, blasting a large chunk of rock into pebbles.

The insect golem's middle shifted, reconstituting and filling in the damage. It swung its arm at Apocalypse. She floated backward out of reach until the insects in the golem's arms stretched between the rocks extending their reach to hit her with a *thump*.

Tumbling through the air, Apocalypse landed in a fountain. She'd seen several in the city. Looking up as she climbed out, this fountain sported a statue of a man eating a baby with more in a sack at his feet. She shook her head, trying to get back in the game. There was no time to sightsee. She flew back up the street to

Knockout. The teenage Angel Morphicon was a pink and turquoise Abrams tank. She fired a round and struck the insect golem in the shoulder, blowing a large section away.

"Are you using kinetic or energy rounds?" said Apocalypse.

"Energy doesn't do much damage to this guy. I've switched to kinetic rounds."

"Do you have enough?"

"I have a full load of depleted uranium in my gravity wells. I'll be good."

Knockout fired, pulverizing some of the stone in the insect golem, but the insects simply flew to the surrounding buildings and harvested new stone.

Poison's golems were working over the insect golem's legs, but when they knocked a stone free, the insects retrieved it and reinserted it. The insect golem punched one of Poison's golems into a building, then picked up the remaining golem and smashed it into the head of the tram. The golem in the building picked up a large stone and hurled it at the insect golem, but it absorbed the stone, making the insect golem's middle larger.

"*Ok, ladies,*" said Apocalypse, "*we need to come up with a new strategy. We can't pound this one into the ground; it just remakes itself.*"

"*We need to target the insects,*" said Poison, "*with what, I don't know.*"

The insect golem picked up one of the opposing golems and slammed it repeatedly into the ground, tearing a leg off. It smashed the damaged golem into the ground and jumped on top, grinding the golem into powder.

"*What if we trap them?*" said Chelsea.

"*In what?*" said Apocalypse.

"*Ice.*"

"*I don't have ice rounds,*" said Knockout as she fired again.

"*I can generate some, but not enough to encase this beast,*" said Poison.

"*I can help,*" said Chelsea. "*Momma-K has been teaching me to control water. I can weave it in between the rocks and freeze it. My mass accelerator can blow it apart. I just have to get close.*"

"*I—*" Apocalypse paused, stopping her mothering instinct from taking over. Chelsea needed to master her abilities, and Kita looked for opportunities, but that didn't mean her daughter needed to go in alone. "*Ok, but I'm going in with you.*"

"*Your Highness,*" grumbled O'Brien.

"*We both have shields and will use them, right, sweet pea?*"

"*Sure, no problem, Mom.*"

"*I will go in and draw its attention. Then Chelsea—*"

"*I can freeze the feet,*" said Poison.

"*Then do it. I'll keep it busy with Dan and the remaining golem. Chelsea, once it engages me, do what you need to do.*"

"*Got it, Mom.*"

"*Karen, attack!*"

"Onca uncia pardus!" Poison cried from a neighboring building. The street was covered with ice and grew up the insect golem's legs, holding it in place.

Poison's remaining golem charged the insect golem and smashed its fists against the enemy's legs, knocking frozen pieces of rock and insect away. The insect golem was unable to repair its damaged legs. It reached over and pummeled the smaller golem but couldn't dislodge it.

Apocalypse and O'Brien moved forward, firing energy beams and a lance of flame. The insect golem swung its arm, extending toward Apocalypse. She stopped her beams and put up her pearly-white shield. The insect golem's hand hit her, sending her bouncing off a pair of buildings, the tram, and through the tunnel under the Zytglogge. She rolled to a stop not far from Knockout. *Woah, what a ride.*

Knockout fired, hitting the insect golem's free leg. The force of the kinetic round shattered the leg. The insect golem shifted to remain upright, momentarily disrupting its attack on O'Brien, who had his heat shield up.

"Hey, Mom, I got what I need!" called Chelsea as she went by with the contents of a nearby fountain held in a large sphere.

"Be careful!" Apocalypse flew after her daughter, trying to get ahead of her so she could be one more thing for the insect golem to swat that wasn't Chelsea. "Chelsea, go around to the back!" ordered Apocalypse as she blasted a section of the insect golem's arm to keep it from swinging at Chelsea.

Apocalypse followed Chelsea around to the rear of the insect golem. Chelsea encased the insect golem's arm and shoulder in water. The golem pulled part of its arm free as Chelsea tried to keep the water wrapped around it.

"Concentrate!" said Apocalypse. "Think about what you're doing. You got this. Freeze what you've got. We'll get more water."

The water around the insect golem's shoulder and upper arm froze.

"Knockout! Do you have a shot?"

"I'm on it! Hold still, you ugly mother——"

"I got it," said Chelsea. She reached into her belt and pulled out a marble. Raising her arm, her elbow flashed with blue light. When the flashing became solid, the blue light streaked down her arm and shot the marble forward into the insect golem's ice-covered arm, shattering it. The force of the blow caused the insect golem to twist and topple, crashing to the cobblestone street and breaking off its damaged frozen leg.

The insect golem spasmed as the rock making it up reconstituted itself into a smaller form.

"Mom! The fire hydrant!" Chelsea pointed to the corner of the building across the street from the Zytglogge. Sticking out of the stone wall was the familiar Y of a fire hydrant.

Apocalypse took aim and blew the caps off the hydrants, flooding the intersection and dousing the insect golem with water. Chelsea flew around the insect golem, freezing it solid. Knockout fired, blowing the insect golem apart.

"Dan, go around and melt the pieces into slag," said Apocalypse. "I want to make sure those Morphicon insects are dead."

"Yes, Your Highness."

"I can help, too," said Chelsea.

"Just don't overdo it. You've expended a lot of energy. Eat some energy balls."

Chelsea sighed. "Yes, Mom."

"Everyone else, spread out and see if you can find a

briefcase." Apocalypse didn't see one lying in the streets. There were some hiding places as she checked behind the archways that led to various shops that lined the streets.

"*I think I found it,*" said Poison. She was inside the Zytglogge clocktower clockface where the Morphicon insects had emerged. She appeared holding a briefcase similar to the one they'd found in the Black Forest.

The Angels met in the center of the intersection, and Poison handed Apocalypse the briefcase. Apocalypse turned the locking mechanism to zero-seven-three-five, and the case opened to reveal a tape recorder. She lifted it out and hit the play button.

"Congratulations on defeating Wing-Ding. A very unique creation, don't you think? I'm sure you're excited to move on to your next puzzle. I won't keep you from it.

"London Bridge is falling down,

"My fair lady.

"You've had a long day. You should go and have a cuppa and see real royalty. Your little empire is but a babe in comparison. Their parliament is filled with antics, but at least it's not a muppet on a string. Have a safe trip. I understand the Chunnel is a wonder. I would stay out of the air. The Swiss Air Force is politer than others. I'll talk to you again in thirteen hours."

Apocalypse made a dark face in response to the criticism of her government. As far as she was concerned English democracy was a mess that didn't get anything done. "I think it's pretty obvious where we're going."

"We have to drive to London?" growled Poison.

"It'll give the others time to heal and us a chance to rest," said Apocalypse.

APOCALYPSE SAT IN THE BACK OF KNOCKOUT AS THEY drove through the night. The French countryside was pretty, but it wasn't the same as Virginia or Maryland. Chelsea was curled up asleep, her head in Apocalypse's lap. She stroked her daughter's hair absentmindedly as the battle of moms raged inside her.

There was little doubt Kita had engineered Chelsea to do great things. Apocalypse just wished she'd been told. It didn't seem right having Chelsea shoulder such a heavy load of the combat. Apocalypse knew part of it was her being a mom and not wanting her daughter in danger. She was only eight. She was supposed to be playing with friends and going to school, not fighting monsters. Apocalypse hadn't objected to the combat training, but Chelsea had only two years of the sword. Kita said she was proficient, but Apocalypse didn't think it was nearly enough.

And then there were the abilities. She and Kita had talked about controlling luck and giving her a hybrid black and white cloud. A new form that allowed access to both types of clouds' abilities. The cloud wasn't fully mature yet and wouldn't be for several more years, but Kita made it so Chelsea could access abilities like the shield, healing, and shifting.

She and Kita had never talked about giving Chelsea abilities like red balls, ice, water, and the mass accelerator. She'd never heard of the last one until

Chelsea used it. *What other abilities does Chelsea have? Would she tell me? What if Kita told her not to? But why would Kita do that?*

Apocalypse didn't want to drive a wedge between her and Kita or put Chelsea in an awkward place. But there was one person who would know. His job was to follow Chelsea everywhere.

Apocalypse leaned forward to the next row of seats. "Dan?"

"Yes, Your Highness?"

"Did you know Chelsea could do what she did today?"

"What do you mean? Her skill with the bow is very good."

"Don't play coy. The abilities she used. No one has ever told me about them."

O'Brien cleared his throat. "The Vicereine wanted her to be prepared to face the world. In her words, 'My daughter won't be kept locked away in a white house, Dan. She needs to be prepared to face the world and conquer it.'"

"I agree, but she *is* only eight."

"The Vicereine believes she's a target."

"I wouldn't let anyone touch her."

O'Brien nodded. "The Vicereine wanted Chelsea to be able to defend herself. I protested, but she made the point of what happens if something happens to me?"

Apocalypse hadn't thought of that. O'Brien had followed her around since she was a little girl and had followed Chelsea her entire life. *Is this wisdom or paranoia on Kita's part?* Apocalypse knew her wife; it was both. "Do you know more of what she can do?"

"The Vicereine has given her a collection of offensive and defensive abilities. Mirroring, fire, water, gravity sphere, ice, wind, lightning, phasing, mass accelerator, luck—are just what I've seen them practice."

Apocalypse's eyes bulged.

"But the Vicereine tells her those are secondary to her sword, bow, and tumbling. She doesn't want Chelsea relying on them to get her out of trouble."

Apocalypse sighed and nodded. Since Chelsea was old enough to walk, she had been in gymnastics learning to tumble. She was good but still learning to use it in a fight like Kita.

"Do you think this is too much for her?"

O'Brien grunted. "If I had my choice, Your Highness, she'd be locked up in the White House, but I think you're doing the right thing using her abilities in an auxiliary role and keeping her from the direct confrontation. This will build her confidence in her abilities and as a member of a team. The Vicereine may have given her everything and the kitchen sink, but you only learn teamwork by working with a team."

"How am I doing?"

O'Brien seemed to be taken aback by the question. "Excellent, Your Highness."

"Come on, Dan. I haven't led a small team since you watched me suffer through OCS. I'm worried I'm out of my element and am going to get someone killed. I already have three in the ward."

"With the monsters we've faced, that's not a bad score. The others are following you and stepping up when needed. That's good. You're trying to use everyone's abilities to maximize our strengths and protect those that need to be protected. I'd say you're doing a better job now than you did against that bunker back in the Georgia swamp."

Apocalypse chuckled. That was a debacle that left half her squad dead and the rest trapped by machine gun fire. All because she had the map upside down.

"Thanks, Dan. I just have to find Kita, get the other girls back, and keep Chelsea and the rest of you safe. I'm sorry you have to go through this."

"The Vicereine made me a demon for a reason. She knew someday you'd be facing more than guys with guns."

"Yeah, she does have good foresight."

"I swear she can see the future."

"She once told me it wasn't the worst that she feared; it was the weird."

"Morphicons are pretty weird."

"Hey!" said Knockout.

"The big ones we've been fighting are weird, not you," said Apocalypse. She leaned back and put her head against the headrest while stroking Chelsea's hair. *I hope this next one isn't too much for her or me...*

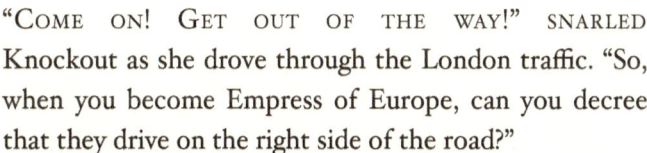

"Come on! Get out of the way!" snarled Knockout as she drove through the London traffic. "So, when you become Empress of Europe, can you decree that they drive on the right side of the road?"

Apocalypse chuckled. She hadn't attempted to make the Indians switch sides of the road. She doubted the English would be receptive to the idea. As far as they were concerned, the EUS was still their lost colonies waiting to return to the Crown.

"Oh, hell yeah. Scanned a double-decker bus for my collection. That's one Bombshell doesn't have," the teenager cried as she drove around the red bus.

"Hey, sweet pea, how much time do we have?" Apocalypse asked Chelsea.

"Twenty-seven minutes," she answered without looking away from the window. She seemed fascinated by London.

Apocalypse decided she should check in with Velositi and the others. "*Hey, Velositi, how are you feeling?*"

"*I am healed and ready if you need me.*"

"*I need everyone I can get. I don't see these monsters getting any easier.*"

"*Zhi is ready as well. Lizzy is still in the ward. The doctor says she will need another day at least.*"

"*Ok. When I get to Big Ben, I'll have them open a rift gate, and you can join us.*"

"*We will be ready and waiting.*"

"*Excellent. See you then.*" Apocalypse leaned back and closed her eyes, feeling some tension drain away. Having two more Angels would make things easier. Especially Velositi. Her leadership skills were second to none.

"Sorry, pal," said Knockout as she swerved to the left, causing Apocalypse to open her eyes and look out the windshield. They were on a bridge, and she could see Westminster Palace and Big Ben next to the river. Knockout pulled hard to the curb after they crossed the bridge.

"Ok, everybody out. We're here," said the teenage Morphicon.

The Angels piled out of the pink and turquoise SUV onto the intersection of Westminster Bridge Road and Victoria Embankment, a street that ran along the Thames River. Once everyone was out, Knockout morphed into her Angelic form.

"What are we looking for?" said Knockout.

Apocalypse wasn't sure. In the past, someone had always come up to them. Across the street was a crowd around a stand under a statue with a sign that read Hop On Hop Off Bus Tours. Those near the street had seen the Angels, and many were taking pictures as traffic drove by.

"Chelsea, Dan, check out Big Ben. Karen, try across the street. Knockout, look at the train station. It has some cafes and sitting areas. See if you can find someone who can give us the clue," said Apocalypse. "*Velositi, you girls ready?*"

"*Yes. We're at the Area Fifty-one beacon.*"

Apocalypse called Rift Command and gave them her location and Velositi's location. After several moments the air in front of her looked like someone tossed handfuls of glitter into the air. A circular door opened, and Apocalypse could see the rift gate complex located under Shiveluch volcano in the middle of the Kamchatka peninsula on Russia's far east side. Velositi and Venom stepped through. Apocalypse gave each a hug. "How are you girls doing?"

"Fit to fight," said Venom.

"I am ready," said Velositi.

"Good. We're searching for our clue. We have about ten minutes left."

"We will have to hurry then."

"Yes. I sent Knockout to the train station. If you could go there and Zhi, help Karen across the street."

"No problem."

"I'm going to go help Chelsea and Dan check the clock tower."

The three Angels split up. It was a short flight to Big Ben's base, but Apocalypse didn't see anyone or a way in. "*Chelsea, where are you?*"

"*We're in the belfry. Fly above the clock face through the windows.*"

Apocalypse flew up the 180 feet and found the Gothic Revival style windows above the polished clock faces. She squeezed through the windows and came face-to-face with the thirteen-and-a-half-ton bell, Big Ben. "Chelsea?"

"We're over here, Mom."

"This thing isn't going to ding, is it?"

"No. We have seven minutes until the quarter bells go off."

"Let's not be up here when they do." Apocalypse knew how sensitive Angel hearing was and didn't want to be deaf for the rest of the day.

"There's no one up here," said Chelsea.

"I wonder if Westminster Palace has an info desk," grumbled Apocalypse.

"We haven't checked the clock's mechanism room yet. The ladder is over there."

The three Angels took the ladder to the floor below that housed the machinery that turned the four-faced clock.

"Wow, this is impressive," said Apocalypse.

"Lots of hiding spots," said O'Brien.

Apocalypse squatted, checking under some apparatus.

"*Hey! We got it!*" cried Venom.

"*Ok. Everyone, meet out in front of the statue on the corner,*" said Apocalypse.

"*That statue commemorates the Boudiccan Rebellion,*" said Chelsea. "*Momma-K said she was once compared to Boudica.*"

"*I haven't heard that story.*"

"*Momma-K threatened to take on her whole army by herself and her people, the Arconians, drew a parallel.*"

"*She would try,*" said Venom.

"*And most likely succeed,*" said Velositi.

"Grab hold, Dan," said Chelsea as she took Apocalypse's gloved hand. The youngster phased the group down to the corner, where they met the rest of the Angels. Venom and Poison flanked a man wearing a Hop On Hop Off polo shirt. Around the Angels gathered a flock of tourists taking pictures and asking for autographs.

"Please give us some room," said Velositi to the tourists, but they refused to listen.

Apocalypse and Chelsea pushed in next to the man.

"What do you have for us?" said Apocalypse.

"Top of the morning to you, Mistress Apocalypse. Doctor Unixilite sends his warmest regards. Big Ben is famous the world over. Its four faces shine across England, but do you know how many times its hands are at right angles in twelve hours? Set the four faces to the correct time before Big Ben strikes noon."

"We have seven minutes," cried Chelsea. "What do we do?"

"Everyone, grab hold of Chelsea. She'll phase us up to the tower."

Apocalypse took her daughter's hand. "Don't worry, we can do it. Have you looked up the positions?"

"Yeah. I've got them. There are twenty-two solutions. We'll never get through them all in time. Hang on, everyone."

The world shifted to black and white as the group flew up to the clock faces. The world shifted back to color when they arrived.

"Just relax. Everyone, take a side, and Chelsea will call out the time to set the clocks to." She hugged Chelsea.

"Should I go in order, or...we only have five minutes."

"Use your skills. Pick which you feel is best."

"Hmmm...ok. Ah, three o'clock?"

"*Three o'clock, ladies.*" Apocalypse flew over and pushed the minute hand while Velositi moved the hour hand. The hand gave more resistance than Apocalypse would have guessed, and it became a fight to get the fourteen-foot minute hand into position.

"*Ready!*" announced Apocalypse.

After two long minutes, the other Angels announced they were set. Nothing happened.

"What do we do?" cried Chelsea. "It didn't work. It was supposed to work."

Apocalypse took Chelsea by the shoulders and looked into her eyes. "Don't panic. We still have time. You just need to try again. Take your time. It's just like the cards and the coin. Concentrate. If you don't get it, that's ok, too. I will figure something out."

Chelsea nodded and sniffed. She closed her eyes.

I wonder what she sees. Apocalypse waited for her daughter.

"*Eight twenty-seven,*" announced Chelsea to the other Angels.

Apocalypse moved the minute hand to the correct time.

"*Ready,*" reported Poison.

"*Good to go,*" said Knockout.

"*All set,*" announced Venom.

Apocalypse held her breath. When Big Ben rang, it caused her to jump. The big bell was joined by the quarter bells as they performed a three-minute concert.

"You did it, sweet pea." Apocalypse hugged Chelsea.

"Yeah, but what are we waking up?"

Apocalypse hadn't thought of that. She turned around, scanning the palace, streets, and bridge for any sign of a monster.

"There!" yelled Velositi.

Apocalypse followed Velositi's finger across the bridge to a dock on the Thames River. On the far side of the pier, a blue tour boat was morphing into a giant Morphicon.

"He's, ah, kind of big," said Venom.

"He's a hundred feet tall," said Chelsea.

"How deep is the water?" said Poison.

"The tides in, so twenty feet or so."

"How are we taking Boaty MacBoatface down?" said Venom.

"I'm thinking," said Apocalypse. "I'm open to ideas."

"It has five system cores, and they are massive," said Velositi.

Apocalypse changed her eyes to see the

electromagnetic spectrum. The five ten-foot cube-like cores sat in its chest, head, and abdomen. "How do we get to them? The chest is twenty-five feet thick."

"Watch out!" said Knockout.

Boaty scooped up a small boat and threw it at the Angels.

"I've got it," said Apocalypse. She aimed her tri-beams at the incoming boat and cut it into smaller pieces that landed in the street and on the front of a cab. "Chelsea, we need to get these people to safety. Gather them under your shield and get them underground into the train station. Dan, go with her. Knockout, hit him from the air with something that can strip his metal away."

"One A-ten Thunderbolt coming up."

"Everyone else, we need to keep Boaty busy until the people are clear."

"The river is too deep for my golems," said Poison, "but I can freeze the river around him."

"If she freezes the river, I can get out there," said Venom.

"Velositi and I will draw its attention," said Apocalypse.

The two Angels flew up to be eye level with the colossal Morphicon. Its square head had no neck and sat on its blocky chest. Its violet eyes glowed brightly when the Angels flew up to him.

"Hey, Boaty!" yelled Apocalypse as she fired her beams into its left eye, causing it to explode.

Boaty brought one arm up to protect its head and swung at the Angels with the other.

Apocalypse and Velositi scattered, dodging the

massive limb.

"Well, I got his attention," said Apocalypse.

"It is too bad our eyes are not our primary visual input," said Velositi.

"What are they for then?"

"A window to the soul. It is our primary way of showing emotion."

The water around Boaty froze, creating an island of ice that ran from the near shore out into the river's middle. Boaty struggled to move his legs, his efforts proving how stuck he was. On the ice near the pier, Venom landed, and millions of insects streamed off her.

"What are you releasing, Zhi?" said Apocalypse.

"Ants. They release formic acid and can burn through metal. It might not be enough to bring him down but will at least irritate Boaty."

"Ick," said Velositi.

Boaty roared and slapped at his ant-covered legs.

"Shit burns," said Venom as she took to the air.

From the east came the sound of jet engines. Knockout came in low, and a loud *brat* sound filled the air as she fired on Boaty, leaving a trail of large holes in its chest from the 30-millimeter depleted uranium rounds she fired.

Boaty roared and slammed his fists down on the ice, causing a spiderweb of cracks.

"That ice is not going to hold him for long," said Velositi.

"We need to do more damage. The thinnest place is his head. Everyone, concentrate your fire on the head. Chelsea, how is the evacuation going?"

"We got everyone inside, but they won't let people

downstairs, and the police are trying to arrest Dan for carrying a gun."

"Then tell the police the people's safety is their problem. You and Dan get back here."

"Sure thing, Mom."

"Velositi, you circle one direction; I'll go the other. We need to get through this guy's head."

"Right."

The two Angels spiraled around Boaty up to his head where they opened fire, leaving large holes and deep gouges. Boaty tried to swat at them, but both easily dodged the massive arms. With a frustrated roar, Boaty struck the ice again, breaking some of it into pieces. He picked up a piece and swung it at Velociti. The Angel backflipped over the frozen bat. Apocalypse fired her beams and cut Boaty's bat in half.

"We need to do more damage," said Apocalypse. "Knockout, aim for the head."

"Got it." The teenage Morphicon was off in the distance, coming around for another pass.

A giant red ball stuck to the side of Boaty's face. Apocalypse spun and spotted her daughter flying up to meet her. Chelsea snapped her fingers, and the side of Boaty's head disappeared in a ball of flame and a shower of liquid metal pieces. When the fire dissipated, a side of the large system core was visible.

"Everyone, aim for the system core!" cried Apocalypse. She focused her beams, turned up the temperature, and fired, cutting deep into the system core's glass structure.

Boaty flailed his arms, trying to hit the Angels. As they ducked and dodged, his left hand morphed into a large cannon. He fired several random shots into the air in the general direction of the Angels. Venom dodged a shot, but it struck the Westminster Bridge, taking a chunk out of the railing and the roadbed.

"Ok, this is getting serious," said Apocalypse. "Everyone, stay high. We have to keep the destruction to a minimum."

"Here I come," announced Knockout. "Make him turn so I can get a clean shot at his system core."

Apocalypse turned and spotted Knockout coming down the river. She was suddenly tackled by Velositi and forced downward. She felt a warm blast go over the top of her.

"Don't take your eye off him," said Velositi.

"Ugh. Thanks."

"Hey ugly, over here," yelled Venom to get Boaty's attention.

The giant Morphicon turned and tried to swat the offending Angel.

"Got him in my sights," said Knockout. She let out a long *brat* as her minigun fired, blowing out large chunks of the system core. The last round blasted through Boaty's head.

Boaty seized, his legs went rigid, and his arms locked to his sides. His body turned to jelly as he morphed. His head sank into his chest, and six cannons appeared, three on each side. His arms morphed into cannons while more cannons extruded from his thighs.

"I suddenly see the property damage amount about to soar," said Poison.

"Is everyone off the street?" said Apocalypse.

"Not everyone," said Venom pointing to a group of

tourists still on a red double-decker bus watching the fight.

"Dan, get them out of here."

"How are we going to get to the remaining system cores?" said Velositi.

"I can get two," said Chelsea.

"How, sweet pea?" said Apocalypse, unsure of what secret power her daughter had.

"My gravity spheres. I just have to get close enough to use them."

Apocalypse bit her lip. They could get her close, but she couldn't activate her spheres behind a shield. A plan was needed. "Ok—Karen, Velositi, and Zhi will keep him busy. Chelsea and I will sneak around behind."

The Angels split up. Apocalypse and Chelsea flew down toward the bridge to act like they were helping Dan. The Secret Service agent was yelling at the bus driver to get off the bridge. The two Angels ducked behind the bus and turned invisible.

"If he makes any move toward you, I'll put my shield up," said Apocalypse.

"It won't take more than a few seconds. The spheres should disrupt the system cores. They cut through everything."

"What is a gravity sphere?"

"It's a sphere of gravity particles that can be collapsed to smaller than a grain of sand. Momma-K says it works good for destroying things or putting kids in time out."

"Has she ever...?"

"No. She said she used to do it to Kylee all the time."

Apocalypse knew Kylee was Kita's last daughter who

betrayed Kita, leading to the destruction of Reality. She hadn't gotten the whole story from Kita, her wife saying it was *complicated*. "Ok, let's go."

They took off from behind the bus. Boaty was swinging his arms at the other Angels and occasionally firing in their direction. The cannon fire was going up over the city away from doing any potential harm.

Apocalypse and Chelsea arrived behind Boaty. His back was blocky but twisted as the liquid metal moved. They turned visible, surprising the giant Morphicon. He tried to twist, but his right leg held fast in the ice as the other tore from the damage done by the ants. His upper body bent some as he flailed with his arms, unable to reach them.

"Go!" cried Apocalypse.

Chelsea stretched her arms out and flexed her hands. Two gray spheres appeared, one around the system core in Boaty's upper right torso and the other in his left abdomen. The spheres were big enough to be partially visible outside of Boaty. The Morphicon spasmed as half its body went limp.

Clenching her fists, Chelsea collapsed the spheres, cutting perfect spherical sections out of Boaty's chest and abdomen. The loss of mass and structural integrity caused Boaty to twist and collapse. His right arm fell off, and his left leg sheared off from the ant damage, leaving him a heap on the ice.

The Angels gathered at the base of what was left of the Boudiccan Rebellion statue. People were coming out of Westminster Palace and Westminster Station.

"You go, *girl*!" said Venom as she offered a high five to Chelsea.

The youngster slapped the hand but looked tired and weak.

"Chelsea, you need to eat," said Apocalypse as she put an arm and wing around her daughter.

"Yes, Mom."

Apocalypse took several of the energy balls—packed with five thousand calories each—and gave them to Chelsea. Her daughter took them without complaint and munched on them as people gathered around the group. "Keep them back. Chelsea needs a break." *She's too young to have this kind of stamina.*

"Everyone, do your best to destroy what's left of Boaty. I don't want him getting up."

"We should be able to get to the system cores easily now," said Velositi.

Apocalypse let the others have at it as she held Chelsea, trying to get both of them to relax. "You did really well today, sweet pea. I'm proud of you. I don't think we could have done it without you."

"Ah, Mom. You would have figured out something."

"It would have been a lot harder. I'm glad Momma-K had the foresight to give you such wonderful gifts."

"You just wish she'd told you, right?"

Apocalypse sighed. "Yes, well, that's between her and me."

Chelsea leaned back in her mother's arms. "You're not going to take them away, are you?"

Apocalypse shook her head. "No. It's too late for that. I want her to make sure you're trained in how to use them properly, and you're only to use them under our supervision."

Chelsea lowered her head. "Yes, Mom."

"It's not that I don't trust you, but until you have full control, we have to be careful. Trust me, there will be plenty of time."

"Excuse me, *Miss* Apocalypse."

Apocalypse scrunched her nose and opened her wings. "Yes?" she said tartly to the bobby standing before her with a briefcase.

"I believe this is for you, miss."

"Thank you." Apocalypse released one arm from Chelsea and took the briefcase. She waited to open it until the other Angels returned.

"What do we have to fight now?" said Venom upon seeing the case in Apocalypse's hands.

"I don't know. I haven't opened it yet."

"I'm tired of this trip around Europe," said Knockout. "We need to find whoever is behind this and punch their nose in."

"We will go where we need to go and do what we need to do," Velositi said sternly.

Knockout bowed her head. "Yes, Mom."

Apocalypse looked up at Big Ben to get the time. She entered zero-eight-twenty-seven on the briefcase's lock and hit the latches. Inside, resting on a foam insert, was another audio recorder. She hit the play button.

"Congratulations on defeating poor MacDuff," said Doctor Unixilite. "You Angels are getting good at such things. I hope you're ready for a doubleheader.

Jack be nimble,

Jack be quick.

How fast does an Angel fly? You have twenty minutes to reach Tilbury Docks and search out the three containers to stop CMX. Good luck."

"I found it," said Chelsea. "It's a dock on the Thames River twenty miles from here. I—I can't phase us that far."

"Twenty minutes to fly twenty miles won't give us much time," said Poison.

"Hey, one C-one-thirty comin' up," said Knockout. She jumped into the air and climbed a hundred feet before morphing into a C-130 military transport.

"Grab hold," said Chelsea.

The young Angel phased everyone aboard Knockout.

"All set. Let's go!" said Venom as she pounded on Knockout's side.

Apocalypse escorted Chelsea to the cockpit.

"Where am I going?" said Knockout.

"It's almost due east on the river," said Chelsea. "Here's the GPS coordinates."

"Got them. We'll be there in ten. Good job, little sis."

Chelsea blushed. "Thanks."

"I mean it. You've been awesome. So, take a break. We'll be there in no time."

"Ok. I could use a minute to sit."

Apocalypse guided Chelsea back to the rear of the plane and sat her in a jump seat. "Have you been eating?"

"Yeah."

"Good. Eat some more."

Chelsea rolled her eyes. "Ok. Mom?" she said around a mouthful.

"Yes?"

"Why are they doing this to us? What did Momma-K do?"

Apocalypse wiggled her nose. *What is the best way to*

answer this? "Momma-K was defending her honor—"

"I thought Momma-K didn't believe in honor."

"Not in the traditional sense, but she has her own flavor of it. Someone insulted her in a way that opened an old psychological wound. Does that make sense?"

"Yeah. What happened to Momma-K?"

Apocalypse removed her gloves and took Chelsea's hand. *How do I explain rape to an eight-year-old?* "When Momma-K was sixteen, a man forced himself on her and made inappropriate physical contact. Someone threatened to do it to Momma-K again."

"You mean she was raped like Nicole? I'm not dumb, Mom. Momma-K explained sex to me so boys couldn't take advantage of me."

Apocalypse felt as if she'd been slammed into park while going sixty miles-per-hour. *Why would Kita have such an important conversation without me? She should have discussed the idea with me first! Chelsea is...is she too young? The world is full of pedophiles, slave traders, and other dangers. Do I live in an ivory tower? Am I unaware of the risks in the world...maybe I'm unaware of the risks to an eight-year-old?*

"Mom, are you ok?"

"I'm... I'm just taken by surprise, that's all. What did Momma-K tell you?"

"She explained how sex works between a man and a woman and then how it is for you. She told me I wasn't allowed to do it until I was sixteen and if anyone asked or tried to force me, to kick them in the crotch and come find her. If they persisted, I was allowed to use whatever abilities I have to get them to back off."

Kita may not be the best parent, but she seems to have beaten me to the critical parts. No, that's not true. She's doing her best to compliment my parenting. She sees the world differently, and I'm glad she does. "That's good. We'll talk about it more later."

"Oh, goodie. Do we have to? It's so gross. I don't want anyone slobbering on me while on top of me."

"When you're older, you'll feel differently. Right now, let's just stick with kicking them in the crotch and running away. But if they persist, you have my permission to crush them with the gravity sphere."

"Cool. So why are they doing this to us?"

"I don't know, but I plan on asking them when we find them."

"Is the CIA working on it?"

"Among others."

"What if we fight one of these guys we can't kill?"

"We're not alone. The entire military around Europe is on alert. If we get in trouble, they'll come and save us."

"That's good to know," said Knockout. "We're here. I'm coming in low over the docks."

The Angels stood up and moved to the door. Poison opened it and leaned out. "Docks are below us," she yelled back to the others when she pulled herself back in.

"Let's go," said Apocalypse. "We don't have much time to find these containers."

"Twelve minutes," said Chelsea.

One by one, the Angels jumped from the plane. Before Chelsea jumped, she opened a pocket dimension for O'Brien.

"See you on the ground, Your Highness," he said as he entered the nether region.

"Last one," called Apocalypse as she jumped. When

she was clear, Knockout morphed into an Angel and joined the others.

"How are we going to find the right containers among all of these?" said Venom.

Below them on the dock were rows of cargo containers stacked four high.

"Look there," said Chelsea pointing to the cranes on the edge of the dock. There was no ship in port. "There are three cranes, each with a shipping container under it. I bet we should start there."

"Good. Let's go," said Apocalypse. The Angels dove toward the dock. The cranes were spaced a hundred yards apart. "Velositi, Knockout, take the far container. Karen, Zhi, take the middle. We'll take the near one."

"Roger," said Poison.

"Of course," said Velositi.

Apocalypse and Chelsea landed by the nearest crane. Chelsea opened the pocket dimension and let O'Brien out. The container wasn't locked, and Apocalypse turned the latches and pulled a door open. Inside the container were dozens of wooden crates. A path between the crates led to the back. There, they found a tablet with the image of Big Ben.

"It smells like diesel fuel in here, Your Highness," said O'Brien.

"It is a port, after all. We have to hurry and disarm whatever is waiting for us. I'm hoping these boxes don't contain our next adversary." Apocalypse touched the tablet. The image minimized to a corner, and four boxes and a number pad appeared. "It needs a code."

"What about the codes from the clock puzzles?" said Chelsea. "They were four digits."

"*Ladies, do you have tablets with pictures of the clock towers on them?*" said Apocalypse to the other Angels.

"*Roger, we have the Zytglogge,*" said Poison.

"*Yes, we have the cuckoo clock,*" said Velositi.

"*Velositi, your code is one-one-one-seven. Karen, your code is zero-seven-three-five. Let me know when you've entered them.*" Apocalypse entered the code from Big Ben on the tablet and received a circular wait icon.

"*Entered,*" said Poison. "*It's thinking.*"

"*Also entered,*" said Velositi. "*Ours is waiting.*"

The tablet went blank, then the message GAME OVER appeared.

"What does that mean?" said Chelsea. "What's going on, Mom?"

The doors of the container banged shut. A shudder went through the container.

"We're going up," said Apocalypse. "We need to get out of here."

Chelsea grabbed Apocalypse's and O'Brien's hands. The world changed to black and white. They made their way to the front of the container and passed through the doors. The world changed back to normal. Above them, the container was lifted into the air by the crane.

"Why is the crane lifting the container?" said Chelsea.

Apocalypse looked down the dock and saw the other two cranes were moving containers out over the water.

"I think that message was to inform us that our antagonist is done playing games. We have to hurry. You and Dan get the middle container. I'll get the far one."

"I can get to the far one faster. You get the middle one," countered Chelsea.

Apocalypse didn't have time to argue. "Fine. Go."

Chelsea grabbed O'Brien's hand and phased away.

Apocalypse jumped into the air and flew as fast as she could toward the closer container. She reached it just as the crane was fully extended over the water. There was a metal *clack,* and the container fell, splashing into the Thames River.

The container didn't sink but rolled to one side. Apocalypse reached the door and tried to twist the handles, but they wouldn't move. As she tried the other side, the back end of the container slipped under the water, causing the front to rise into the air.

"*Karen, Zhi? Are you ok?*" called Apocalypse.

"*We're ok, just trapped in the container,*" said Poison.

"*I'm at the door. I'm trying to get it open.*"

"*We'll never reach the front.*"

"*Then I will come to the back and see if I can cut a hole.*"

Apocalypse leaped over the top of the container and flew down to the water's edge. The back end was wholly submerged, and she couldn't see anything through the murky water. She aimed her fist at where she thought the top of the container was. Her plan was to cut the top corner sections away, giving the other Angels enough room to wiggle out. She set her beam to high and fired. The water boiled and steamed as she made her cut.

"*Kimmy, is that you?*" said Poison.

"*Yes.*"

"*Did you cut through the top?*"

"*Yeah. Can you get out?*"

"*More water is pouring in. It's too fast. We can't get out.*"

"*Just wait until the water level equalizes,*" said Chelsea. "*It should be easy to swim out then.*"

"*Something started beeping,*" said Venom.

"*That can't be good. We need to get out of here,*" said Poison.

"*Try to get out the hole. I'll pull you through,*" said Apocalypse. She dove into the water, following the container's corrugated top until she reached the area she cut. "*Ok, I'm here.*"

"*We're trying. I've got an edge.*"

Apocalypse ran her hand along the edge going by feel as she sought out Poison's hand. She moved along the cut, searching. She bumped something with her hand. "*Karen, Is that you?*"

"*Yeah.*"

"*Hang on. I got you.*" Apocalypse grabbed Poison's wrist. She braced her feet against the container and pulled against the rushing water. She felt Poison slowly slide out. "*Zhi, where are you?*"

"*I have a hold of Karen's skirt. I'm pushing from the other end. Don't worry about me. Keep pulling!*"

Apocalypse braced herself and pulled harder. She couldn't tell how far she had to go, but she was nearly standing.

"*Ok, I think I'm out. I don't feel the push of the water anymore,*" said Poison.

"*We have to get Zhi out.*" Apocalypse took a step backward, pulling Poison with her.

"*I'm on the container. I've got Zhi's arm.*"

"*Guide me to her.*"

Poison pulled Apocalypse downward to her other arm. Apocalypse found it and moved along it until she found Venom.

"*Pull!*"

Together, the two Angels pulled Venom until the resistance suddenly gave way, and they fell backward against the container.

"*Damn. My hair is going to be a wreck,*" said Venom.

The sudden upward force caught Apocalypse by surprise. She was launched upward out of the water. She tumbled through the air and landed hard back in the river. She tried to swim, but her legs and wings refused to work. She pulled with her arms towards what she thought was the surface. In the murky water, it was impossible to tell how close she was until she broke through. The daylight and air were a relief after the foulness of the water. She leaned back and floated on the surface, her mind slowly registering the pain in her wings and legs. *What happened?*

"*Mom? Where are you?*" Chelsea sounded worried and upset.

"*I'm in the river, sweet pea. I think I've injured my wings and legs.*"

"*I'll come find you.*"

Apocalypse raised an arm and fired a broad red beam skyward so Chelsea could find her.

"Mom. I'll get you back to the dock."

Apocalypse felt herself rise into the air. Chelsea was moving a section of the river with her on top of it. Her daughter set her down on the dock. Apocalypse sat up. She tried to move her wings but couldn't. Her legs each had a piece of metal stuck in them. She grabbed one of the pieces and pulled it out. Blood seeped from the wound. She put her hand over it and healed it.

"Mom, are you going to be ok?" said Chelsea, standing back, looking worried.

"I'll be fine. I just need to heal this wound and figure out why my wings aren't working."

"They don't look right."

"I might have dislocated them. Don't worry. It's not hard to fix. How are the others?"

"Velositi and Knockout are looking for them."

Apocalypse made a face. "What happened?"

"Velositi said the containers blew up. Were—were they trying to kill us, Mom?"

Apocalypse pulled the other piece of metal out of her leg. It was going to be a bloody affair. It had sliced her artery. While she worked on that, she thought best about how to answer her daughter. The creatures today had been designed, though not very well, to kill them. The container traps were another thing. *Whoever came up with this idea underestimated us, especially Chelsea. But Chelsea had a lot of the same abilities as Kita. The original idea must have been to capture Kita and kill the rest of us. How do I explain that to an eight-year-old?* "Yes, dear, they were trying to kill us. Someone doesn't like us very much, and I plan on finding out who. This is why Momma-K gave you all these abilities. To keep you safe and protect the rest of us."

"What did we do to them?"

"I don't know. My guess is they didn't plan on us having you today. It was good luck Doctor Unixilite wanted you to come along."

"I wanted to come along."

Apocalypse smiled at Chelsea. "Even better." She stood up. "Dan, can you help me with my wings? They need to be popped back into place."

"Yes, Your Highness."

As O'Brien pulled on Apocalypse's right wing, Knockout arrived with Venom.

"She's kind of awake."

"Place her on the ground. I'll examine her. Ouch. I think you got it, Dan. I'll have to let it heal on its own." Apocalypse knelt and ran her hand over Venom. Inside her hand was a medical scanner that let her see with several different types of images. "Zhi, you have some dislocations and soft tissue damage, which I can heal. Hold still." Apocalypse slowly moved her hands over Venom's chest and abdomen, healing the internal bleeding. Her ability to heal soft tissue was given to her by her cloud—an alien lifeform known as an A'ahegre, brought by Kita that Apocalypse had bonded with. When she was done, she did her best to pop the dislocated bones into place. She was glad for the reinforced skeleton. She could heal the damage of dislocation; she couldn't heal broken bones. The bionanites could do that, but according to Kita, the process was slow. "Ok, give that some time to heal."

"Thanks. What a ride." Venom coughed several times, finishing with coughing up something bloody. "Ah. I can breathe again."

"Dan, can you pull on my other wing? It hurts like a bitch."

O'Brien pulled on the wing, stretching it out.

Apocalypse felt something pop. "Got it." She opened and closed her wings slowly. They still hurt, but they worked.

Velositi landed with Poison in her arms. A big piece of metal was sticking through her chest.

Apocalypse checked her breathing and heartbeat.

Both were shallow and slow. "We need to get her to the ward." She called Area 51 and Rift Gate Command. "Place her on the ground. I'll see what I can do for her."

Velositi placed Poison on the concrete dock. Apocalypse knelt and scanned the stricken Angel. As she finished one side, the rift gate opened, and a medical team exited.

"She has internal injuries from an underwater blast." Apocalypse stepped back to give the team room to stabilize Poison and get her loaded on the stretcher. Once they were ready, they hurried back through the rift gate. Before the gate closed, Sapper stepped through.

"How are you feeling, Lizzy?" said Apocalypse.

"Good to go and ready to rock and roll. What do we do now?"

Apocalypse wasn't sure. Someone had to be watching and report their survival to Doctor Unixilite. She was tired of dancing to his tune. *Is it in his plan that any of us survive? If it was me, I would count on it, but the game is over. It's time he reacted to us.* "We're going to find out what rock Doctor Unixilite is under and kick it over." She held the gate. "Come on. We're going to Area Fifty-one. We'll see if anyone has found anything."

APOCALYPSE TIED BACK HER HAIR AS SHE ENTERED THE briefing room on the first level of the Majestic Twelve bunker at Area 51. She felt better after a shower and a change of clothes. It had taken three washings to get the smell of the Thames River out of her hair, and she didn't think it would ever come out of her clothes. Satisfied her hair was under control, she flipped the hood of her jacket over her head and joined the other Angels on the far side of the stage. "How is everyone?"

The other Angels turned to greet her.

"Sounds like I missed an epic fight," grumbled Sapper.

"It was definitely harder without you."

"I think everyone is fine," said Velositi. She was joined by her three daughters: Knockout, Bombshell, and Stunner. Ryan, Sprokkit, and Bernoot were there as well.

Bernoot's eyes dimmed. "Yo! We got to get Nicole back. I'll be having a panic attack if we don't." He was a soldier that arrived with Velositi. Nemesis had been his liaison before becoming an Angel. After returning from helping the Russian people, Nemesis had taken back the job, and the pair remained close.

Can a Morphicon even have a panic attack? "Don't worry. We'll get her back."

"Yes, and retribution for Leaf as well," said Sprokkit. "Her death was untimely."

"We will get what is ours and more. Whoever this Doctor Unixilite is, he can't hide. My people have been looking for him for the last two days."

"We helped the CIA out as best we could," said Ryan. "The phone number traced back to a town in West Germany called Boxkel, near Frankfurt. The CIA was going to send someone to check it out."

"Boxkel is very interesting," said Sprokkit. "From satellite images, it is a small village. But its internet traffic and electrical consumption are very high. Something is there they do not wish us to see."

Apocalypse wrinkled her nose. "Then we'll have to pull back the curtain and have a look."

The door across the stage opened, and Chelsea and O'Brien entered.

"Did you get clean, sweet pea?"

"Yeah. That stuff was gross. I'm glad my hair is short. I'd hate to be Momma-K. She'd be in the shower for two hours."

Apocalypse chuckled. She had no doubt that Kita had some trick of physics to keep her massive mane of hair clean. Probably the same way she braided it. "Sprokkit and Ryan were just telling us what they found while we were out playing games."

"I'm tired of playing games. I want Momma-K back."

"Hell yeah," said Sapper.

"We're about to have a meeting with the Security Council and intel chiefs to tell me what they found. You get to stand by me and listen in."

Chelsea flipped her hood up. "Oh boy, another teachable moment."

The other Angels laughed.

"You're the only eight-year-old I know that gets to learn to lead the world," said Stunner.

"Trade you."

Stunner looked at Velositi, whose eyes dimmed. "I think I'll stick to the lab. You'd be better than me anyway."

"It doesn't matter anyway. The throne isn't hereditary. The world breaks up into states when Mom dies."

"Like that's ever going to happen," said Sapper.

"Or I abdicate the throne," said Apocalypse. "I may

decide to leave and not come back. But that is a worry for another day. Let's worry about today. Captain," she called to the crew running the communications array, "tell everyone I'm ready."

Faces appeared on the small screens flanking a large one displaying everyone's location. Defense Secretary Brice Mayfield and CIA Director Charlie Rosenstein were the only ones Apocalypse cared to speak to.

"Brice, Charlie, tell me you have some good news for me."

Mayfield spoke first, "Your Highness, we traced the number you gave us back to a West German IP address located in the town of—"

"I know that much. It sounds like a reasonable candidate. I want to know what's there."

"We sent someone to investigate," said Rosenstein. "The town is unusual. It is not on any map, and satellite images show it wasn't there eight years ago. From the pictures our operative sent, the town looks pristine, almost like a movie set. The people are reported as being friendly, helpful, but at the same time, they have simple answers to questions, if they answer at all. There is no sign of any industry or commercial operations that could generate the level of activity we're seeing. One other thing: our operative missed his last check-in."

"That sounds suspicious."

"Yes. The operative said the town didn't feel right, both figuratively and literally. All the structures he touched were warm—"

"Warm!" exclaimed Apocalypse. "Can a Morphicon take the shape of a building?" she looked at Velositi and the other Morphicons.

"Theoretically, it is possible," said Sprokkit. "It would not be a very good disguise. So many systems and materials inside a human structure to mimic, it would be hard. Running water comes to mind as something we cannot do."

"So why would they do it?" said Knockout.

"We'll have to go ask," said Apocalypse.

"Are we sure this is the right place?" said Velositi.

"If it's not, we take out a Neophorm base and deliver a blow to Europe as retaliation for the death of Leaf. I'll go after another if they don't hand over Kita and the other girls. Brice, I want the military on standby. I authorize Operation Nail Driver. Get everyone moving. We'll move as soon as everyone is ready."

THE RIFT GATE OPENED ON THE WIDE DIRT TRACK leading into the small West German village of Boxkel. Six thatch-roofed homes built in the *Fachwerkhäuser* style lined the dirt road. Each was surrounded by a green lawn and shrubbery. Apocalypse led the Angels into West Germany.

"Very picturesque," said Sprokkit.

"Yeah, you could almost see Hansel and Gretel coming out of the forest," said Sapper.

When no one came out to greet them, Apocalypse said, "Spread out and check the homes."

Apocalypse took her daughter's hand, and they walked toward the last house with O'Brien trailing.

"It's pretty here, Mom," said Chelsea.

"Yes, it's very nice. Too bad it's not real."

They walked up the flagstone pathway to the house. Apocalypse took off her glove and placed her hand against the wooden door. It didn't feel like wood but felt like a Morphicon, warm and metallic. Opening the door, they found furniture suitable for an old woman's home. Touching the antique couch was a shock to the senses. It wasn't velvety, nor did it give like she expected.

"Hey, Mom, I found something," Chelsea called from the kitchen.

Apocalypse entered the small kitchen and moved in next to O'Brien, standing in front of the pantry. Looking at the floor, a trapdoor was cut into the boards. "Cellar?"

Chelsea grabbed the pull ring and lifted the door. A ladder disappeared into the darkness. Apocalypse shined a red beam from her fist so they could see.

O'Brien looked down the hole. "It's too deep to be a cellar. The rungs look industrial."

"It's big enough for Angels, but not Morphicons," said Apocalypse. "*Did anyone else find anything?*"

She received a round of negatives from the others.

"*Meet me in front of my house. We found a trapdoor that leads underground.*"

Outside, the Angels and Morphicons met on the dirt road.

"We found a trapdoor, but it's only big enough for Angels," said Apocalypse.

"There must be another way in," said Stunner. "If this has an underground complex, they must have a way of getting supplies inside."

"We have the satellite images," said Sprokkit. "We can search the surrounding area for an entrance."

"Yes. You girls go ahead, and we will meet you inside," said Velositi. "Knockout, go with them."

"Ok, Mom," the teenage Morphicon sighed and shrank three feet, so she was just under six-feet-tall.

Apocalypse led everyone inside to the trapdoor. She went to place a foot on the first rung when O'Brien stopped her.

"If you don't mind, Your Highness, I should go down first."

Apocalypse shrugged. "Of course, Dan," she said with a smile.

O'Brien climbed down fifteen feet before Apocalypse followed him. The ladder led to a small room with an elevator door. She hit the button next to the door, and the panels opened. It wasn't large enough to fit everyone.

"I'll go first," said O'Brien as he burst into flame, burning his flesh away leaving a flaming skeleton.

"Me, too," said Sapper.

"I'll go too," Knockout.

"Fine," said Apocalypse, "but if you run into trouble, I'm coming to save you."

"What about me?" said Chelsea.

"You're to find Velositi and get help."

They loaded into the elevator. The door closed, and Apocalypse waited, lighting the darkness with her beam.

"I'm proud of you," Apocalypse told Chelsea. "You've done well during this adventure."

"I just don't want anything to happen to Momma-K."

"I don't think anything has happened to her. I can feel her cloud."

"Yeah, but you can feel her cloud from anywhere."

"Yes, but if we ever stop feeling it, then we know something bad has happened."

"Something bad *has* happened." Chelsea hugged herself tightly.

Apocalypse put her arm around her daughter. "There's bad, and then there is *bad*. This isn't that bad. Momma-K is alive, and we will find her."

"Promise?"

"I Promise. I won't stop looking until I do."

"*Kimmy, Lizzy. It's all clear down here.*"

"*Ok. We're coming down.*"

Apocalypse guided Chelsea onto the elevator and hit the down button. The doors opened onto a corridor that made a sharp left turn after a hundred feet. The walls and floors were dull metal. The other Angels waited at the corner.

"*All clear,*" said Sapper.

Apocalypse and Chelsea caught up to the others. Down the adjoining corridor, glass walls lined both sides.

"Good, let's go," said Apocalypse.

They walked down the corridor. The windows looked down on two workshops. The workshop on the left was filled with Morphicons.

Apocalypse zoomed in her vision on one. Each Morphicon had square holes in its chest. "I bet these are waiting on system cores."

"As long as we don't have to fight that many," said Sapper.

Apocalypse's quick count said there were over a hundred.

"I think I'd rather fight those than that," said Chelsea motioning through the other window.

On the floor was a giant Morphicon in the process of being constructed. Large printing machines worked on a shoulder and a leg. On the back wall was a large three-story door.

"You suppose they take it out laying down?" said Sapper.

"They must," said Apocalypse, "if they want to get it out."

"At least he's not as big as Boaty," said Chelsea.

Apocalypse nodded. "*Velositi, we found a door big enough for you. We're...*"

"*Northwest, Your Highness,*" said O'Brien.

"*Northwest of the house. There must be an exit somewhere.*"

"*Thanks, Kimmy. We'll keep looking in that area.*"

The Angels reached a door at the far end of the corridor. Apocalypse and Chelsea were waved to the corner as Sapper and O'Brien stacked up on either side of the door in preparation to breach it and clear what lay beyond.

O'Brien opened the door on a silent count, and Sapper charged through, going right as O'Brien followed going left.

"Clear!" called O'Brien.

"Clear," said Sapper.

Apocalypse and Chelsea moved inside to find a seating area and a coffee table with a glass top and a map of Europe set underneath. The map flashed and showed a video of Morphicons of various sizes fighting alongside European forces as they created what the video called "Fortress Europe."

"Someone is thinking ambitiously," said Apocalypse.

Around the room were houseplants, a coffeemaker

on a table, and a large Morphicon-size door at the rear.

"What do you suppose they do in here?" said Sapper.

"It's a waiting room," said Apocalypse. "I bet European dignitaries are brought here to be shown the power this Doctor Unixilite offers."

"That is correct, *Frau* Apocalypse," Unixilite's voice filled the room from all directions. "I have struck a deal with the European leaders. Soon they will have an army capable of countering the Empire's."

"I think we've shown today you're nowhere near there."

"Like all science, trial and error. Yesterday was a minor setback. I was unaware of the power the little Angel possesses. What I have learned I will apply, and next time you will not be victorious."

"I'm here for Kita. Your capture of her was luck. Once she's free, you'll never win."

"Kita is already free. She could leave if she wishes."

"Let me see her!" Yelled Apocalypse.

"I don't believe she wishes to be disturbed. She is meditating on a problem."

"You're going to have a problem in a minute. Let me have her, or I will tear this place apart."

"Why don't you sit and relax. Once she's ready, I'll see if she's interested in contacting you."

"Damnit!" Apocalypse smashed her fist through the video table. "I *am* the Dragon God. I will not be denied."

"Destroy the room if you must, but you are *not* going anywhere. Your friends outside will be found and brought inside."

Apocalypse sneered. "Lizzy, Dan, get that door

open." She pointed to the large door in the back of the room.

"Right," said Sapper.

They examined the door and the area around it.

"There's no switch or any way to get it open," said O'Brien.

"Nothing," Sapper confirmed.

"I'm not out of tricks yet," snarled Apocalypse. "We'll use our clouds. You take Dan, and I'll take Lizzy."

"Hang on, this is a chilly ride," Sapper said to O'Brien.

Apocalypse dissolved into her white cloud form. She wasn't a pure white cloud; she had a small part of Kita's black cloud in her to keep the white cloud's urges and desires at bay. Kita had discovered this in her youth. A newer innovation was Chelsea's cloud. She was a hybrid cloud made up of equal but separate amounts of black and white clouds. This allowed her access to the abilities of both cloud types.

Chelsea floated over O'Brien and settled on top of him. He disappeared in the shapeless, depthless mass of energy. Apocalypse did the same to Sapper. Together they floated through the solid metal door into a room filled with oversized workbenches and equipment.

"Where are we, Mom?" said Chelsea in a high, monotone voice given to her by her hybrid cloud.

"I don't know, sweet pea," Apocalypse answered in the high, melodic voice of a white cloud. "This room isn't meant for humans. It's sized for Morphicons."

"Yes, it is. Do you think humans are the only ones who perform science?" said Unixilite. This time his voice came from across the room.

Apocalypse dropped Sapper, and Chelsea did the same with O'Brien. The two clouds changed to Angels.

"You did not lie when you said you were full of tricks. Kita didn't tell me about that one. What did you become that allowed you to pass through a solid door?"

"We're not telling you," said Sapper.

"Knowing it can be done is ninety percent of the challenge. I will discover it in time."

"Where is Kita?" demanded Apocalypse as she floated above the workbench to see a room filled with workbenches, laboratory equipment, experiments—including parts of Morphicons—and 3D printers slowly moving around constructing new Morphicons. Unixilite stood by a workbench on the far wall. He was thin for a Morphicon but still eleven feet tall. His blocky exterior was white, and he wore a helmet with three cones running along the spine.

"I said she is safe. Meditating happily. We've had some fascinating conversations about the nature of the universe. She promised to look for a few answers for me."

"Why would she help you? Does she know what you did to Leaf?"

"I explained the tiny Angel's death was an accident. I *am* sorry. I just wanted to learn where your boundaries lie."

"So you killed her?" snapped Sapper.

"I gave the order to cut her throat. I have punished the human who was overzealous in carrying out my order."

"You're still responsible. And whatever Kita's up to, I don't care. I will not let Leaf go unavenged." Apocalypse raised her fist and blasted a hole through Unixilite's chest.

Unixilite raised his hands. "I am a scientist, not a warrior, but I am not without my defenses. I have your friends, both Angels and Morphicons, and I will trade their lives for my freedom."

"I say we kill him, and we'll figure out how to get the others out on our own," said Sapper.

"I will warn you that I am all that stands between you and war. My army of Morphicons is more powerful than any that Savacron had."

"I have my own army of Morphicons that serve me throughout the world. *And* my military has been fighting Morphicons for over fifty years. We know how to kill you. What we saw yesterday are nothing special, just bigger targets for us to hit."

"I have delivered on my promise to the Europeans; they have an army that can stand up to yours."

Apocalypse felt a funny feeling all over. *Liar.* Another of her cloud abilities was to sense when someone lied. Apocalypse folded her arms. "I'm willing to gamble. Mine is waiting for the command to go. Release my friends, and you could still walk out of here functional."

"If I die, your friends die."

Truth. But is that immediate, or do I have time? "If my friends die, you will take a long time to die."

"I am a Morphicon of science. All I wish to do is study in peace. Savacron refused to let me, and my deal with the Europeans is nearly complete. My discoveries can become yours. I know you have a lab in the desert of Vegas. Imagine what I could do for you."

"Release my friends, and we'll talk."

"I will release the Morphicons." On a screen behind Unixilite, Velositi and the other Vehlixen appeared. They were trapped between two giant sets of doors. The door behind them opened. "You are free to go," Unixilite told them. "Please return the way you came."

"Velositi, Kimmy. Do as he says. We'll meet you at the evacuation point."

Velositi turned and gave a thumbs-up.

Apocalypse glared at Unixilite. "How do I get you from here to Area Fifty-one?"

"Do not worry, Empress. This facility is more than it appears. It is a Morphicon, and I am its system core." He tapped his helmet. "After you leave, I can morph into an aircraft, and with your aircraft guarding me, I can fly to Vegas."

Apocalypse smiled as her vision switched to the electromagnetic spectrum. "That's all I need to know." She raised her fists, and bright red beams cut Unixilite into four sections, missing his five system cores.

"Why'd you do that?" cried Chelsea.

"Oh, man. I'm glad you did it, or I was going to do it," said Sapper.

"First rule, sweet pea, is if a person has betrayed someone else and they offer to join you, they'll be just as quick to betray you when the going gets tough. Plus, I don't need another grumpy Morphicon scientist. Sprokkit is bad enough."

The Angels flew to Unixilite's body.

"*Velositi, I need you to come back. Unixilite is incapacitated, and I need Sprokkit to look at this place.*"

"*I would love to, but we can't get past the door.*"

Apocalypse kneeled down and picked up Unixilite's

head. She knew it contained one system core, enough to give his head life. "Wake up."

Unixilite's eyes turned on, glowing a soft blue.

"You're not dead yet, but only your continued usefulness is keeping me from putting a beam through your head. Now, open all the doors between my friends and here."

"It's...tooooo late, Angel. The Euro-peans are, on their...waaaay. They'llllll be...here in min-utes." Unixilite's voice was slow, and his words broken.

"You think I'm a fool, Morphicon? My forces are waiting for the word to attack. I'll have planes, helicopters, and paratroopers here in minutes." Apocalypse set Unixilite's head on a counter. "*Secretary Mayfield, broken lance. The Empress and Princess are in danger. I'll send you my coordinates. Execute Operation Gravedigger.*"

Upon hearing the code phrase, O'Brien took Chelsea by the shoulder and guided her next to her mother. He then put up his heat shield.

"*We're on our way, Your Highness. Aircraft will be overhead in five minutes. The Five-Oh-Five air assault division is lifting off now from East Germany. The rest of the units in Operation Gravedigger are moving to seize European objectives now.*"

"*Thank you, Secretary. The Princess and I will await their arrival.*" Apocalypse looked down at Unixilite. "I can't tell you how nice it is to have an Empire willing to do my will. Soon, it will be the entire world. Can you imagine? Probably not. I bet things aren't computing well in there. Now, let my friends in, and we'll see about discussing your future. Also, wake Kita and let the other Angels go."

The clapping caught Apocalypse by surprise. She didn't let her shock show, but both Sapper and O'Brien pointed their weapons in the direction of the sound.

"Bravo, love, bravo," Kita stepped from behind a workbench dressed as the Vicereine.

Apocalypse motioned for O'Brien to lower his shield. When he did, she glided over and gave Kita a hug and a kiss. "Are you alright, angel?"

"I'm fine. The drugs wore off a while ago. I'm proud of you. You conquered the world. I am impressed."

"I'm not there yet."

"All that's left is the body count. The outcome is inevitable." Kita looked back at Chelsea. "How are you, sweet pea?"

"Momma!" Chelsea glided over and gave Kita a hug.

"I'm proud of you, too."

Chelsea's eyes widened. "Really?"

"You performed exceptionally in your first real combat. You've learned well. I'm impressed. I think it's time you get your angelic name."

"You mean it?" Chelsea clapped her hands and bounced up and down.

"You're one of the Angels now," said Apocalypse.

Kita reached out and touched Chelsea's nose. "Boop! You are Jynx. Forever will fortune be in your favor."

"Yeah!" Jynx hugged both her moms.

"And I think it's time to go home."

"It'll be a while before the military gets here," said Apocalypse.

"As much as the White House has been a nice place to live, I mean my home."

"You mean?"

"Yep." Kita snapped her fingers.

Apocalypse appeared in a terrarium, looking at the tallest tree she'd ever seen. Above them was a night sky—or space, she wasn't sure. Water flowed through the trees down a stone-lined stream. Curved metal walls formed the base of a transparent ceiling.

"Hello, everyone. Welcome to your new home," said Kita, drifting upward.

"What happened to Earth?" said Ryan. He was standing next to his girlfriend Sarah. Both looked lost.

"Kimmy conquered it. So, I thought it was time to bring you here. I have some things to do with Kimmy, but Lizzy will be happy to show you around."

"Oh, come on. I just got back."

"You can help them pick rooms, show them Roost's cantina, rec room, simulators, labs, and workshops. Everyone, follow Lizzy. Things will be new for her, too. I had to make the ceilings and doors tall enough for Sprokkit."

Kita drifted back to the floor. "Why don't you go with Lizzy, Chelsea?"

"What are you and Mom going to do?"

"We have some unfinished business to take care of. Go with Lizzy and pick out a room. Any one you want. She'll show you which one is ours so you can be as close or as far as you like."

"I will take her," said Velositi. "I assume these rooms come with all the creature comforts for Morphicons?"

Kita rubbed the back of her neck. "No...but as soon as you tell me what those are, I can make them."

Velositi chirped laughter as her eyes lit up. "We do not have any. I will have to experiment. I do know I like giant beanbag chairs."

"Find a room with a view you like, and we'll figure out the rest later."

"Sounds good. Come, Chelsea. Let us see what the view is."

Kita turned to face Apocalypse. "Shall we go, my love?"

"And where are we going?"

"Your final test."

"I thought I was the teacher's pet: I get an A regardless."

"True, but if you want to become what you seek, you have one last task."

Apocalypse stuck out her hip and put her fist on it. "I just finished conquering the world. What more could you want?"

"Follow me and see." Kita turned and walked down a dirt path back into Roost and around a corridor with a long window showing a beautiful green and yellow nebula.

Apocalypse gasped. "Are we in space?"

"Yes. Someday I plan on turning all that stardust into a sun and planets. The original Roost orbited my homeworld. It was my home for years."

"Are you going to cry now, Mom?" teased a female voice that wasn't quite human.

"Hello, Athena. I missed you too."

"Who is she?" said Apocalypse.

"Kimmy, meet Athena. Athena, meet Kimmy, your new step-mom. Athena is the AI that runs the station. She also has a body around here somewhere."

"Currently, I'm checking out a fluctuation in the power generators. Hello, Kimmy. This is an adventure I must hear. I noticed we had lots of new faces—and I had a new sister, though she is small."

Kita chuckled. "That's because she came from an egg, and I had to change how fast she grew so she could be gestated."

"YOU DIDN'T!" exclaimed Athena.

"No, no. I didn't carry her. Kimmy did."

"It wasn't as bad as you make it seem," said Apocalypse, annoyed at Kita.

Kita stopped in front of a door. A glowing plaque read UNIVERSE ROOM. The door slid open, and Kita entered. Apocalypse followed and stopped next to Kita, who was standing in front of a purplish-red glowing ball. Computer terminals and storage servers lined the room.

"I've been able to keep Universe Eight Thirty-two stable," said Athena.

"That's...That's my universe?" said Apocalypse.

"That's it," said Kita. "Cool, huh?"

"It's incredible. I can't believe we were in it. I mean, this place looks like it could come from it."

"That's because Roost did come from a universe very similar to it. There are many layers of universe physics to make it possible, both the universe it came from and the mother universe. Now, you have a choice to make."

Apocalypse looked at Kita warily. "What choice?"

"You want to be a god like me, right?"

"Yes. You said you'd help me. I'll fight you if I have to."

"You won't win that one," said Athena with a chuckle.

"She's proven she can fight. Just like I had to prove I could fight by defeating Kerri, she took on three different giant Morphicons and won."

"Because I know what a Morphicon is," Athena drawled sarcastically.

"To become a god, I had to give up everything. Now, it's Kimmy's turn. Can you give up everything to become a god?"

"You mean give up you and Chelsea?"

"I mean, give up your universe. Like me, you must destroy your past to fulfill your destiny."

Destiny? I never thought of having a destiny. A plan, yes... and I succeeded. The Earth is mine...but there is more...but at what cost? My homeworld, my past, my people, my friends...Am I willing to sacrifice all of them to become a god? "What about Leaf? She's still in there."

"That's a choice you'll have to make."

"You want me to be like you?"

Kita smiled. "No. I want you to be free."

"You said before we could copy it and keep my universe."

"I did, and I can. You would still be Emperor, rule Earth, and go on from there. I'm just offering another path...one you've never known. Freedom to find out who you are."

The freedom to find out who I am? But...I thought I knew who I was...Do I? What am I if I strip away my titles? If I'm not an empress, who am I? I'm a mother? But am I really? I could be better. I'm a wife. Kita doesn't complain about me. That's all been second to being Empress. What am I if I can't be an empress? A not very good wife and mother. I've always had others to rely on...Velositi handles Kita, and the staff managed Chelsea. But Kita wants me to be more than a wife and mother; she wants me to be a god. And a god can be anything. What do I want to be? I want to go on adventures and see the cosmos like Kita. I want to see it with Chelsea. I want the power my daughter has and the knowledge my wife has. And now I have the time to learn it all.

Apocalypse looked into Kita's eyes. "I don't know who I am without what's in this universe. I've put my everything into being Empress to the detriment of you and Chelsea. I want to fix that. I want the knowledge you have and the power our daughter has. If I have to destroy this universe to get it, so be it, but Leaf is on your head. I know you can save her if you want."

A corner of Kita's mouth ticked up. "I can and will. What I can't save is the time she spent in the universe if you destroy it. She'll never miss it."

"Then destroy the universe. I will join you and become a god. My first task is to become a better mother and wife."

Kita raised an eyebrow. "I thought you did a fine job of that."

"I could do better."

"Our first task will be getting you installed on the main computer that governs Reality. I will show you how to operate it."

"How long will that take?"

"Out here, time doesn't matter anymore. We'll be together from now to infinity."

SPECIAL THANKS TO THE FOLLOWING PATREONS!

Adam Dunsmuir
Xrebelion
K.V. Wilson
ParadoxicMouse
Skye Miller
Andre Matos
Joshua Le Tourneau
Natalie Nicholls
5m7kabedfr76
Lolena
Mark Gardner
Vivenne Sullivan
Sarah Ilbrink
Noble Seven
Monica and Shirlee RichardsonMiller

ABOUT THE AUTHOR

L. Fergus is an Amazon Bestselling author with Birthright, Razor's Pass, and Rebirth. All titles were #1 new releases in LGBT Science Fiction. Before Amazon, L. was a Wattpad Featured Author and #1 writer of science fiction. The Fallen Angel Saga has more than four hundred thousand reads. The books Birthright, BykeChic, and Rebirth have won over twenty awards, including Best Overall.

L. lives with four dogs: Rust, Moxy, Stormy, and Valor, and four cats: Jupiter, Crater, Pluto, and Forest Fire.

If you want the most up to date stories consider becoming a patreon at www.patreon.com/FallenAngelKita

Join L. Fergus' mailing list at FallenAngelKita.com for news about upcoming book releases. Follow L. on Facebook at Facebook.com/FallenAngelKita, Twitter @FallenAngelKita and contact L. at L@FallenAngelKita.com.

Did you enjoy EARTH 832?
Tell the world what you think!

Leave a review on
Amazon or Goodreads